Cheers for Catheen Schine's

She Is Me

"*She Is Me* is a droll and profound meditation on the fluid relationship between motherhood and daughterhood. . . . As ever, Schine entertains as she enlightens, demonstrating her enviable talent for balancing humor with emotional heft."

— Kera Bolonik, *Chicago Tribune*

"In this marvelous story, Schine brings a smart, fresh eye to the condition of marriage, adultery, and motherhood. Each thread of this tale weaves through a tapestry of honest observation, tremendous humor, and a cast of characters whose poignant puzzlements and yearnings you won't easily forget."

— Elizabeth Strout, author of *Amy and Isabelle*

"Cathleen Schine is a genius at poking fun at her readers, but she always lets us in on the joke. . . . She has a mastery of the lightly clever and the devastatingly subtle, and she captures the random jukebox of the brain perfectly. . . . *She Is Me* joins Schine's other work in being simply elegant, whip-smart modern fiction."

— Emily Gordon, *Newsday*

"A sweetly disarming testament to the unpredictability of romantic impulse. . . . Schine writes with deep, gentle empathy. . . . She interweaves bright literary gamesmanship with potent, difficult mother-daughter emotions."   — Janet Maslin, *New York Times*

"Deeply funny and wonderfully satisfying — a social satire with its arms around truth, grief, and family love. This is a glittering Schine: fun made literary, and the rarest of pleasures."
— Elinor Lipman, author of *The Inn at Lake Devine* and *The Pursuit of Alice Thrift*

"*She Is Me* is sly, smart, and darkly comic. . . . At the same time, the novel is knowing, compassionate, deeply poignant, and suffused with a tender and earnest kind of love. In the end, it is a heart-breaking story rather than a scandalous one."
— Jonathan Kirsch, *Los Angeles Times Book Review*

"Clever, charming, and uplifting. . . . Schine takes a refreshing and often very funny look at love, aging, and loyalty in the complicated lives of three women in a tight-knit family. . . . She deftly mixes humor and pathos."
— *Publishers Weekly*

"In *She Is Me*, a typically delightful Cathleen Schine heroine — a brilliant intellectual naïf — enters a typically delightful Cathleen Schine situation — a densely compacted *ronde* of generations, love affairs, movie scripts, and misunderstandings. But the book's central matter, of death and renewal and the responsibility of each generation for the next, gives it a mysterious grace and authority, with results far from typical even of any of Schine's earlier comic novels, dark but somehow full of comic light."
— Adam Gopnik, author of *Paris to the Moon*

"*She Is Me* is funny in a subtle, even sly way. . . . Schine gracefully weaves dark themes of illness, adultery, passion, betrayal, and loss into a fresh and surprisingly cheerful family comedy."
— Diane White, *Book*

"Schine writes with the speed and punch of a seasoned comic, conveying character in a single line of dialogue. But this sly novel is a silver cloud with a dark lining. . . . Just when we've settled in for froth and sparkle, Schine ambushes us with feeling."

— *The New Yorker*

"The beauty of Schine's book lies in the way it brings together the two meanings embedded in its title. Schine's women are mothers and daughters, but they're also Emma Bovary–quality adulterers. Schine allows them to be many things at once, and when we're done reading about them, most other women in most other novels seem a little emotionally impoverished. . . . Schine has given us such a rich portrait of ordinary life. She loves the chat of families, their intimate gossip. Her elegant writing has a down-home appeal: you dig in happily and eat it all up. But neither she nor her people are complacent. Schine's novels are literary — this novel is literary — because they are anything but formulaic: she and her characters are grasping their way in the dark."

— Claire Dederer, *New York Times Book Review*

"Schine sets up her characters brilliantly. . . . Throughout the book is a tremendous enjoyment of life, an enjoyment that none of the characters are ready to relinquish even in the face of terrible illness."

— Melinda Bargreen, *Seattle Times*

"Cathleen Schine is one of our best and most elegant writers. Few satirists can cast such a sharp, yet sympathetic — often evanescent — light on human frailty and desire and move us so deeply. Witty, penetrating, and riveting at every turn, *She Is Me* may well be Ms. Schine's finest novel."

— Nicholas Christopher, author of *Franklin Flyer* and *Veronica*

ALSO BY CATHLEEN SCHINE

The Evolution of Jane

The Love Letter

Rameau's Niece

To the Birdhouse

Alice in Bed

She
Is
Me

A NOVEL

Cathleen Schine

BACK BAY BOOKS
Little, Brown and Company
New York • Boston

Back Bay Books / Little, Brown and Company
Time Warner Book Group
1271 Avenue of the Americas, New York, NY 10020
Visit our Web site at www.twbookmark.com

Originally published in hardcover by Little, Brown and Company, September 2003
First Back Bay paperback edition, September 2004

Copyright acknowledgments appear on pages 265–266.

Library of Congress Cataloging-in-Publication Data

Schine, Cathleen.
    She is me : a novel / Cathleen Schine. — 1st ed.
        p. cm.
    ISBN 0-316-78609-8 (hc) / 0-316-15942-5 (pb)
        1. Adult children of aging parents — Fiction. 2. Motion picture
industry — Fiction. 3. Parent and adult child — Fiction. 4. Mothers
and daughters — Fiction. 5. Los Angeles (Calif.) — Fiction. 6. Women
screenwriters — Fiction. 7. Women — California — Fiction. 8. Aging
parents — Fiction. 9. Grandmothers — Fiction. 10. Adultery —
Fiction. I. Title.

PS3569.C497S54 2003
813'.54 — dc21

                                                        2002041639

10 9 8 7 6 5 4 3 2 1
Q-FF
Text design by Meryl Sussman Levavi/Digitext
Printed in the United States of America

To Janet

She
Is
Me

one

Motherless children have a hard time, but what about the rest of us? Elizabeth thought. *Motherless children have a hard time, when your mother is dead. . . .* She must have sung out loud because her mother, Greta, slapped her hand lightly and said, "That's enough music."

Elizabeth put her arms around her mother.

"Thank you for coming," Greta whispered. "You're a good daughter." Tears appeared below the rims of Greta's sunglasses and ran down her cheeks.

"Mom, she'll be okay," Elizabeth said. "Don't cry. You're a good daughter, too."

Then Elizabeth began to cry. And wished she had sunglasses.

"It's so fucking hot in here," Greta said, patting Elizabeth's back in an almost unconscious, ritualistic gesture of comfort. "Why do they have the heat on? They'll make us all sick." She turned to the doctor's receptionist. "First, do no harm!" she said.

The receptionist, a middle-aged black woman with long, squared-off plastic fingernails, looked up.

"Maybe you're having hot flashes," Elizabeth said. She wiped sweat off her forehead with the back of her hand. "Maybe we're all having hot flashes."

The clacking of the receptionist's manicure on the computer keys resumed.

Elizabeth listened to the pitter-patter of plastic against plastic, the rhythm of work. Order. A peaceful resolve. One foot in front of the other. One fingernail in front of the other.

She imagined her grandmother's skin. Her grandmother was so proud of her skin. It was white, as white as the shoulders of a heroine in a novel. It was soft and scented by Ponds cold cream. How many times had that cheek been presented to her to kiss? How many times had she seen it approaching, in the slow motion of a horror movie? Once, she ran away from the advancing cheek, and her grandmother cried. When Elizabeth got older, she loved to kiss her grandmother, loved the old-fashioned delicacy of her face. But as a child she'd sometimes felt suffocated by her grand-mother's cheek, by her strong, grasping fingers, by the demand. Elizabeth did not like demands. Unless it was she who made them.

"Poor Grandma," she said. She shed a few tears. Then stopped herself. Then sniffed.

Her mother stood up. She took several tissues from a box on the receptionist's desk. "Here."

"Filthy tumor," her grandmother had said when they'd found out. "Why couldn't I have it on my goddamned ass?"

Elizabeth blew her nose. She wiped the back of her neck with another tissue. She sat in the waiting room, sweating, a dirty tissue in each hand.

* * *

Now, Lotte, shut up, Lotte said to herself. You son of a bitch, you've had a good life. And there's life in the old mare, yet.

She adjusted her hat, patted her hair. Beautiful hair with a natural wave. The haircutter came to *her* now. Fifteen dollars, that was all, no charge for the house call. Of course, she gave him a big tip. He was a darling, and so devoted to her. Well, that's just the kind of person I am, she thought.

Her daughter, Greta, was talking to the doctor. Handsome? Like a matinee idol. But such a waste on such a cold, cold fish. A top man, of course, world renowned, best in his field, with that flashlight, like a miner, on his forehead. Two assistants to go through before you could speak to him, and then he was abrupt, rude, let's be frank, all they wanted was money. Butchers. Even so, this gorgeous stiff with a pole up his high-priced ass had stayed to talk to her, had laughed at her joke, had called her by her first name and told her she was as sharp as a tack.

"What about chemotherapy?" Greta was saying.

Greta wore ridiculous clothes for a grown woman. She wasn't at all bad looking, and she'd never put that weight back on, God bless her. But Greta neglected herself. Lotte wondered how she, Lotte Franke, née Levinson, practically brought up in Levinson's, her family's department store, how she, an actress — a dancer, anyway, and on Broadway, don't forget — how she had raised a daughter who could appear in public in such dreary clothes.

"You're dressed for the rodeo," Lotte said in the car on the way home.

In the backseat, Elizabeth laughed. "Grandma, have you ever seen a rodeo? I mean, how would you even know?"

"I'm wearing jeans, for heaven's sake," Greta said. "Not chaps."

Lotte began to cry. "I don't want a hole in my face."

"Grandma, Grandma, they cover the hole," Elizabeth said. She took Greta's shoulder. "Don't they?"

"Plastic surgery," Greta said. "And they're *blue jeans,* Mother, just like everyone else on earth."

"You see?" said Elizabeth. "Plastic surgery. Like a movie star."

Elizabeth was a wonderful girl. Subdued, but chic. If she would just let her hair loose, instead of pulling it back like a librarian. "Beautiful, wavy . . ." Lotte said, clucking disapproval.

"We did go to a rodeo once," Greta said. "Remember, Mother? Lake George? It was so hot Daddy drove in his boxer shorts?"

"My Morris," Lotte said with a sigh. What a nightmare that trip was. And the filth! "*You've* got real style," she added, turning to Elizabeth. "That's genetic."

A little makeup would be nice, too, though. Spruce things up a bit. Too serious, these young people. Working so hard. They all looked haggard.

"If it's so genetic, what the hell happened to me?" said Greta.

"You," Lotte said. She raised her shoulders in a shrug. "For the rodeo, you're not bad." She suddenly lifted both her large, bony hands. She clasped them together as if in prayer. Her bracelets clattered. "What would I do without you?" she said. "Without you two? My family. My family . . ." She trailed off. Leaned her head back. She was so tired. They were going to cut up her face. She might as well take the pipe.

Her face. Her beautiful skin that everyone admired. All her life they had admired her soft, white skin. Never even a pimple. She sat up straighter, gazed down at her wedding ring, not the original simple band, but a thick tire of gold studded with diamonds. Now, stop your moping, Lotte.

Life can be delish with a sunny disposish. . . . She ran the old song through her head, tried to smile. She'd done it at the Roxy. Or was it the Orpheum? She could hear the sound of her shoes on the stage, the chalky dust that rose like little clouds and settled on the black patent leather. A sunny disposish. But she was so tired. Couldn't she just die and be done with it? It was about time, any-

way. She was old. It would be so much easier. For Greta. For Elizabeth. For all of them.

"But I'm just not ready yet," she said, only half to herself.

～

The 405 goes north and south, the 10 goes east and west. Elizabeth
chanted these words in a silent singsong.

So, I take the 10. No, no. The 405. Take it through the pass that
takes you over the hill and into the Valley to the 134, which turns
into the 101.... There was something unnerving about driving
somewhere new in L.A. Everyone kept a map in the car, even
people who had lived their entire lives in the place. Elizabeth
had not lived her entire life in Los Angeles. She had learned to
drive on the North Shore of Long Island, where she had grown
up. She still felt the ocean was placed all wrong in California. Go
west, someone would say, but you couldn't even follow the setting
sun if the sun happened to be setting, because no one meant
"west," really. They meant toward the Pacific Ocean, and the shore
jutted out in peninsulas or formed bays, or did whatever else it
could think of to make "west" mean something that had absolutely
nothing to do with the location of the long white beach and the
crashing surf. When she had first started driving in L.A., she'd gotten herself a compass, but a compass was useless in this strange
land.

"And the women!" her grandmother had said, when Elizabeth
told her how strange L.A. felt. "With their *tztizkes* hanging out!"

She squinted in the glare of the beautiful sun. Yellow flowers
that looked like a child's crayon drawing lined the freeway. She got
off at the correct exit. She held the directions she had downloaded
from the Internet and tried to follow them.

After 1/8 of a mile, turn left.
Continue for 1/3 mile. Take second right.

The instructions were overly detailed, confusing and uninteresting at the same time. That was the definition of a boring person. But Elizabeth was not bored. She was frantic. And how much was one-third of a mile added to one-eighth of a mile?

She arrived in plenty of time. But she was worn out, her underarms damp, her head throbbing. And she had to pee. She didn't really understand why she was here. Why she had been summoned. She couldn't compete with women who had *tztizkes* hanging out.

She found the correct gate on the third try. A uniformed man came out of a glass booth.

Elizabeth said, "Elizabeth Bernard for —"

"He's expecting you," said the attendant.

A concierge in a brass-buttoned blazer took her in a small elevator paneled with exotic wood to a large waiting room paneled with exotic wood.

"Eliz —"

"He's expecting you," said the receptionist at the first desk.

"He'll be a few minutes late," said a second receptionist.

"He apologizes," said the first.

Maybe I can just have the meeting with these two, Elizabeth thought. They were both purposefully unglamorous, she noticed. She forgot about peeing. She sat in a chair and looked out the windows at a flowering tree. The waiting room was historic, she knew. The style of the studio boss who ruled here in the 1930s had been left intact. Towering silver doors etched with art deco designs. Crystal statuettes. Curving, undulating wood. Why am I here? she wondered again. I don't belong here. I belong in a cramped office correcting papers about the Lacanian implications of *How to Marry a Millionaire.*

The silver portals swung open.

"Come in!" said a man in a suit and tie, the first man in a suit and tie Elizabeth had seen in the week she'd been in L.A. He was waving her in, grinning, excited.

She followed Larry Volfmann down three steps into an office as soft as a thigh — carpeted, upholstered, and pillowed.

Larry Volfmann is a millionaire, she thought. What would be the Lacanian implications of marrying him?

"How's your trip? You like L.A.? First time out here? Takes some getting used to . . ."

He talked so fast it was difficult for Elizabeth to convey that her parents had lived in L.A. for years, had moved there when she was in college.

". . . started out as a bunch of Indian villages, then towns, now they're all linked together, so, you know, it feels like it has no center because it actually has no center . . ."

Elizabeth wondered again what she was doing there, summoned before this great man. She had heard that all powerful men in Hollywood were short and was a little disappointed to see he was actually of average height. He didn't have a tan, either. Or wear a baseball cap.

"Mr. Volfmann —"

"Larry . . ."

He handed her a bottle of water.

"Larry, it's so good to meet you. I'm a little stunned, of course —"

"Happiness," Larry said, interrupting. "Passion." He waved a magazine at her. "Intoxication." The magazine was *Tikkun,* the issue with her article about *Madame Bovary.* "Happiness, passion, intoxication. I like it!" He shrugged as if to say, I *like* happiness: sue me! "I like it," he said again, tapping the page.

"Well, those are Flaubert's words," she said. She smiled, modestly, she hoped. "Not mine."

And don't think you can con me or co-opt me or impress me,

either, just because I'm a dreary academic, just because I'm impressed that you somehow manage to read *Tikkun.* I don't read *Tikkun.* Who has time to read anything? And you probably have even less time than I do, although I bet you don't have to run home after work and make dinner and play with Brios and Duplos and Play-Doh. Maybe an assistant read it. No. What assistant would have the balls to recommend an academic article in a down-at-the-heels Jewish monthly? This has to have come from the eccentric boss himself.

"No," Larry said. "Not Flaubert's words. *Emma's* words."

Surprised, Elizabeth examined the eccentric boss himself. He looked a little like a boxer — the dog, not the athlete. Dark eyes, a bit jowly, but fierce. High-strung. And he was right. Happiness. Passion. Intoxication. They were Madame Bovary's words, the words Emma Bovary read in books, over and over.

"The words her marriage failed to make her understand. They're Emma's soul, her quest, her destiny, her tragedy . . ." He was still waving the magazine around.

Elizabeth smiled. A man of business, as Larry Volfmann so clearly was, was discussing her humble article. As she smiled, her pleasure at being noticed by him transformed almost effortlessly into a warm sense of personal superiority. Okay. I get it, she thought. You're smart, you're serious. You went to college. You're sensitive. You studied literature. But somehow, life took a funny turn and here you are, a man with a literary mind stuck doing action movies at Pole Star Pictures. The head of Pole Star Pictures, who earns more in one week than I earn in a year, but you haven't given up your soul. . . . She continued to smile at him and nodded to convey thoughtful attention the way she had learned to do with ardent students. He tilted his head, as if he'd been petted. She wondered if he was muscular like Fritz, the boxer dog who lived on the third floor in her building in New York. He was a little bow-legged, she had noticed. Like Fritz. And, to be fair, he might make a lot of money and be driven in a limousine, but he was right. Emma Bovary was so fucking compelling. It didn't matter how obvious one's response was, how banal, how romantic, how innocent. All of that just somehow made Madame Bovary — so compelling in her own romantic, innocent banality — all the more compelling.

"'The Way Madame Bovary Lives Now: Tragedy, Farce, and Cliché in the Age of Ikea,'" he read. "We'll have to change the title, of course."

She stared at him, speechless, until he began to laugh and she realized he was making a joke.

"It's tough," he said. "I mean, it will be tough to make it fresh. Because, you know, every movie is really *Madame Bovary*, right? *Madame Bovary* 'R' Us!" He laughed. He was having fun.

The phone rang.

"What?" he answered, tough and rude, just like an executive ought to be. "If you could remove your tongue from my ass and say whatever it is you want to say . . . Uh huh . . . Right. Do it! I like it!"

He slammed the phone down, put both elbows on the desk and his chin in his hands, and stared expectantly at Elizabeth.

"So . . . sort of like *Clueless* meets *American Beauty?*" she said. After all, he was offering her cash money, and quite a bit of it.

"Don't patronize me, Professor Smarty-Pants," he said. "I don't know if you can write a script even half as good as either of those. I don't know if you can write a script at all, do I? I'm going out on a limb for you —"

"No, I just meant —"

"I know what you meant, I know what you meant," he said, leaning across the desk at her, almost lying on it. He moved one hand, as if waving away smoke. "History. Ancient. Gone. . . . I'm not looking to you to marry two pictures we already saw. No *marriages,* honey. I want . . . *adultery!*"

"I just —"

"I want new! I want to stray, roam, betray the conventions. And find me . . ."

He paused. Slowly, seriously, he said, "Find me Emma Bovary."

Elizabeth felt the cold beads of water on the Evian bottle. When students assaulted her with their enthusiasm, she learned to watch them and nod while trying to decipher their barrage of critical theory and undergraduate sentimentality. But this growling man was not a student. His enthusiasm was not youthful. Critical theory was not a phase he would eventually have to grow out of. And she was not his teacher.

Elizabeth took her wet hand from the Evian bottle and put it on her forehead. I really want to do this, she thought, surprised. And she suddenly very much wanted to please Mr. Larry Volfmann, too.

"Familiar but fresh," he said.

"Fresh."

"But *familiar.*"

"But . . ." She hesitated.

"Fresh?"

"No. I mean, yes. But . . ."

Volfmann glared at her. "But *what?*"

"But I'm an academic."

"You'll get over it. Look," he said, pushing *Tikkun* at her, "I have a feeling about this. Trust me."

And I don't even have tenure, she thought.

"I've always dreamed of doing this project, but how the hell do you update *Madame Bovary* when every picture with an unhappy young wife *is Madame Bovary?*"

"I don't know," Elizabeth said.

"Then, I'm in the gym," he said, paying no attention, "and I'm reading, and . . . here it is!" He smacked the magazine. "Concept. Clarity. Class." He smiled at her, his boxer jowls lifting. "You've got the common touch."

I certainly do not, Elizabeth wanted to cry out, offended.

"In spite of yourself," he added.

"Oh. Thank you," she said.

Larry Volfmann leaned back, his hands behind his head. He spun around, 360 degrees, in his leather chair.

"You on?" he said.

"Well, but, I don't really have any experience . . ."

Shut up, asshole, she told herself. Way to talk yourself out of a shower of fucking riches.

"No. But you've got . . ." He thought for a moment. "*Seychel*," he said. "You know what that means?"

She nodded. But he continued anyway.

"Common sense. I mean, that's the translation. Good, common sense."

"Yeah. That's good," Elizabeth said. "Yeah. I like that."

"*Seychel*," he said.

"Thank you," Elizabeth said. She realized she liked him, even though he had read her paper on Flaubert in *Tikkun* and wanted to pay her a lot of money to write a screenplay for an updated *Madame Bovary*, to turn poor Madame Bovary into a "project." She liked him even though he was buying Emma Bovary as if she were a new sweater, cashmere, but still; and buying her, Elizabeth, as if she were . . . what?

Oh, come on, now. You mean you like him *because* he's buying you. Don't be a prig about selling out, you prig.

"It's oddly comforting to be a commodity," she said.

"Back at you," he said.

Greta remembered when Elizabeth was a baby, her beloved first child. When she woke up in the morning, her first thought had always been of little Elizabeth. To call it the first thought was not quite accurate, though. It was the continuation of last night's thought, which was a continuation of that day's thought, which was simply a continuation of the thought of the day before. Elizabeth had filled Greta's consciousness. She was a beautiful baby with intense, dark eyes and, even then, a worried scowl that could burst into a smile so unexpected and bright it caused complete strangers to laugh out loud. Elizabeth's eyes were still big and dark and round. She stilled scowled, too often for a grown woman. But she smiled, too, and when her big, wide smile appeared, it still broke through like a glorious surprise. Elizabeth's whole face lifted into an expression of such benign, open joy that those around her knew the world was good and fair and our reward would come in this life; we would not have to wait for the next. Witnessing the transformation from pensive baby moodiness to generous baby joy had felt like a gift. It had always been Elizabeth's unconscious, secret power. It still was. When she'd left the house earlier to go to this mysterious meeting of hers, she had turned her head just before the front door closed and the smile had been revealed and the people, or Greta, who was the only one present, had rejoiced.

Greta had existed in the baby's beauty, in her moods, in her needs. Now, she realized, she existed in Lotte in the same way. Her mother's comfort, her spirits and moods, her demands, and her sad, vulnerable needs had been transformed into the air she breathed, a steamy atmosphere as real as the mist that poured from Lotte's humidifier, which Greta was careful to clean every day.

Lotte's voice had wormed its way into Greta's head. Lotte's pain was as clear to Greta as if she felt it herself. The disappointment Lotte felt with each failed treatment, each unsuccessful doctor's appointment, weighed heavily on Greta's chest. Lotte's joy, the intermittent, glorious moments when she struggled up from her illness and courageously enjoyed a new pair of shoes, a huge, garish sunflower, or a cookie — this was Greta's joy.

"It's like having a two-year-old," she said to her husband. But how could Tony know what she meant?

"You have to separate yourself from her a little bit," he suggested.

Greta looked at him, disturbed. Separate?

"Why is that a goal, I wonder?" she said. "I know it is. I know it's what we're always supposed to be doing, all our lives. The therapists so rule. But why?"

"Self-preservation?"

Preservation? Should she zip herself up in a plastic Ziploc bag and preserve herself in the vegetable bin in the refrigerator? Even though she wasn't the one whose face was rotting?

"Don't you think 'self-preservation' is just a nice contemporary phrase for selfishness?" she said.

"No," Tony said. "I don't. People need boundaries."

She hated the way he said "boundaries." It sounded as though it should be written with a capital B. Tony often seemed to capitalize his nouns.

"People *need* Boundaries," he said again.

Perhaps People do, she thought. Tony would know. He was an authority on People. He looked authoritative, too, standing there, his rather large head with its pleasantly crow-footed blue eyes and firm, reassuring, smiling lips.

"Fuck people," she said.

Elizabeth walked out of Larry Volfmann's office still gripping her bottle of water, now empty, now warm. Most people thought Elizabeth willful, but she often felt her will was not entirely her own. She was a person who appeared arrogant and unmovable not because she made up her mind and then stuck to it but because she found it so difficult to make up her mind to anything at all. Elizabeth waited, and waited, and waited, hoping for that elusive bit of evidence that would finally and utterly convince her.

Sometimes there was no alternative before her, and then she

would rush down a path as if pulled by gravity. It made people think she was ambitious and energetic. But I'm passive, don't you see? That's why I studied so hard in school — too lazy not to. And now this. I'll do this because Larry Volfmann told me to.

"Elizabeth?"

Elizabeth realized she was still standing in the waiting room with her empty plastic water bottle. A young man stood in front of her, short, preternaturally tanned, his thinning blond hair gelled into alarming spikes.

"I'm glad I caught you," he said.

Elizabeth was not glad, somehow, although she did feel caught.

"I'm Elliot." He took her by the elbow and led her to another office. "Elliot King."

"Look," said Elliot King. "I'm sorry."

He sat at his desk and put his feet up, motioning her to a chair.

"I'm just a businessman," he said.

Elizabeth sat and looked past the soles of his Adidas at the businessman who was sorry. His brows were knit. He put a pencil to his lips.

"I have to warn you about Larry," he said.

"You do?"

"I love him dearly," he said.

Elizabeth nodded.

"He's the boss," he said.

She nodded again.

"The studio head."

"Right."

"I love him dearly." Elliot stared at her. "But I'm just a businessman." He threw the pencil onto the table, where it skipped like a stone. "Elizabeth Bernard," he continued, "your head is spinning, right?"

She nodded.

"Heady stuff, movies," he said. "Like champagne, right? You

want to be in the business, right? Because it *is* a business. A business you want to be in. But who doesn't? Every kid wants to be in the entertainment industry. But let me tell you something." He leaned back so far that Elizabeth could see into his nostrils. "As a businessman. As the man who picks up the pieces." He snapped his head forward and stared at Elizabeth with obvious hostility. *"Madame Bovary?"* he said. *"Who* are we kidding?"

Elizabeth did not know what to say. Was this planned? A loyalty test? She shrugged, hoping that did not commit her either way.

"Elizabeth, Elizabeth, the man is sincere, don't get me wrong. I love him dearly."

Elliot's phone rang. He picked up the receiver, motioning for her to wait. He nodded, grunted once or twice. "The murders are *boring,* I told you that," he said.

Elizabeth tried to look intelligent and interested and comfortable, but she was hot with embarrassment.

"I love you dearly, you fuck. Just give me a cooler murder, maestro."

He hung up.

"Business," he said apologetically.

Elizabeth shifted. She was having trouble focusing on Elliot. She had not eaten and she was feeling faint and far away. She felt her belly was sticking out and wished she had not worn this shirt. She wondered if she would ever find her way home.

"I know this industry," he said. "I know the marketplace. I know your patron, too, Professor. I love him dearly, but the man is like a dog with a bone when he gets these 'literary' ideas, gnawing and slobbering all over them and then, what? Drops them in the dirt. Look, I'm just a businessman, but, whim or no whim, Larry Volfmann is a businessman, too, and movies are a business, and bad business is bad business. And Madame Bovary . . . who I love dearly, by the way . . ."

He held his palms out.

"You get my point?"

Elizabeth said, "I'm a little confused, actually."

"Need I say more?"

Greta was on her knees weeding when Elizabeth got home. Her daughter did not look sunny anymore. Greta stood up. "How was Mr. Wolfman?"

"Volfmann."

"Wolfman, Volfmann . . . Did you hit traffic?"

She put her hand on Elizabeth's cheek, leaving a smudge of dark, rich dirt, and wondered if this tall grown woman dressed in black who drove a car and plucked her eyebrows could really be her daughter, her little whining Elizabeth, her baby.

"Mom . . ."

Yes, she decided as Elizabeth wrinkled her face in an unattractive, hostile way. She could.

"Mom, I got a job. Then this asshole told me not to take it —"

"Volfmann?"

"No. The other one. Elliot King?"

"Oh! His mother is my client!"

"So that settled it —"

"His mother wanted a waterfall, totally wrong for the space, but I must admit the pergola really does look great —"

"So, I need an agent," Elizabeth said. "I'm supposed to write a screenplay." Then she smiled.

Greta was suddenly elated, and wondered, not for the first time, that the moods of her children were such powerful masters, causing her own moods to do their bidding so readily. She felt herself about to clap her hands in a show of excitement as she had done when Elizabeth was a child, but caught herself and pulled back before any damage was done. Elizabeth did not like being "infantilized," as she put it.

"I'm so proud of you, darling," Greta said, instead.

"God, you don't seem very excited," Elizabeth said, and headed for the kitchen, pouting.

Greta followed. Her son, Josh, now off in Alaska on a geological dig, had always been less talkative than Elizabeth, but his feelings were easier to read. Josh had been a cheerful boy, boisterous as a child, usually outside running or digging holes like a dog. Sometimes, he would come to his mother and say in a plaintive voice, with no explanation, "It's ridiculous." That's how she knew he was unhappy. It was a simple, direct communication, and she could then go about solving the problem. But Elizabeth had never been direct. Greta sometimes thought of her daughter as a ski slope in the Olympics, the ones full of moguls and poles with shimmering orange flags.

"Anyway," Elizabeth said, sitting at the table, "I'm suddenly a screenwriter. Can you believe it? I've been anointed. I've been plucked from the toilers of the academic field to write a movie. Every undergraduate's dream. It's bizarre. The guy is serious though and I kind of liked him, even if I'm just a whim . . ."

Greta watched the clouds gather over Elizabeth's mood.

". . . which I suppose I have to admit I am."

And Elizabeth's eyes narrowed. Then she sighed. Then she put her head down on the table. Then she picked her head up and looked at the ceiling.

"Elizabeth . . ."

"Oh, you don't understand."

Greta looked at her daughter's neck, the curve of it as Elizabeth gazed miserably at the ceiling, her whole posture a relic, perfectly preserved, of long ago, before every spelling test, every paper or exam. Elizabeth had been an absurdly earnest and conscientious student. My poor baby, Greta thought, and, she couldn't help it, she smiled.

Elizabeth caught the smile from the corner of her eye and her scowl focused on Greta.

"It's not that big a deal, Mom, okay?"

"Don't be such an ass," Greta said.

"He said it was his pet project," Elizabeth said. "People abandon pets. He'll send his limo to dump me and Madame Bovary by the side of the road. Or have his assistant drown us in a burlap bag. Then he'll buy himself some goldfish." She stood up and opened the refrigerator.

"Just enjoy the moment, darling," Greta said.

Elizabeth gave her a savage look. "Lots of brilliant people come to Hollywood and fail." She took an apple from the fridge and riffled through a newspaper that lay on the counter. The phone rang beside Elizabeth's elbow, but she seemed not to notice. "Like, say, Bertolt Brecht," she said.

"Goldfish," Greta said. "God, that reminds me. I have to get koi for that Ripley woman's fish pond." She reached past Elizabeth, picked up the phone, and heard her mother's voice, irate, no "hello."

"I can't get this screwy machine to work," Lotte said.

"Brilliant people," Elizabeth was saying, ducking under the curling telephone cord, throwing herself down on a kitchen chair and biting her nails. "And I'm not brilliant . . ."

"Goddamnit, everything is so complicated, they used to give you a switch. One switch. It went up, it went down . . ."

"Mama," Greta said into the phone, "what machine?"

"It went on, it went off . . ."

"The TV? The dishwasher?"

". . . or coming to Hollywood," Elizabeth said.

"Fine," Greta said, turning to Elizabeth. "Fail from New York! Who cares? . . . What machine?" she said again into the phone.

"Don't use that tone of voice with me," Lotte said. *"I may be old, but I'm still your mother . . ."*

"You're so supportive," Elizabeth said, pacing up and down the kitchen.

"Stop regressing!" Greta yelled at Elizabeth's back. "And don't you start with me," she added, into the phone.

Lotte began to cry. It was a terrible sound, high and unearthly and somehow unclean and unnatural, too, the howl of the wind on a moonless night, a bird of prey plummeting to its death, a wolf caught, squeezed without mercy by its bloodthirsty throat. Greta had heard it all her life, and she had never gotten used to it. It frightened and enraged her. It turned her stomach with terror and murderous rage. She dreaded that weeping, as exaggerated as Lucy Ricardo's, as loud as thunder, as eery as lightning.

"Mother, please, don't . . ."

"All the machines, the buttons . . ." Lotte was wailing. *"My own flesh and blood . . . It's inhuman, Hitler should have had to push so many buttons . . ."*

"What machine?" Greta said again, very calmly, very slowly, as she watched Elizabeth sit down again. Your mother is very old, she told herself. Very very old. Pretend she is a child. Just like your child, your highly competent, adult, big horse of a child sitting at the kitchen table biting her fingernails and spitting them on the floor. "Stop that!" she said to Elizabeth. No, no. Patient. Be patient with your child, as if she were a child. Be patient with your mother, as if she were a child. "Which machine is bothering you, Mama?"

"What?" Lotte said, the crying over, her voice back to normal. *"For God's sake, darling. I've got it. I'm not senile."*

Elizabeth went with her mother that afternoon to pick up Lotte for another doctor's appointment. In the face of death, she thought as they waited with Lotte in the examining room, what difference did it make if you wrote a screenplay? If a tenure was on track or not? If your three-year-old slept in your bed and you really didn't mind?

"Ultimately everything is meaningless," Elizabeth said.

"Don't be maudlin," her mother said.

"What?" said Lotte. "What did she say?"

"Nothing," said Elizabeth.

"Nothing," said Greta.

Lotte sat on the examining table. Elizabeth was leaning against the door. She felt it push against her and she stood back to let the doctor in. This was the third doctor they'd tried since she'd been in L.A.

"Well! Mrs. Franke!" said the doctor, yet another broad, tanned, unsmiling specialist with his headlight strapped to his forehead and a pair of reading glasses balanced on his nose.

Her grandmother looked white and bony beneath the blue paper gown. It crinkled noisily as she held out her arms, then surrendered to the metallic burst of Lotte's bracelets. "You're handsome," she said, shaking her finger at him, "for a butcher!"

The doctor smiled a thin smile. He began to examine the red spot by her left nostril.

"Does this hurt?"

"Hitler should have my pain."

He poked some more.

"The gangster," she said.

"Never even had a pimple," she added.

"Who? Hitler?"

"That dirty son of a bitch," she said.

"Me," she said finally when the doctor made no further response. "Me. I never had a pimple in my life. Not one. Look at this skin."

"That's what I'm doing, Mrs. Franke."

"Call me Lotte," Lotte said.

"Loosen up, Doc," Lotte said.

"Cheer up, what are you, Dr. Karoglian?" she said.

"Kevorkian," Elizabeth said.

The doctor, who had studiously been ignoring everything but his patient's tumor, turned to Greta and said, "Your mother is a pistol."

"Aha!" Lotte said. She smiled triumphantly. "You, Dr. Whatever-Your-Name-Is, said a mouthful."

* * *

It was almost six by the time they got home. Elizabeth clumped up the stone steps into her parents' house, a three-bears, wood-shingled sort of place nestled into a hill in the Rustic Canyon section of Santa Monica. Greta's elaborately designed garden billowed around Elizabeth as she climbed the steps and navigated the mossy path that led to the front door. Her mother designed gardens for a living, and her own garden, changing styles every few years, was now a carefully planned jumble of roses and heather and lavender.

"Through the moors and highlands, fells and dales, the downs, the heaths, the copses . . ." Elizabeth said.

"*Such* a vocabulary," said Grandma Lotte proudly.

Elizabeth left them and went out to the patio in the back. There were more steps, leading up the almost vertical hillside to the pool, and she heard Brett and Harry splashing and playing up there. Daffodils swayed in the breeze, hundreds of them. She was a little homesick for New York, there at Santa-Monica-on-Thames. The daffodils reminded her of springtime in Sands Point, Long Island, where she had grown up. But the smells were off. It still smelled so strange to her at her parents' California house, even though they'd lived there for more than ten years. Like an exotic desert spice cabinet, in spite of every British blossom her mother planted. The smell of one particular flower — she hadn't been able to locate the culprit yet — intruded now and then, a nauseous scent, like dog shit, wet dog shit, waiting to jump her when she least expected it.

She heard Brett coming down the stairs, singing "Yankee Doo-dle" to Harry.

"I'm a foreigner here," she said. "Even though I grew up here." She was sitting with her back to the stairs. She didn't get up or turn around. She liked that moment of uncertainty, not knowing exactly where they were, but knowing they were there.

"You didn't grow up here," Brett said. He was right behind her now. "Your parents moved here when you were in college."

Elizabeth felt his hand, cold and wet from the pool, on her neck. She reached back and held it. Something began tugging on her hair and Brett walked into view, holding Harry, whose hair was slicked to his head, his face shining, his wet eyelashes even darker and longer than usual. His fist was clamped around a lock of her hair, pulling it loose from the clip.

"Let go, Harry," Brett said. "I feel like a foreigner, too, sometimes."

"You are a foreigner."

Brett had grown up in South Africa. His father was an outspoken liberal there, a cancer researcher and university professor in Cape Town, and they had been forced to leave when Brett was eight. The family moved to Rochester, a cultural and climatic change that was reflected in Brett's accent, which shifted from the soft, sweetly off-kilter British accent of English-speaking South Africa to the flat, nasal tones of upstate New York, depending on which word he had learned in which place.

He had been Elizabeth's student, which was how she met him. Brett stood out from the other students not only because of his height but because he was so obviously older, a couple of years older than Elizabeth. His hair flopped down from a middle part and he kept jerking his head to the side, like a teenage girl, trying to get it out of his eyes. He'd had a goatee then, too, and had looked wonderfully poetic to Elizabeth. Even so, there was no reason for him to be attending a seminar called The Poetics of Adultery. He'd already gone through law school and worked for a year at a firm in New York when he decided to go back to school to get a graduate degree in philosophy. Elizabeth met him outside her classroom, where he sat on the floor, a disturbed look on his face, listening to a squawky news broadcast on a small radio.

"My father's uranium has been stolen!" he said, pointing at the radio.

Brett was not like anyone she'd ever met. His career was upside down. His accent was motley. His father's uranium had been stolen.

He wore a gray checked shirt and a pale-blue plaid tie. He had a long face and a narrow, prominent nose. His eyes were narrow, too, and dark. But his mouth, which was wide, and two deep dimples softened the sharpness and gave him a demeanor of distracted gentleness. Elizabeth fell instantly in love.

"Why are you taking my class, anyway?" she asked him some months into the relationship. "It's not required. It's not related to what you're doing. It's not even a graduate course."

She realized as she asked the question that she hoped he would say he had seen her, admired her from afar, and registered for the course in order to get to know her.

"Well, it's so early in the morning, your class. So it seemed prudent, didn't it?"

"It did?" Elizabeth said.

"In a getting-oneself-out-of-bed sort of way."

"But now you've got yourself into bed," Elizabeth said, indicating the rumpled sheets and pillows around them.

"Yes," Brett said. "It all came out right in the end."

Elizabeth remembered that day so well. Brett had suggested they get married. He had often suggested it since. And just as often she had suggested they wait.

"Let go, lightey," Brett said now to Harry. "You'll hurt Mommy."

Harry was shaking his head no. How did Harry know that what sounded like "lit go" when Brett said it had the same meaning as "let go" when Elizabeth said it? How the hell did he know what "lightey" meant? Children were very intelligent. He was three, skinny for a toddler, which she liked, though before he was born she admired only stocky, sturdy toddlers. She reached for him and stood him on her lap, wondering at the almost desperate surge of love, as if they had been apart for forty years rather than forty minutes.

"Brett," she said, pronouncing it "Brit."

Brett hated his name. "Shut up, won't you?" he said.

Elizabeth asked Harry if he needed to pee. He glared at her.

"Should we call Daddy 'Bob'?" she said.

Harry shook his head. He smiled from behind his pacifier. He pulled the pacifier out with a pop.

"No," he said. He plugged himself up again.

Elizabeth put her face against his cool forehead. She rather liked "Brett." A cowboy name. Harry's hair stuck to her lips. She drew in the damp scent of his little body, felt his curled hand pushed against her breast. She listened to him breathe.

She closed her eyes. She heard the birds, the dogs barking next door. She felt the cool air. God, she thought. There is a God after all.

"Don't cry, Mama," said a small voice.

Elizabeth opened her eyes.

"Sad?" he said. He offered her his pacifier.

"No, no." She wiped her eyes. "Mommy's having an epiphany."

When Greta came out and saw little Harry curled in Elizabeth's lap sucking on his pacifier, she thought how cute he looked, his cheek creased against his mother, his wet hair stuck to his forehead. His swim diaper was swollen with pool water. She suddenly remembered the soggy weight of Elizabeth's postnap diaper and the threatening furrow of her brow, like a dark storm cloud on the horizon.

Greta kissed Elizabeth on top of her head and pulled playfully at Harry's pacifier, as if it were the plug in the bathtub.

"It *doesn't* hurt their teeth," Elizabeth said.

"I haven't said a word."

"Good. Don't."

"Look at you, Elizabeth! You're curling your lip the way you used to when you were little," Greta said. She smiled at the memory, which for some reason comforted her. "I think pacifiers are cute, if you really want to know," she said. "Like Maggie Simpson."

"That's hardly the point," Elizabeth said.

"No, that's hardly the point." Greta sat across from Elizabeth and

Harry. Harry reached out for her, then crawled wordlessly across the low wooden table between them and settled in Greta's lap. Greta held him and remembered Elizabeth as a child so clearly it was confusing. Elizabeth's curly brown hair, her mouth round and talking at full speed or silent and extended in a determined pout, her manner ridiculously arrogant, her cheeks pink and vulnerable.

"What are we going to do?" Elizabeth said, tears coming to her eyes. "I feel so helpless." She reached across the table and took her mother's hand.

Such an unlikely combination, Greta thought. The misanthropic sentimentalist. Skeptical of the world at large, Elizabeth could nevertheless be foolishly, innocently, and thoroughly zealous toward the world up close. It struck Greta, not for the first time, that Elizabeth was a sort of inside-out version of her father. Tony was an exceptionally kind person, though it was necessary that the objects of his kindness be generalized, categorized, and named as part of some group, like "the Elderly" rather than his parents, or "Empty Nester" instead of his wife, or even "Awkward Adolescent" when that term fit Elizabeth and Josh. Groups of complete strangers were, of course, ideal. Tony had briefly succumbed to the lure of Mao in college, and he still retained a great compassion for and interest in the needs of the People. It was a shame, Greta thought, that he was so vague about any person in particular. Elizabeth, on the other hand, was as loyal as a dog to her friends and family, as wary as a dog toward the rest of the world.

"You're just like Daddy," Greta said, and Elizabeth looked so pleased that she did not have the heart to add, "in reverse."

For the next six months, Elizabeth flew back and forth to Los Angeles in a frantic shuttle that accomplished nothing, never did anyone any good, and still seemed vital. She met once with a young agent who was the nephew of one of her mother's clients and willing to sign up just about anybody, but most of the monthly visits were a simple attempt to help her mother out.

Now, sitting in her own living room, a long, dark rectangle with windows facing an air shaft, she dialed her grandmother's number, sure that Greta would be there as well. She always was. It was a bright, sunny day outside, but the room was so dark that Elizabeth could barely see the toys mounded like the banks of a river along the walls. Her mother answered Grandma Lotte's phone.

"Grandma's pretty good today," Greta said. "I just gave her a shower."

"A blessing," Elizabeth heard Lotte say in the background.

"What about you, Mom?" Elizabeth said. "You're exhausted."

"How's Harry?"

"You can't keep running over there every five minutes, sleeping on Grandma's couch, cooking for her and for Dad . . . And you're working, too . . ."

"What am I supposed to do?" Greta said. "Grandma has to eat, she needs to shower . . ." Then her tone changed abruptly from a tense and defensive rumble to a tight, higher-pitched sound of controlled, straining rage. "Mother, I told you before," she was saying to Lotte, "the pills are lined up on the dining-room table. In order. Look. See? You check off the box on the pad when you've taken it. . . . No, you will not die of liver disease because you took your Tylenol twenty minutes early . . . Yes, I will fix your lunch as soon as I'm off the phone with Elizabeth . . ."

"Mom? Hire someone?" Elizabeth said, as she always did.

"Easier said than done," Greta said, as she always did.

"I want Jell-O," Grandma said.

"It's like having a two-year-old," Greta said into the phone to Elizabeth.

"I'm three," Harry said. He had picked up the extension in the bedroom.

"Yes. You're Grandma's big, good boy."

Elizabeth was glad she could bestow solace in the form of Harry, because her mother would accept little else. Whenever Elizabeth went out there, she of course took Harry with her. Greta was so happy to see him that she seemed to cling to him, pressing her cheek against his head the way she still did with Elizabeth sometimes, so perhaps the trips really were restorative in some way. Her mother was not feeling well, rushing to the bathroom every minute with nervous diarrhea, but when Elizabeth offered to take Grandma to the doctor or to spend a night with her or to cook her a special dinner, or even to heat up a can of soup for her, Greta would agree gratefully, then insist on coming along and doing it all herself.

"Poor Elizabeth," she would say, doing all the work Elizabeth was supposed to take off her shoulders. "You've got Harry to look after."

"What about Brett?" Elizabeth said on one occasion when Brett had come with them.

"Yes, you've got him to look after, too."

"Mom, that's not what I meant."

two

It was late February, and Elizabeth stared at the Christmas tree in the living room, which was somehow still standing in the corner, a sad, desiccated betrayal of her ancestors as well as a fire hazard. The phone startled her.

"Mommy has to go in for a test," her father said. He rarely called Greta "Mommy" to the children anymore, though Elizabeth and Josh called their mother "Mommy" far more often than one might have expected from two adults.

"You do?" Elizabeth said. She assumed her mother was on another extension. Elizabeth tried to call them only when she thought one or the other might be out, though there was nothing she could do when they were the callers. She hated it when both of them were on the phone. It was like talking to neither one. Her words were projected into uncertainty, into thin air.

"I do," Greta replied from the ether.

Elizabeth had no idea what they were talking about. Was her mother becoming a real-estate agent or something? Did she need to renew her driver's license?

"Don't worry," Tony said.

"It's nothing," Greta said. "I told him we didn't have to call you. I told you not to call, Tony."

"She has a right to know."

"There's nothing to know," Greta said in a sharp voice. "That's why they do a test. If we knew, we wouldn't have to do a test, would we?" Then she began to cry.

"Right, yes, that's right," Tony said. His voice was soft, soothing. "To rule it out," he said. "Just to rule it out."

Gradually, Elizabeth was able to ascertain that her mother had a lump. Elizabeth listened to them discuss the lump (in her colon), the test (to rule things out), and the timing (as soon as possible). Their voices, joined together in their customary telephone duet, seemed even farther away than usual — one strange, garbled, disconsolate articulation.

~

The night before she was to fly out to be there for the biopsy, Brett held Elizabeth as she fell asleep, her cheek sweaty and crumpled against his chest.

"Imagine hearing that your mother might have cancer and responding with an overwhelming sense of crankiness," she said. She was ashamed.

He kissed her forehead. "You're not cranky," he murmured. "You're angry. And why not?"

She felt his lips, still pressed lightly against her skin, shift into the faintest of smiles, a smile she knew well — his modest (for he was modest) but honest (for he was that, too) appreciation of his own easy temperament, his good humor. Elizabeth knew she gave him too many opportunities to display his patience. Perhaps it was one of the things he liked about her. She hoped so, hoped his amused forbearance would not wear out before she could morph into a more balanced, even-tempered sort of person, something she was always aspiring and planning and attempting to do.

"Thank you," she said. She held on to him. He was wearing pajamas, one of his quaint customs. She had never known a man who wore pajamas, not even her father, who wore boxer shorts to bed. She buried her face in the clean, starchy smell of the pajamas.

"I love you and your pajamas," she said.

"I love you and yours," he said, stroking her naked body beneath the sheet.

Elizabeth welcomed the surge of desire, an enormous wave of physical emotion. She smiled at the image of a wave, imagining a tidal wave with pickup trucks and mobile homes and shacks on its foaming crest.

"Thank you," she said again, pulling him against her.

He kissed her throat. "You're very, very welcome," he said, his voice soft and husky and muffled.

Later, rolling away from him, she said, "You're making me sweat," though he was already asleep. She listened to his breathing. She heard the familiar gurgling with each exhale. It sounded almost like speech. She tried to synchronize her own shallow, rabbity breaths to his.

She flew out to L.A. the next morning and took a taxi to the hospital. She sat for hours with her father waiting for the verdict, sure that the tumor would be benign and certain that it would not. Her father was wearing his white lab coat with his name stitched across the left breast pocket, like a bowler or a gas-station attendant or a security guard. Or a doctor. His ID was clipped to his lapel. DR. ANTHONY BERNARD.

Elizabeth wondered disloyally why Dr. Anthony Bernard had

not noticed the lump on Mrs. Dr. Anthony Bernard, had not wondered about the stomach cramps and the diarrhea. Of course, he
rarely saw patients anymore. He had left the bedside to become an
impassioned and brilliant fund-raiser for his hospital. Admirable,
Elizabeth thought. But a lump is a lump.

"She'll be all right," she said, as if that would relieve him of the
guilt she had just assigned him, or relieve her of the guilt of as-
signing it. "Don't worry, Daddy."

He took her hand and kissed it. His lips were chapped. She dug
in her bag for lip balm and handed it to him. In his white coat, he
looked particularly helpless to her, as if the coat, labeled in black
stitched script, were the real Dr. Anthony Bernard.

They called Josh in Alaska when they got back to the house, and
surprisingly he was at the base camp. He was four years younger
than Elizabeth. He loved rocks and was so happy among them that
Elizabeth suspected they loved him back.

"It's malignant," she said. "It's stage C."

There was silence on the other end.

"It's encapsulated, though," she said. She repeated it. "Encapsulated." Encapsulated was good.

Her father was pacing up and down the house. He kept bumping his shin on the same sharp point of the coffee table. "Shit," he
said, each time, back and forth. "Shit."

Elizabeth couldn't breathe. Her father had said "shit." Her throat
had grown smaller and smaller. Her father never said words like
"shit." Funny. How could a throat shrink? How could her father
say "shit"? She realized that now that her throat was shrinking,
she could not swallow through such a narrow passageway. And
how was the air to get from her nose to her lungs, her lungs to her
mouth?

"I'll be down tomorrow," Josh was saying. "Tomorrow morning.
As soon as I can get there." Elizabeth had forgotten she was on the
phone. She handed it to her father.

"Z-z-z . . ." she said.

"What?" her father said. "Jesus, you're white."

"Z-z-a-a . . ." she tried again. She pointed to her throat. She felt her eyes widening until they hurt. "Z-z! Z-z!"

"Josh? Call you back. I think Elizabeth wants a Xanax."

It was afternoon by the time Josh arrived at the house the next day. Elizabeth sat at the top of the steps waiting for him. Harry had fallen asleep under the coffee table in the living room and she just left him there. She kept the front door open and sat on the top step and crushed lavender between her fingers and breathed in the sickeningly powerful perfume and waited for Josh. Then, there he was, getting out of a cab, and she wondered why she hadn't gone to the airport to get him. She waved and stood up and watched him make his way up the stone garden path past the fat, blowsy roses. His skin was dark with sun and wind and, for all she knew, dirt. He had shaved his head before heading out into the field, and now, three months' grown out, his hair stuck up in shaggy tufts. He caught sight of her and ran easily up the steps, grabbed her around the waist, put his face against hers, and burst into tears.

They wept, holding each other, for so long . . . or was it? How long? Half an hour? Three minutes? Elizabeth had no idea. She held on to Josh. He was sturdy and had the big, comfortable hands and feet of a puppy. He was the only one who could understand. The only other one. Greta was their mother. No one else's. Josh called Elizabeth by her childhood nickname, Tizzie, and he patted her back as she patted his.

"Poor Mommy," Josh said. "Poor Mom."

"Poor Mommy," Elizabeth repeated. They meant it. But what they both also meant, and knew they meant, was: Poor us. Poor Josh, poor Elizabeth.

"She'll be okay," Elizabeth said.

"I know," Josh said. "Of course she will."

And they believed this, too. Because, Elizabeth realized, it was inconceivable that she would not.

~

In the early morning, the fog hovered as low as the rosebushes. It was Greta's happiest time. The raggedy city had disappeared into a softened, silver light. She could sit on her steps in front of the door and drink her coffee in peace. Greta liked to be alone. It was only when she was alone that she forgot to be lonely. Everything around her, the dewy flowers, the grit beneath her feet, seemed perfectly articulated and beautifully balanced, with her own body as one more balanced, articulated part of the morning. This hour in semi-darkness was the only time she had for herself. Or maybe it was the only time she liked for herself. These were surplus hours, the hours no one else wanted. She could claim them in good conscience, knowing she wasn't depriving anyone of anything.

Tony was still asleep. Josh had moved back into his old room, and he was sleeping, too. Elizabeth had gone back to New York with little Harry, and even they, in a time zone that put them three hours later, might still be in bed. Lotte certainly would be asleep now. She had always been a late sleeper, claiming the habit as a casualty of her days in the theater. Greta remembered sitting on the threshold of her parents' room watching her mother sleep, her face distorted, smashed into the mattress, her arm hanging off the bed like the arm of a dead person. Greta would stare and stare at the motionless body until she had convinced herself that her mother was dead. Then she would start to cry, to wail, and Lotte would awaken from death with a start and comfort her hysterical daughter.

But that probably won't work this time, Greta thought. For either of us.

~

Back in New York, Elizabeth taught her classes and worried. She put Larry Volfmann and the movie version of *Madame Bovary* out of her head, partly because the distant drama of her mother's and grandmother's struggles, the day-to-day pleasures of Harry and Brett, and even the demands, delights, and frustrations of her students took up whatever room there was. But also because, after her visit with Volfmann and Elliot King, after finding the young agent who was the nephew of one of her mother's clients and willing to sign up just about anybody, she'd heard nothing more about it for months.

Then one day in April, as the daffodils were blooming in the park, Elizabeth got a call from her new, young, undiscriminating agent saying, with unconcealed surprise, that Larry Volfmann really did want to sign her up to write a screenplay and had offered a reasonable amount of money, which to Elizabeth sounded like a completely unreasonable amount of money, coming to three times her salary as an assistant professor.

"What should we do?" she asked Brett.

"I think we should celebrate with a bottle of champagne," Brett said.

They put Harry to bed and ordered in sushi and broke out a bottle of Veuve Clicquot '95 that Brett had been given as a thirtieth birthday present. It had been in the refrigerator for three years. They sat on the couch and ate off of trays, as if they were watching television, but they didn't put the television on. Elizabeth was glad to be next to Brett, to feel his thigh against hers.

"Does champagne really go with sushi?" she said.

"I think we should talk about moving out there, Elizabeth," Brett said. "At least temporarily."

"I guess champagne goes with everything."

"You love movies and you hate teaching," he said. "What does this suggest to you? And it doesn't matter to me."

"Everyone loves movies."

"Then perhaps everyone should shake the chalk dust from their shoes and head west." Brett kissed her cheek. "And I can work from home there as easily as I can work from home here. At least you won't be flying back and forth every minute."

How could he suggest such a thing? Just pack up and leave their home? Their overcrowded, overheated, overpriced apartment? Their friends? The ones she neglected now that Harry was around, those friends?

"You know I'm right about this," he said.

"Just tie the mattress to the roof and drive west?" She wondered what it was like to be so calm and so generous. Was it glorious? Or was it a monstrous burden?

"And we can get married," Brett said.

Elizabeth did not comment. They had had this conversation before. She supposed they would have it again. Her friends, who always said they wanted to get married and yet never did, could not understand her reticence. Neither could she.

"You don't have a child yet," she would say to them, as if that explained it.

"To you," Brett said, raising his glass. "To Elizabeth in Hollywood, long may she reign."

They polished off the bottle quickly. But Elizabeth found it difficult to eat anything at all.

"Can I have your salmon?" Brett said. His chopsticks were poised over her plate.

"I would be close to my family," she said. "They need me."

But the idea, at that moment, sickened her. She could almost smell her grandmother's cold cream, taste the lipstick her mother left behind on the rim of a glass of ice tea. Her father's feet, one toenail longer than the others, rose, enormous, in her imagination. To all this would be added bedpans, phlegm, sweat-soaked sheets, stiff limbs from which pale, wrinkled, dry flesh hung uncertainly. One oughtn't be one's brother's keeper. Or one's mother's. Certainly not one's grandmother's. Surely that was what the Bible meant.

"My mother," she said. My mother might die. What would Elizabeth do without her mother? What does anyone do? It was unimaginable. She felt suddenly greedy for her mother, a desperate acquisitive need for Greta. She could hear Greta's laugh, a loud caw, and she could see her gold inlays sparkling in the California sun as Greta tilted her head back, her mouth open, and laughed and laughed.

∼

They moved to Los Angeles as soon as the term ended in May.

"I hope you're not doing this for me," Greta said when Elizabeth called to tell them. "I don't want you to make that sacrifice."

"God forbid anyone should make a sacrifice for you, Mom. No, I'm not doing this for you. Relax. This is for work."

Of course I'm doing it for you, you idiot.

"It's for her work," said Elizabeth's father, on another extension as usual. He was emphatic.

"I can still hear, Tony," said Greta.

"I told you before, it was for her work," Tony said.

"I'm not deaf and I'm not senile."

"Work. I told you before."

Elizabeth waited until they were done. She could tell her mother was not completely convinced. But she could also tell that her mother had decided she didn't need to be completely convinced.

"Well!" Greta said. "Truthfully? I'm so glad you're coming. So glad," she repeated, her voice drifting into a weak near whisper that Elizabeth had never heard before. "My little girl. My sweet Elizabeth . . ."

Was she crying?

"Elizabeth can help you, can't you, honey?" Elizabeth's father said.

"She doesn't have to take care of me —" Greta said, indignant now.

"With Lotte. She can help you with Lotte."

"Yes," said Greta. "Right. Grandma will be so happy to have you here. And Harry! We'll have Harry all the time!" She paused. "Just don't worry about me, sweetie." Another uncomfortable pause. "There's nothing to worry about, anyway."

"Of course there's nothing to worry about," Tony said. Too fast, Daddy, Elizabeth thought. You agreed too fast.

"I can look after myself," Greta said. "You come and concentrate on your work."

You're my work, Elizabeth thought. You. You will be my work.

In her bedroom, Lotte leaned against the pillows and watched the girl exit. A nice girl, although she was so tiny. Practically a midget. And with that big ass on her . . .

"Maria!"

The girl turned around, holding Lotte's breakfast tray.

"Yes, Mrs. Franke?"

"Maria, you must lose a little weight if you ever want to find a man."

Lotte watched Maria blush. Silly young woman.

"Honestly, Maria! Don't be a goose. I speak my mind!"

"But, Mrs. Franke . . ."

"I have a lot of experience, my dear."

Maria said, "But, Mrs. Franke, I have husband!"

Lotte surveyed Maria. Well then, she thought.

"You better lose that behind to keep him!" she said.

Maria giggled and left the room. Lotte hated having her here. On principle. It was one thing to have a housekeeper to tidy up and vacuum, to keep house. It was another to have a nursemaid, a housekeeper who was really a keeper, as if Lotte were an animal in the zoo.

"I'm very lucky, my dear," Lotte called after her. "Very lucky to have you!"

True, absolutely true, Lotte thought. Fat ass or no, Maria was sweet and quiet and she made the smoothest, most delicious Cream of Wheat.

"But, Maria, darling, I'm afraid I just can't afford an attendant right now. You're a lovely girl. I'll miss you."

Maria returned to the doorway. She looked baffled.

"But Mrs. Greta, she pay me already. Don't worry about nothing, I take care of you."

She came to the bed and took Lotte's hand in hers. She smiled, encouragingly, soothingly. Sad, stunted little dwarf, Lotte thought. Trying so hard. It was a shame Maria should have to go through this. Greta should have thought before exposing a poor, desperate immigrant to such disappointment and embarrassment.

"You're very sweet," Lotte said. She pulled back her hand. "You will kindly leave at once."

By the time Elizabeth arrived at her apartment, Lotte had showered and dressed. She hadn't fallen in the shower, a point of considerable pride, but the effort had been tremendous. Each step, each turn had involved a slow, concentrated physical attention, as if she were dancing in slow motion. Pulling on her girdle had been even worse. Greta sometimes teased her about wearing a girdle. Lotte barely heard her when she did. The girdle was simply a part of her day. Like brushing her teeth. Or eating. But today, she could almost hear Greta's voice: "Don't forget your truss, Mother!"

Lotte couldn't bend enough to reach down to her feet to pull it on, so she had dropped the corset on the floor in front of the chair she sat in. Then she reached out her feet and slid her toes in. But then the girdle just lay there, motionless around her ankles. She couldn't reach it. She stared at it awhile, a dingy, white elastic object that just then reminded her of calamari, which she loathed. What if Elizabeth arrived and found her this way? Staring at an inert girdle on a shag rug?

Lotte closed her eyes. *Knees! Knees! Knees! Knees! Movin' up and down again. . . . Don't you dare to frown again. . . .*

She opened her eyes. It is a curse to grow old, she thought. She looked around. A box of Kleenex. Bottles of pills. An empty glass. The remote control for the television, it should rot in hell with all its buttons, who could manipulate such a contraption? Her cane. She reached for the cane, hooked the handle into the girdle, and pulled it within reach.

"Everything but my shoes and stockings," she said when Elizabeth arrived with Harry.

Elizabeth bent down and pulled socks onto Lotte's feet, slipped her shoes on, tied them.

"I got them from a catalog. Kenneth Cole."

Harry was hugging one ankle. If only Morris had lived long enough to meet his great-grandson.

"Grandma's pretty shoes," Harry said, stroking her shoe as if it were a pet.

"Only three years in America and listen to him!" Lotte said.

"They're not bad, not bad, Grandma. *Très chic.*"

"You have taste, Elizabeth. Look what a wonderful little boy you produced."

As Elizabeth held Harry up so Lotte could kiss him, Lotte noticed Elizabeth's shoes, rather clunky affairs, but fashionable, and nodded her approval. And that Harry! He was magnificent. Brilliant. End up a professor like his mother. A Ph.D., no money, too many opinions. She grabbed Harry's face and pushed her lips against his cheek, over and over.

"Driving me nuts," Harry seemed to say. He wiped the kiss from his cheek in a manner Elizabeth recognized.

"Where's Maria?" Elizabeth asked. "Late lunch?"

"Maria? It has nothing to do with me, dear," Lotte said. "Nothing at all."

Elizabeth made dinner for her grandmother, called her mother with the news of Maria's departure, called Brett to tell him they would be late, undressed her grandmother, helped her into her nightgown, then tucked her into bed. She was exhausted and wondered how her mother could stand it. It seemed as though she'd been with Lotte for months, not hours. I'm sorry, Grandma, she thought. I don't mean to be disloyal. You can't help it if you're old. Old and selfish and stubborn. And a wave of love for Lotte brought tears to her eyes, tears of irritation and tenderness, the familiar poles of family feeling, wrenching and urgent. Thank God I'm here to help, she thought, and then, the next minute, Why didn't I stay safe in my apartment in New York?

Instead, here she was, driving to her new home in her new car. The car had been an embarrassment for both Elizabeth and Brett. They laughed at how self-conscious they were about their choice. But they admitted to each other, late one night, as if confessing an unusual sexual desire, that it mattered.

"What tools we are," Brett said.

Elizabeth thought of her essay on *Madame Bovary*. Brand names have replaced the cliché, she had written, as the instrument of banality.

"Slaves," she said. "We're slaves."

Then, full of excitement, the slaves discussed what kind of car they would get. Not the academic's customary secondhand Volvo station wagon, though they reread Stanley Fish's essay "The Unbearable Ugliness of Volvos" for the occasion. The Volvo was a safe car, which suggested they were responsible people and caring parents; it was expensive, which showed they were doing quite well; secondhand signified they were still of the people; Volvo meant East Coast and superior, understated taste; and the choice of a station wagon indicated they needed to cart stuff around but were not willing to be sucked into the gas-guzzling SUV rage. But Brett *wanted* an SUV, and Elizabeth wanted a *new* car, and neither of them actually liked the big, boatlike Volvo station wagon they test-drove, so they leased a Subaru Forester instead.

Where to live in L.A. had been easier than what to drive. They rented a little house in Venice Beach, just a few minutes from Greta and Tony's house in Santa Monica. The real-estate agent called it a bungalow. Elizabeth liked the sound of the word "bungalow." It was a bona fide Arts and Crafts bungalow, the agent said, which gave the house some architectural panache. It also gave it lower ceilings and smaller windows than they would have liked. On the other hand, the beautiful, rather wild-looking garden in front was cool and refreshing. Arts and Crafts bungalow, said the real-estate agent. And Elizabeth and Brett moved into a house with its very own brand name.

"A brand name," Brett had said. "It's a sign."

Elizabeth drove up the alley behind the house and asked Harry if he wanted to press the clicker to open the gate, but he was asleep. She carried him inside and handed him, wordlessly, to Brett, and got herself a beer from the refrigerator. The phone rang.

"Sweetheart? Did I take my pills?"

"Yes, Grandma."

"You didn't write it down."

"I'm sorry."

"You have to write it down. That's our system."

∿

Greta crouched in the dirt of her garden. None of her neighbors were awake. No one would notice her. She was getting up earlier and earlier. The light was just spreading itself thinly through the trees. She checked her PalmPilot for the dates of Lotte's doctors' appointments. She checked her own doctors' appointments. She wondered how on earth she would be able to keep track of so many oncologists, dermatologists, radiologists, surgeons, gastroenterologists, gerontologists . . . Then she felt the heat of sickening shame and wondered how she had managed not to see a doctor until she had a huge malignant lump. She hated to go to the doctor, that's how. Being married to one ought to have been enough.

Tony would rumble out of bed soon wondering what was for breakfast. Greta never understood why he had to ask this question each and every morning since he made his own breakfast and it was always toast with low-fat cottage cheese. Well, sometimes they had bagels around. Or low-fat cream cheese. Maybe that's what he meant. Then he would read the newspaper, where he would discover what would become his Topic of the Day. He didn't realize he had a Topic of the Day (unless, during an argument, Greta ungraciously pointed it out to him). And he was able to speak with considerable intelligence on any number of topics. But he had a habit of pouncing, as Greta saw it, on one hapless victim each day, and then parading it around, like a terrier with a rat between its jaws, waving it, shaking it at everyone he met, even after its neck had long been broken. One day it would be the Middle East, another Latin America. Sometimes the Economy, others the Electoral College, SATs, Oprah, Oil, Automotive Safety. Tony was interested in everything and gave everything its day in his court. Greta had never read the paper very carefully. She lacked "curiosity," according to Tony, and perhaps he was right. But now, especially, his energy and obsessive attention to the worries of the world exhausted her.

She wondered when Elizabeth would show up today. She came by practically every day. Elizabeth had become relentlessly considerate. It frightened Greta, emphasizing the gravity of her condition, and it moved her.

Later, when she went in to sit with Tony over coffee, he read the *Wall Street Journal*. The stock market appeared to be today's Topic.

"It's like the weather," she said. "You have no control over it. The forecast is never accurate. It's crucial and meaningless at the same time . . . and you never invest anything anyway."

"There are real opportunities in the technology arena," he said, his voice warm and loud with pleasure, with almost boyish excitement. "Yes, it's true, the NASDAQ reflects the realization of just how overvalued technology stocks were in the high-flying nineties . . ." This is my first break after my first six weeks of chemotherapy, she thought. ". . . and true, I know, I agree that within the rarefied atmosphere of the tech bubble . . ."

She was so relieved that she still had hair.

"Even so, there is every indication that the well-managed global information and communications companies will grow as these huge new markets open up . . ."

She'd slept in a nauseated stupor for three days each week after watching all those chemicals drip into her arm, but she was beginning to feel a little better today.

"I mean, the Developing Nations are *hungry* for information," Tony said. "Don't you think?"

"I have to go to my mother's," she said.

Tony put the paper down.

"Don't say 'take it easy,' *please*," she said.

"Sorry."

Greta shrugged. She sipped some coffee. It took some of the metallic taste away. She couldn't stand water anymore. And it used to taste so good. Bottled water of course. God knows what was in tap water. You could get cancer from tap water. She wondered if she would die. Everyone dies, she reminded herself. But will *I?*

"Do you really have to go?" Tony was saying.

Greta was still trying to finish up the last few jobs she had started. Soon she could stop work completely until she was better. Would she get better? They spoke of five-year survival rates. And even the odds for that were not what one would hope.

"You won't be able to keep this from your mother forever," Tony said.

"Watch me." Why should her mother spend her last months worrying about Greta's last months?

He made a sound that fell somewhere between a laugh and a sigh.

"I have to interview the new companion," she said. "Then I'll come right home." She had noticed that she was required to justify her behavior these days; every outing, every move. As if she were a child. People tried to make things easier, she knew. But they were not very good at it. Yet. Perhaps they would improve with practice.

Her mother was probably thinking exactly the same thing.

"I hope to God this one works out," she said. "She's a little older, anyway. Someone Mother can talk to. In English."

Tony folded the paper, took a breath. She waited for the lecture: take it easy; don't be so hard on yourself; it's okay to be scared. "Just don't . . ."

"Overdo it?"

"Sorry again." Tony took off his reading glasses and rubbed his eyes. He looked annoyed.

"I won't," Greta said, to comfort him.

Dr. Charles Bovary . . . Dr. Charles Bovaine . . . Dr. Chuck Bovaine . . .

Chuck? Good God. She might as well call Charles Bovary "Brett."

Poor Chuck. Fasten your seat belt, Chuck. Emma's comin' round the mountain, Chuck. She's comin' to git you. She's comin' to marry you, Chuck, she's comin' to destroy you. You best be gettin' outta town, I'm thinkin', Chuck.

Poor stupid, clumsy Chuck doesn't see what's coming, doesn't see what's in front of his nose. Chuck has no imagination. Emma has only imagination. Emma doesn't see what's in front of her either.

If having an imagination means imagining all the things you don't have — imagining, in fact, the impossibility of your own happiness — is an imagination a good thing? Emma Bovary imagined herself into two affairs, ruinous debt, and an appalling, agonizing, bile-soaked suicide. Elizabeth thought with longing of that other Emma, bossy but decent, self-deluded but not self-involved. Jane Austen's Emma, clean and witty and dry. But Emma Bovary? Extravagant, desperate, humid Emma Bovary?

See them clouds, Chuck? Storm's a brewin'.

Elizabeth played around with the screenwriting program. It had so many features. It was the program that had suggested the name Chuck. All you had to do was type in a few letters and it offered alternatives. Chip. Chester. Charlemagne.

She left the attic office and passed a tranquil, napping Harry in his bed. Brett was glued to his computer in their bedroom. He had worked at home for the last two years. After graduate school, he taught for a year, hated it, and started a consulting firm that followed and evaluated the impact of every law passed in every state, every regulation in every agency, that might affect the various nonprofit organizations who became his clients. Brett was the whole firm. He had an impressive business address at Rockefeller Center, though anyone arriving there would find only a mailbox.

"Piecework," Lotte said once, when Brett's business was explained to her. "My Morris's mother took in piecework."

Elizabeth liked having him around all the time, especially now.

They had more room than they'd had in New York, and she could leave Harry at a moment's notice if she had to. But mostly she just liked knowing he was there. They had lunch together, they brought each other cups of coffee.

"Coffee?" Elizabeth asked him.

He shook his head no and waved, a combination "hello, thank-you, stop-talking-to-me-I'm-thinking, go-away" wave, without turning from the screen.

In the kitchen, Elizabeth spooned out coffee for herself, lost for a moment in its scent. Coffee and ginger ale were all Greta could drink now. Elizabeth went with her to the chemotherapy sessions. They were less frightening than either of them had imagined. For one thing, they took place in the doctor's office, not the hospital. Elizabeth would sit in the waiting room reading *Travel and Leisure*. Greta would come out twenty minutes later. It was just a drip, she said, and it didn't hurt. Afterward, though, everything tasted like aluminum foil, she was queasy, and the fatigue was as heavy as death itself.

"They give you poison," Greta said. "Odd, isn't it?"

Outside, a dog barked. A little propeller plane from Santa Monica Airport buzzed overhead. The house faced a small walkway. In the back, there was an alley for cars. In 1900, Venice had been planned as a vacation spot for middle-class Los Angeles city dwellers, a series of summer cottages at the beach built around canals. A lovely idea, Elizabeth thought. Canals and walk streets. The walk street in front of her house was lined on either side by the front gardens of pretty little bungalows. If it weren't for Harry, who treated the walkway as his own, rolling toy trucks up and down, she wasn't sure if she would ever go out there, since she was always driving up the alley to park in the back, and coming into the house through the back door. She wondered if any of her neighbors ever saw their front gardens.

There was no traffic noise, not even Harry's simulated engine roars, which meant that from the kitchen Elizabeth could hear the old men (it must have been their beagle who'd been barking) next door talking by the open window of their kitchen. They were identical twins in their eighties and often sat on their porch wearing matching green caps that said SKIDMORE BASKETBALL.

"Beautiful girl," one said.

"That Cher," said the other.

Elizabeth heard Harry singing in his bed, waking up from his nap, a nap he would soon have to abandon altogether as he started out on life's narrow rocky path at nursery school. He sang with his pacifier in his mouth. He would have to give that up, too, she supposed.

Harry stopped singing. She heard a shuffling. He appeared in the doorway.

"I'm a cat," he said, and began making hideous high-pitched squealing noises.

"Why are you screeching, kitty?"

"I can't answer," he said.

"Why not?"

"Cats don't talk."

He ran to the television and turned it on.

"Tommy!" he cried, pointing at a cartoon baby.

Tracy? Britny? Barbie?

Barbie, Elizabeth thought. I will name her Barbie. A brand name. An icon among brand names. A brand name with a wardrobe. Barbie the pilot, the bathing beauty, Olympic skater, equestrian, career gal, African American. Nobody could say Barbie lacked imagination.

Harry wanted an apple. Harry lined up his blocks on the floor. Harry had cities to build. Which meant Elizabeth had cities to build, too. Her workday was over. Her workday was just beginning.

She sat on the floor with Harry, who was intent, his vision as grand as Robert Moses's.

"That's great, sweetie," she said periodically, reaching out to steady a tower. Barbie and Chuck, she thought. Poor Flaubert. Chuck, a chiropractor, rushes off to his office late one night. He has to perform an emergency adjustment on a burly, prosperous ex-hippie microbrewer! The brewer's beautiful daughter drives her father to the dedicated chiropractor! Dad is bent over in pain! She helps him, in all his tormented bulk, into the office! But, *mon dieu!* She is very beautiful, this daughter!

Elizabeth picked up her mug from the coffee table. Beautiful in which way? she wondered. A drop rolled down the side of the mug onto her pants. Beautiful how? Elizabeth would have to decide, and she was not used to dispensing beauty, only interpreting it. Should Barbie Bovaine possess the dark-eyed mysterious beauty Flaubert gives Emma Bovary? Or the blond, blue-eyed prettiness favored by Americans? Perhaps she is stylish and cosmopolitan and dark, but lives in a blond, robust, homespun town? Yes. Dark hair, black hair. Swollen lips, like a model. Which she bites, like Emma Bovary. And beautiful white fingernails, like Emma. Small, lovely feet. No heroine within spitting distance of Emma Bovary could have anything but small, lovely feet.

Elizabeth rubbed one of her own feet against her other ankle. Sandpaper. A wide swathe of sandpaper. That was Elizabeth's foot.

She listened to the construction noises of a neighborhood on the way up. The house was oddly cool, not at all what she had expected. Even the attic. Two shimmering green parrots sat on a telephone wire. A flock of them lived in the palm tree next door, the progeny of pets who had escaped.

"The Way Madame Bovary Lives Now: Tragedy, Farce, and Cliché in the Age of Ikea." It wasn't a bad paper. She had an old college friend who was an editor at *Tikkun* and desperate for last-minute copy.

"Some piece on peace has dropped out, I wonder why, don't you have something, anything, in a drawer?"

Elizabeth had just finished this paper, and though *Tikkun* was not a suitable academic journal and would not help her get tenure, she was not sure she was a suitable academic or that she really wanted tenure.

Is adultery tragedy? Or is it farce? Was that the part of the paper that interested Volfmann? Perhaps he had liked the part about cliché. The word "cliché" originally described a metal plate that clicked and reproduced the same image, over and over, mechanically. Elizabeth flipped through Flaubert's collection of clichés, *The Dictionary of Accepted Ideas,* looking for inspiration. But most of the entries did not translate well, more because of the passing of time than the shift to English. Rather than a dictionary of familiar clichés, it read like the historical document it had become. What remained fresh and clear were not the expressions themselves but the forms used to express the clichés. These were timeless. The knowingness and importance of tone that was merged with the emptiness of the information — the portentous commonplace — this was instantly recognizable. "**Horizons.** Find them beautiful in nature, dark in politics; **Enthusiasm.** Called forth exclusively by the return of Napoleon's ashes. Always indescribable: the newspaper takes two columns to tell you so."

But the very idea of cliché, the repetition of machinery in a printing press, the horror at repetition, had become itself a cliché.

"I don't want *The Man in the Grey Flannel Suit,*" Volfmann had said. "I want cutting-edge banality."

"So . . . a farce . . ."

"I don't know," Volfmann said, shaking his head. "Cutting-edge banality seems like tragedy to me."

Elizabeth didn't know what to make of Volfmann. He talked about the bottom line and demographics and grosses. He was crude and yelled at people on the phone. But he was smarter than she was. She saw that right away. And she wondered if that made her like him more, or less. Because she did like him.

She suddenly remembered him closing his eyes, just for a moment, as he listened to someone on the phone. When he opened them, he'd looked right at her, caught her watching him, and she had blushed.

Farce, farce, tragedy, tragedy, squawk, squawk. One parrot seemed to be raping another parrot. The coffee was no longer hot. Her mother had colon cancer. Her grandmother had skin cancer. Adultery was neither tragedy nor farce. It was simple self-indulgence. Madame Bovary was an ass.

She went into the bathroom, turned on the water, and leaned her forehead against the cool tile.

"Madame Bovary is an ass," she said to Brett at dinner.

"A piece of ass," he said.

"Why can't people be content . . ." she said.

"Ass is a donkey," Harry said. "Grandma said."

". . . and appreciate what they have?"

Brett sighed. She saw his foot tapping.

"Am I boring you?" she said. She felt the blood rising to her cheeks as it always did when she was even the slightest bit emotional.

"I'm trying to decide if being content and appreciating what you have is a romantic notion," he said, smiling, "or an antiromantic notion."

Larry Volfmann called Elizabeth the next day. He wanted her to meet a director who was interested in the project. The project? she thought. You mean the page?

"Edgy little comedy," he was saying about the director's first and only movie. "*Doll.* You ever see it?"

Elizabeth had not seen it, but she thought she might have read a review. Maybe she heard her students talking about it. "The girl is obsessed with her doll? Or something?"

"Yeah. It's sexy. Nuts. But sexy. Sundance audience award. Didn't make a nickel. So, Sunday. At the Malibu house. Bring the family."

Elizabeth hung up, full of excitement. She lived in Los Angeles and was going to have a meeting with a director at a beach house in Malibu. She pressed the mute button and the sound of the television came back up. She was watching *The Magic Box,* an old English film she'd never heard of about an Englishman who was the true inventor of the movies. He has just succeeded in projecting the world's first motion picture, a scene of his cousin and son walking toward him on the street. It is projected onto a sheet. It is two A.M. but he runs out into the deserted streets of London and grabs a policeman. He has to show it to someone!

Elizabeth loved old movies and watched them constantly. It was rare that she saw one on television that she hadn't already seen. She watched Robert Donat haul the bobby up the narrow stairs, sit him down, and turn on his primitive projector.

I'm making a movie, she thought. Just like Robert Donat.

She realized the heavily whiskered cockney policeman was a very young Laurence Olivier.

"Laurence Olivier," she said to Brett, who had come in the room and sat beside her. He was carrying bagpipes he'd just gotten on eBay.

I'm not making a movie, she thought sadly. I'm watching a movie. There is a big difference. I'm so good at watching movies.

"I'm not sure the skill of watching movies translates into writing movies," she said to Brett.

"Don't worry," he said gently. "You can do it." He blew on the long, black stem of the bagpipe. "Nothing happens," he said.

"What if my beginner's luck runs out?" she said. "I've never given any signs of being a screenwriter."

"Now is your chance."

But don't you see, Elizabeth thought, I don't want a chance. I don't like chance. Chance is too chancy. I want to write the same paper over and over and teach the same class to succeeding generations and have them file past my deathbed, black-and-white images superimposed on my grizzled, worn self. Like Mister Chips.

"Mister Chips never wrote a screenplay," she said.

"Well, neither have you. Yet. So relax."

"And I'm so flattered and excited by the attentions of a rich and powerful person," she said. "Which offends me on my own behalf."

Brett said nothing. He flipped through a book. *Piping for Dummies.*

"That's what's wrong with this place," she said. "You see yourself too clearly."

Brett usually teased her when she made declarations of this sort. She waited for him to say, "I've often heard that said about L.A., the city of authenticity." Instead he looked at her in a way she could only describe as searching.

"Why are you looking at me like that?"

"Don't forget me."

"What?"

He stuck both hands in his hair, trying to push it back, making it stand up ridiculously. "I don't know. Forget it."

Sometimes Elizabeth noticed how handsome Brett was. His eyes were soft, pale gray. His hair was soft, pale blond. Unconsciously, at least she thought it was unconscious, he wore pale gray sweaters or soft pastel shirts. He was the most harmonious of persons, melodious and silvery, a willow in a soft breeze.

Elizabeth smoothed his hair. "Forget you? You're nuts."

She kissed him. "Mrs. Norman Maine," she said. His arms were around her. They pressed into each other. Forget you? Forget this feeling? Never, she thought. Never ever. His hands moved up inside her T-shirt. She felt them on her breasts, then pulling the shirt up over her head. She stiffened for a minute. What if Harry . . .

"He's with your father, remember?" Brett said, not even bothering to ask what was the matter, and pushed her down on the couch.

"Baby, I love you," she whispered afterward. "How could I forget you?"

∽

"Even before I was on the circuit, *with* my mother as chaperone," Lotte said, "there was Talented Children of America . . ."

Greta sat across from her mother at Lotte's little dining-room table. Josh sat beside her, anxiously touching Greta's arm now and then, as if to make sure there was still flesh and bone beneath the sleeve of her sweater. He had urged her to stay home, to rest or retch or whatever the chemo dictated. But she had washed her face with icy water, dressed as nicely as she could manage, and he had driven her over to visit Lotte, who was, as usual, without help. Lotte fired anyone they hired to help take care of her. Her reasons shimmered with the extravagant implausibility and inevitability of Greek myth. "She watches me, day and night, watching, watching . . . how can I trust a woman who watches?"; "She sleeps, like a lump. For this I'm paying?"; "She prays. It frightens me, a religious fanatic in my living room."

On a plate in front of her, little sandwiches were neatly stacked, Lotte's specialty, each with a single slice of slimy turkey breast. Greta felt ill. She prayed that Lotte would not now describe how she had become a Talented Child of America.

"You know how they were in those days?" Lotte said. "Don't ask. Off to the doctor! Four years old! The doctor with his red face. And that nose of his . . ." She paused. "Bulbous." Then, leaning toward them, confidentially, she whispered, "He drank." Then she resumed. "The doctor says, 'Constipation?'" She paused, again. "Dancing lessons! The doctor prescribed dancing lessons."

"A star was born," Greta said. She tried to smile.

Lotte was no longer clear, if she ever had been, what sort of an organization Talented Children of America was. What she remembered were thirty or forty children, every Sunday, dressed in their Sunday best, exhibiting their talents.

"Anyway, who cares?" she said, slumping, suddenly tired.

Greta forced herself to get up. She got a glass of water for her mother.

"I care," she heard Josh say.

I don't, Greta thought, surprised at the thought and the bitterness behind it. But her mother's stories had become too familiar to hold any mystery, any promise. And Lotte's theatrical pretensions were still, even now that Greta was a grown woman who was the mother herself of a grown woman, a source of embarrassment to her.

She brought the water back to the table and absentmindedly took a sip of it herself, then gagged until her eyes watered.

"That drunk," Lotte was saying, handing Greta a tissue, "with his dirty rotten red nose . . ."

Los Angeles had no center, as Larry Volfmann had said. But what did? Not life, that was for sure. Life was a queasy twisting path, circling back on itself, but circles did not mean centers. To Elizabeth, a circle usually meant she was lost, and she was frequently lost in L.A. But today Brett was driving. She could daydream and squint at the bright sun without worrying about missing a turn. Being in a car was so relaxing, so private. When she did drive, she particularly liked to be caught in traffic. In traffic, there was plenty of time to consult the map and the compass. You listened to the radio. To CDs. The sky was blue. The air conditioner was on. The cars moved at a gentle pace. No honking.

"Just shooting," Brett responded when she tried out this theory on him. "Maybe we should get married in the fall," he added.

"Shh," Elizabeth said. She pointed at Harry, asleep in his car seat behind them. "And then when you're late," she continued, "you just call on the cell phone and say, 'Oh, I'm stuck in terrible traffic.' Of course, you're just late, but you have observed the proper formalities."

"Your parents would like it. Your grandmother would definitely like it. *I* would like it . . ."

Elizabeth put her sunglasses on, then took her sunglasses off and cleaned them on her shirt.

"What's the big deal?" Brett was saying. "We're as good as married as it is."

"See? So why bother?"

Brett scratched his chin. Elizabeth saw he had forgotten to shave. Or had he done it on purpose? To look like a movie star now that he was in Hollywood?

"You can buy vodka in the grocery store here," she said, a little manically, she realized, to break the silence. "I love that. Don't you love that? I even like Lincoln Boulevard."

They were on their way to Malibu, driving along Pacific Coast Highway, cliffs to the right of them, beaches to the left, but Elizabeth thought fondly of Lincoln Boulevard, a street as undistinguished as any other swath of strip malls cutting through any city, town, or suburb in the country. But there was something special about Lincoln Boulevard's dismal monotony, its density or maybe just the intensity, that made Elizabeth feel that here, in this dazzlingly grim tunnel of billboards and ghastly neon signs, here the culture of America had been born.

The traffic was at a standstill in front of them. Brett slammed down the brake, hard.

"Jesus," Elizabeth said.

Harry was still miraculously asleep.

"Jesus, Brett."

"I just don't see what you have against fucking marriage," he said.

Elizabeth thought this over, as she had done so many times before.

"I don't, either," she said, sadly, returning her attention to the road.

The house was right on the beach, a big, airy, modern house of glass and polished wood, the floors a pale gray concrete that mimicked the sea. It was not a mansion, which both relieved and disappointed Elizabeth. It was a house — a rich man's house, but still, a house.

The director of *Doll,* that edgy little comedy that made such a splash at Sundance, sat on a chair constructed of polished chunks of wood, its cushions wooly sheepskin. At first Elizabeth thought the frowning woman curled up and biting her lip must be Volfmann's wife. Then she was introduced.

"I have no idea how I got here," Daisy Piperno said, holding out her hand. "Do you?"

Elizabeth shook Daisy's hand.

"No," she said.

Daisy smiled. Her hair was black. Her face was a little bit round and pouty looking, with dark arched eyebrows and narrow, sleepy brown eyes. Those eyes rested on Elizabeth. That was how Elizabeth experienced it — they rested on her. And yet the other features of Daisy Piperno's face were almost ludicrously animated. She bit her lip and looked around her, this way, that way, craning her neck, screwing up her face.

"Emma Bovary bites her lip," Elizabeth said. "Like you."

The agitated twisting stopped. Daisy turned her head and gazed again at Elizabeth. It was an unhurried appraisal, a look of thorough and sedate curiosity. Elizabeth blushed.

"I know," Daisy said.

What on earth made me say that? Elizabeth thought. Had she

offended the auteur? She caught Volfmann's eye. He gestured like a parent urging a shy child to join the birthday party — Go on, go on, have a good time. Brett appeared at her side and Harry pushed his way between her legs. "Mommy, it's a Flintstones chair," Harry said, pointing at the chair Daisy still sat in. "And there's scary men."

Daisy laughed. Elizabeth noticed several African masks on a shelf, one of which looked a little like Larry Volfmann.

"Hey, Harry," said Volfmann. "They're not real men, Harry."

Harry shrugged. "Pretend scary men."

"Like me?" Volfmann said.

"You're not a pretend man," Harry said. He was disgusted. He went off in search of a television. On the way his elbow bumped a vase full of flowers, which fell to the cement floor, spilling and shattering. Harry began to cry. He began to scream. Elizabeth picked him up. His face was sticky with tears and mucus. Volfmann hovered apologetically above them. Brett hovered apologetically beside them. Elizabeth, calming Harry, both mortified and defiant on his behalf, glanced up at Daisy. Daisy was still watching Elizabeth with her strange expression of contented scrutiny.

"You can dress us up . . ." Elizabeth said.

"Harry, want to look for whales in the telescope?" Volfmann said. Elizabeth gratefully watched him carry a happy Harry away to the telescope set up at the window. She wondered if he had children. How old would they be? How old was he? Older than Brett, younger than her father, an age that was not part of her world.

Elizabeth cleaned up the mess with paper towels she found in the kitchen.

"You missed a piece," Daisy said. She pointed at a sliver. She had not moved from the big chair. For someone so jumpy, she seemed oddly lethargic.

Brett kneeled beside Elizabeth with a wet paper towel, getting the smallest slivers. It was a routine they knew well, were good at after so much practice. He leaned across the gray, soggy paper towels in their hands and gave her a kiss. He smiled, unperturbed. She envied him. Her face was burning with embarrassment, with a sense of personal responsibility and despair for the broken vase, the spilled water, the flowers strewn across the floor.

"I guess they should live in Milwaukee," Daisy said.

Elizabeth looked up from the floor. "Who?"

"The Bovaries," Daisy said, lighting a cigarette.

"Os!" Harry said. He was back, staring with a fascinated admiration at Daisy's lazy, drifting rings of smoke.

three

It was four A.M., earlier than even Greta liked to get up. But she sat in her garden, surrounded by roses dripping with fog. She sat on the wet ground, the damp seeping through her robe. She had woken up, stifling, sure she was choking. Quietly, careful not to wake Tony, with whom at that moment she felt she could not bear to exchange even one explanatory word, Greta crept from her warm, soft bed to the cool, sodden garden. The cold felt good: the freshness of the hour and its damp perfume.

I have cancer, she thought.

What she craved, what all this talk of cancer had reminded her of, was a cigarette.

"Oh, come off it," Elizabeth had said when Greta confided this craving to her daughter. Greta heard the fear and tension and boredom. She recognized that tone. Elizabeth sounded the way Greta sounded with her own mother. Impatient, desperate, disgusted. "You're totally perverse. You haven't smoked in twenty-five years."

"Twenty-nine."

"But, okay, now you've confessed," Elizabeth said, her voice softening. "You can relax and put it out of your mind."

Greta wanted to explain that she had not confessed. She did not feel guilty, did not need to unburden herself about cigarettes. She had simply wanted Elizabeth to know what she knew, if only for a moment, for the moment that she wanted a cigarette: She wanted Elizabeth to know that she was still alive. She wanted Elizabeth to know that she still had the wherewithal, still had the power, to do as she pleased, even if she pleased to start smoking again.

But I don't really have power, Greta thought. I am a slave of this illness. It tells me what I can eat and when. It tells me that I can sleep, that I must sleep, or that I must not. It tells me that if I smoked even one cigarette, I would vomit.

At least I have my hair, she thought. She tucked a strand behind her ear. Maybe the chemo would turn it from the indistinct light brown it was now back to her childhood blond. She had so many treatments to go. There was still plenty of time.

Plenty of time. She repeated it to herself. She heard a mockingbird sing. She heard her own breath.

What would Lotte say if Greta did lose her hair? Would her mother shake her head in bemused disappointment, the way she did when Greta turned up in her gardening clothes? Lotte was tall, particularly for a woman of her generation. She had loomed, a giantess of a mother, in Greta's life. Greta suddenly remembered walking along the sidewalk in the St. Louis suburb she'd grown up in. She had reached up for her mother's hand and Lotte had smiled down at her as if from a mountain. What a funny little memory. So ordinary. A girl reaching for her mother's hand. Greta could hear the leaves swishing beneath her feet, swirling around her ankles. Autumn leaves. Her mother had towered, out of reach, as high as the trees, her beautiful blond hair so comfortable, so at home among the golden leaves. Lotte had not been a bad mother, just an eccentric one, taking Greta out of school sometimes when she wanted company at a movie matinee, refusing to allow Greta to ride a bicycle, fainting noisily whenever Greta scraped her knee or got a bee sting. Greta had learned not to tell her mother when she fell, to wash the cut or extract the stinger herself, to steal bicycles out of neighbors' garages for an afternoon, then put them back before anyone noticed. And she had seen a lot of movies. Her father had been the tender, affectionate parent, her favorite when she was a child. But she had come to appreciate Lotte over the years. Eccentricity has its value. Lotte loved her, and she was, if nothing else, amusing. Amusement was something Greta valued more and more.

She wondered if Elizabeth thought of her the way she thought of Lotte. With annoyance, pleasure, contempt. With awe. With good-natured condescension and longing. With such need that it frightened her. With dread. What a horrible idea. Yet wasn't that all just another way of saying Greta loved her mother?

Lotte was the palest person Greta had ever met. She saw, for a moment, her mother's large, pale feet. Did they really tag toes at the morgue? Did everyone go to the morgue? She didn't want her mother to die. She didn't want to die. She dug her own bare toes into the dark soil. The sprinklers went on and she let the spray wash over her.

Larry Volfmann was appalled by Elizabeth's initial attempts at screenwriting.

"What the fuck have I done?" he said, shaking the one measly page of dialogue at her, as he had earlier shaken the issue of *Tikkun*. "What is this? Only one page and I'm already bored? What's with the first wife? She's history, she's nobody, *she's* not the Madame Bovary we're interested in. You've got one hundred pages to tell your story, you understand? One hundred fifteen tops . . ."

"Well, but it's not an action picture, it's —"

"I know what it is. And it's not *this*." He looked sadly at the sheet of paper. "I was sure that here was someone I could count on not to be literal minded . . ."

"I'm not even a screenwriter . . ."

"You wrote this. You wrote it under contract. You're a screenwriter, all right. A *bad* screenwriter."

She was so angry that for a second she had nothing to say. She wondered why she didn't just walk out. Oh, yes, she reminded herself. This is what comes of being a whore.

"You're scaring me," Volfmann said. "How can you write like a hack the first page out? It's like your screenwriting program did this."

Elizabeth thought of her screenwriting program, so polite, so attentive, so quiet. She wished it was sitting on the soft sofa beside her. Better yet, instead of her. It would have just the right response.

"You don't know anything yet — how can you have absorbed so much banality so fast?" Volfmann began pacing around on his thick carpet. "I hire a virgin, I get a . . ." He stopped himself.

"Whore?" Elizabeth said.

"*I* didn't say it."

Elizabeth stood up, grabbed the paper from his hand, crumpled it, and threw it in the wastebasket. "I don't know you well enough for you to be this rude," she said. She headed for the silver doors.

"Oh, calm down." Volfmann sat, leaned back in his chair. "Don't go delicate on me, for God's sake. You think screenwriting is beneath you so you write beneath you. You think it's formulaic hackwork so you write formulaic hackwork. You think it's easy, so you write shit. Big fucking deal. It happens."

Suddenly, he leaped to his feet, his face dark red.

"But I don't want shit!" he screamed.

Elizabeth stared at Larry Volfmann, who was right about her, but had also pounded his desk and stamped both his feet.

"I see you are very upset," Elizabeth said, softly but firmly, using the method she'd learned in a women's magazine for dealing with three-year-old temper tantrums. What an asshole, she thought, meaning Volfmann and then, on second thought, herself. "You are very angry at me. You feel I have let you down." Acknowledge the child's feelings. Okay. Done. Now, she was supposed to suggest they have a snack. "Would you like a bottle of water, Larry? I think I would."

Volfmann nodded his head without looking at her, just as Harry would have, although there was no visible pouting and no sniffled up tears. He pulled two bottles of water from a small hidden refrigerator.

"You know, some writers have a gift," he said.

Elizabeth smiled, waiting for the healing compliment. "A gift," Volfmann continued, "for putting in every scene that shouldn't be there, and leaving out every scene that should. Don't do that to me, Elizabeth. Don't make a fucking fool of me. Okay?"

Elizabeth drank from her bottle of water and thought this over. She noticed a loose thread on his expensive jacket.

"Yeah," she said finally. "Okay."

~

INT. SUBURBAN BEDROOM — NIGHT

CHUCK BOVAINE, a mild-looking young guy, sits on the edge of his wife, GAIL's, bed. She is a little older, vegetarian gaunt, her face marked by perpetual anger. Her arms are entwined around his neck, but less lovingly than like a poisonous vine.

                    GAIL
I can't swallow and I can't breathe! Clinical depression, Chuck. Get it? Why can't you help me, you passive-aggressive piece of shit? Not a word, not a pill . . . Everyone said I'd be miserable with you . . .

                    CHUCK

Honey . . .

                    GAIL

They were right, they were so right . . . You make
me sick.

Chuck, defeated, begins to extract himself from the vines.

                  GAIL (cont.)

Don't you leave! How dare you leave me alone?

Chuck dutifully puts his arms around her.

                    CHUCK

I'm here . . . I'm here, honey. See? Don't worry . . .

                    GAIL

You're here? I'll say you're here . . . What're you,
hovering around waiting to see me die?

                    CHUCK

Hey, come on, now, calm down, baby . . .

                    GAIL

Who is she?

                    CHUCK

What?

                    GAIL

Who is she? That's all I'm asking.

                       ∽

INT. SUBURBAN BEDROOM — NIGHT

> CHUCK BOVAINE, a mild-looking young guy, sits on the edge of his wife, GAIL's, bed. She is a little older, vegetarian gaunt, her face marked by perpetual anger. Her arms are entwined around his neck, but less lovingly than like a poisonous vine.

GAIL

Z-z-z . . .

CHUCK

Xanax?

∾

Elizabeth had been working at her parents' all morning. She had listened with envy to the sound of Harry and Josh splashing in the pool. At lunchtime, Harry had been so tired he fell asleep beneath the kitchen table beside the cat. Harry usually preferred the coffee table in the living room, but Elizabeth left him where he was. She went into the living room and sat down next to Josh on the couch. Josh had a finger hooked in a tear in his T-shirt. His hairy legs and big feet were stretched on the coffee table. He was staring into space.

"You okay?" she said.

"It's ridiculous," he said.

He sounded sad in the same way he had sounded sad when he was a child. That Josh was a man with hairy legs still surprised Elizabeth. She tried to imagine how her mother felt looking at Josh, how Elizabeth would feel when Harry was a man.

"Who wants an orange?" Greta said, appearing from the kitchen.

"Don't wait on us," Elizabeth said.

"Me," Josh said at the same moment.

Greta handed him a plate of oranges cut in quarters.

"The smell seems to soothe my stomach," she said. "This week, anyway."

"*I* am generous enough to give you the pleasure of waiting on me, your only son," Josh said.

They sat on the couch for a while, the three of them in a row. No one spoke. Elizabeth listened to the sound of her brother eating. The orange scent was fresh and energetic. She closed her eyes. She was angry at her mother. She was angry at her brother. Didn't they get what was going on? Elizabeth was conscious of a tangled sense of superiority and exclusion. She felt a hand on hers and opened her eyes. Josh clutched her hand. Her mother's eyes were closed and she seemed to be sleeping. Josh's face was contorted and red. He was crying, without making a sound.

When the doorbell rang, Greta opened her eyes but did not even attempt to get up. Josh, the plate of orange peels balanced on his stomach, wiped his eyes with his fists and looked helplessly at Elizabeth.

Elizabeth opened the door to a young man with wavy dark hair, rather long, that would have been considered romantic in a far-off era and stylish in another. Elizabeth did not recognize him until he smiled and blinked, and she saw that it was her brother's best friend, Tim. When he was in high school and lived with his mother, Laurie, next door, Tim had been an ordinary-looking nerdy kid. Now he looked like he'd wandered from a poetry slam to a nineteenth-century English vicarage. And back.

Elizabeth envied Josh having his friends around. She had been the first of her friends in New York, was still the only one, to have a baby, which had distracted her from friendship, to say the least. But even when she was neglectful of them and rarely saw them and forgot to call them, she always knew her friends were there, going to bars and breaking up with their boyfriends, quitting their jobs, moving to Brooklyn. Only now that she was three thousand miles away did the distance from her friends seem real. Maybe she could be friends with Tim.

"I brought your mother a book," Tim said. "From my mother. She said it's soothing."

He went into the living room and threw himself on the couch beside Greta, who was awake from her nap. Tim hugged her and kissed her hand, which made her laugh. Elizabeth remembered how easy he had always been with her mother. He handed Greta the book, *An Unsuitable Attachment* by Barbara Pym, and made small talk while Josh sat glumly on the other side of Greta, and Elizabeth watched, fascinated, from the doorway. Tim's manner was trusting and open, like a child's, and as smooth as a ladies' man. He leaned his head on Greta's shoulder. He took a tiny Snickers bar from the pocket of his T-shirt and tossed it to Josh. But then he stared at Josh for a minute, stood up and circled the room, his hands in his pockets, his shoulders hunched, and the ladies' man disappeared.

"Are you okay?" Elizabeth said. "What's with everyone today?"

"Well, *I* have cancer," Greta said. "Since you asked."

Elizabeth was shocked at her mother's tone. Cold. Angry. It had not occurred to her that her mother might be angry. That's my job, she thought.

"Yeah, she does," Josh said. He unwrapped the candy bar and bit into it.

"Thank you both," Elizabeth said.

"And that's what's wrong with everyone," Greta said.

Tim started laughing. "Shit," he murmured. He sat down again.

Greta patted his head affectionately as she left the room with her book.

Tim slid from the couch to the floor.

Elizabeth sat in the indentation he had left behind. She pushed Tim with her foot. "Why are you sitting on the floor?" she asked. "It's no safer down there."

Tim took hold of her foot. Elizabeth looked down at him and

she felt herself overwhelmed by a feeling of intense, vast, dizzying relief at being touched by someone who didn't need her. His hands massaged her foot. It was a casual, easy gesture that bestowed peace, as if he were a priest giving her absolution, or a trainer patting a skittish horse. She wanted to thank Tim. You are a priest, she wanted to say. And I am a mess. But she was afraid she might burst into tears.

He tapped her polished big toe.

"Nice color," he said.

~

On a gray July morning, as she and Lotte made their slow painful progress, like a tractor trailer laboring up a steep hill, across yet another waiting room toward yet another receptionist in yet another doctor's office, Greta clenched her teeth and was silent.

"Hmmph! Look at the *posterior* of that one," Lotte whispered. Her whisper was like a loud hiss. "And she shows it off?"

Greta did not look. Presumably the one cursed with the remarkable posterior was a large woman in stretch pants, her mother's favorite target for this particular comment.

"Maybe nothing else fits," Greta had once said. "Maybe that's all that's comfortable."

"It's a disease," Lotte had said. She strung out the word "disease," just as she had "posterior," as if they were equally revolting, as if they were synonyms. The letter "s" itself seemed damning. She might just as well have been spitting as talking. "A disease."

"It's a disease," Greta heard her mother say now.

Greta sat Lotte down, balanced the cane against the chair. The cane was looking a little shabby, scratched and dented with use. So unlike Lotte. It depressed Greta.

"Maybe it's time for a new cane," she said.

"Where'm I going? Carnegie Hall?"

Greta turned toward the desk.

"My pocketbook!" Lotte cried. The alarm in her voice made the receptionist look up. Greta smiled and rolled her eyes at the woman, then immediately felt disloyal to her mother.

"Here, Mother. I've got it." She handed Lotte her bag and continued to the receptionist's desk. Behind her, she heard Lotte mutter, "Stupid stick. A new one, yet?" Then came the sound of Lotte shaking out her bracelets. She would hold her arms out in front of her as if waiting for a child to jump into them, then shake the bangles, of which there were many, straightening them with a burst of jingling. Lotte characteristically shook out her bracelets whenever she settled into a new room, as if communicating with any other members of her species that might be lurking in the brush.

"We're here to see the radiologist . . ."

"Name?"

"Dr. Lyman."

The receptionist, a beautiful black woman, looked up. Now here was someone Lotte could appreciate. "No, *your* name," she said, smiling at Greta, an encouraging smile. God, what people she must deal with to be so kind right off the bat: the dying, the walking dead . . .

"My name?" Greta said. "But, it's my mother . . ."

The receptionist put her hand out and patted Greta's hand. "What's your *mother's* name, honey?"

When Greta finally sat down she realized she was shaking. My mother, she thought. My Lotte. How would she help Lotte if she was sick herself? How would she help Lotte if she had no hair?

She ran her fingers through her hair, which was, indeed, thinning.

I want my mama, she thought.

She took Lotte's hand, whether to comfort Lotte or to comfort herself she didn't know.

The surgeon had already tried to get rid of the tumor once, in his office, with something called a Mohs procedure. But the tumor was back with a vengeance, spreading across the landscape of Lotte's face, and now he wanted to remove a piece of Lotte's nose. Should the beautiful Lotte's last days be cursed with half a nose? Before such a drastic step, Greta thought they ought to try radiation. Greta tried to remember if radiation also made you lose your hair. She would have to make sure to ask the doctor that. Privately, when Lotte was out of the room.

"Life Saver?" Lotte offered Greta the frayed paper tube of candy. Greta shook her head no.

"I don't like green, either," Lotte said.

The bed was big for the little bedroom. The walls felt close. The twins next door had such bright outdoor lights. Scraps of Latin music arrived periodically from somewhere farther down the street. Elizabeth stared at the ceiling and tried to understand which wall faced north, which east, which west, which south. She had no sense of direction. It was a source of anxiety even in New York, with its lovely grid of numbered streets and avenues, its lovely song: the Bronx is up, the Battery's down; although Elizabeth often found herself wandering in aimless circles even in New York, hoping she might accidentally arrive at her destination. In L.A. of course it was a thousand times worse. She got up, looked out the window for the North Star. But she had no idea what the North Star looked like, really. It was in the Big Dipper, perhaps. But where was the Big Dipper? In the evenings, when she looked out the window toward the ocean, she expected to see the sun setting. But it set much farther to the right, which was supposed to be north.

She lay down again and tried to take her mind off her location. But the reason she had started thinking about her coordinates was to help her take her mind off her grandmother and her mother. She had already repeated to herself every scrap of Harry dialogue, partly because she held on to Harry's words as if they were spoken by the Buddha (she knew it was ridiculous, and she tried to keep her worship private) and partly because she liked to relate Harry anecdotes to Greta and Lotte to amuse them. Harry said this, Harry said that. North by northwest. Her grandmother was going south.

Two of her friends' mothers had gotten breast cancer, and they were both fine. A professor of hers had died of a brain tumor. She knew a boy in college who'd had colon cancer and he was healthy now. She ran through every person she'd ever met who had or knew someone who'd had cancer, friends who'd just lost a parent or a grandparent. She tried to stop herself, but then she began to think of the people she ought to have called, those friends in New York she'd lost touch with. She knew she'd become careless of her friends even while it was happening. But after Harry was born, people seemed superfluous to her. Sometimes even Brett seemed superfluous. Only Harry was real, a constant presence, a magnificent sun shedding light on the bleak satellites around him. She had seen it happen to others, and she'd sworn it would not happen to her, that self-satisfied, glazed parental worship.

Who was the sun now? She could see only Lotte, a glittering constellation, and Greta, bright and clear as the Milky Way in the desert sky. No central star. No center. No north, no south, no east, no west.

She turned all the pillows over to their cool sides and attempted again to switch her thoughts. She tried to sort out some of *Mrs. B,* but found herself thinking instead of Volfmann, his short graying hair and canine visage, his glowering eyes. Bedroom eyes, she thought, irrelevantly, for they were hardly that. The thread hanging from his jacket. She should have reached over and plucked it.

She kicked the sheet off. Her mother did not look bad, she told herself. She actually looked rather good. She had lost weight, which was okay, and had not lost hair, which was a blessing. She had switched her uniform from jeans and T-shirts to stretchy yoga pants and T-shirts because she needed to lie down so much and wanted to be more comfortable, a fashion decline that was not really appreciable.

Elizabeth had always liked the way her mother dressed. She never fussed. She was identifiable. She was predictable. Lotte's relationship to clothes, on the other hand, was creative, proprietary, demanding. She was a clothes hobbyist, Elizabeth thought. And then realized, No, it went beyond that. Lotte could have been an artist, if clothes were paint or graphite or marble. She could have been a racehorse breeder if clothes were horses. For Greta, on the other hand, clothes were just clothes. Elizabeth had always relied on that quality in her mother, on her pragmatic vision. Elizabeth had always relied on her mother, period.

She began to cry. When she finished, she got up, washed her face, and found Brett at his desk. She sat on his lap and wrapped her arms around him. He would know what to say to make her feel better. He always knew. Brett kissed her and reassured her. He spoke in a gentle singsong, as if he were telling a wonderful bed-time story. "Those statistics include every ancient crumbling old ruin who ever got sick," he said. "Greta is young. She's in good shape. 'Fifty percent' means fifty percent *do* recover. *That's* Greta's fifty percent."

Elizabeth listened, her chin on his head, waiting. Brett's calm had always struck Elizabeth as a thing of beauty, a miracle of physical grace. His tranquility soared before her, as exquisite as a dancer, and she waited for that moment in the ballet when it would lift her in its arms and let her soar, too.

"And I'm here," Brett was saying. "I'll take care of you. I'll watch over you. I'll feed you and bathe you and tuck you in at night with a martini. I'll do whatever it takes."

Elizabeth listened and thought how much she loved him. And still she waited for the feeling of calm.

Brett brought her back up to bed. He held her and made love to her and she waited.

He fell asleep on his back and she waited some more, confused. She stared at his long, narrow profile and wondered, Where is the calm?

She waited for hours. She watched Brett sleep. She looked at the clock. It was three A.M. No calm. She began to worry. No calm? No calm. She began to panic. It was four. No calm. Her grandmother was dying. No calm there. It was five, and her mother was dying. It was six in the morning and she was helpless. There was no calm. There never would be. How could there be? Her grandmother was dying and Elizabeth couldn't save her. Her mother was dying and Elizabeth couldn't cure her. And no one could help Elizabeth. No one. Not even Brett.

"Did you sleep okay?" he asked her in the morning.

"I don't know," she said. And she avoided him all day.

Elliot King called Elizabeth and Daisy in for a meeting. He made them wait for half an hour.

"He's a prick," Daisy said. She was curled in the leather chair, her eyes closed, looking like a cat, or a snake. Elizabeth tried to decide which. She wondered if Volfmann would be at the meeting.

"Do you ever get lost," she said, "even though you live here?"

"No." Daisy opened her eyes. Her gaze spread itself lazily over Elizabeth. "I'll take care of Elliot," she said. "Don't you worry, Cookie."

Elizabeth smiled and leaned back, lulled by Daisy's eyes, by being called Cookie. She felt as if she had been handed a cookie and some nice cold milk to drink.

When Elliot finally arrived, Elizabeth was disappointed to see Volfmann was not with him. Then Daisy said to him, "The man behind the curtain!" with such warmth that Elizabeth realized she was jealous. I'm Cookie, she wanted to say. Not Elliot.

Elliot, wearing a tight, shiny, stretchy T-shirt that showed off his perfectly formed, proportionate, and therefore pint-size muscles, thought over Daisy's greeting for a split second, weighing it. His scale pronounced it good, for he smiled.

"Look," Daisy said, her tone confiding, her voice low, "you are the only one who *really* gets this project."

Elliot pursed his lips, an unconscious smirk, as if he couldn't help but reveal his glee at having gotten away with something.

"So, where are we, Elliot?" Daisy said. "Where the fuck are we?"

Elliot talked about demographics. He talked about content creation. That was what Elizabeth and Daisy were engaged in. Content creation. He had two assistants, young and eager, a boy and a girl. Better than graduate school, Elizabeth thought. She heard the word "dramedy." Her mind drifted to a passage in *Madame Bovary* in which Charles's conversation is described as being as flat as a sidewalk. On which everybody's ideas trudged past.

"You're a wizard," Daisy was saying.

Elliot shrugged his shoulders modestly. Then, as he escorted them out, his face became sober and grim.

"*Madame Bovary*," he said. He sighed as he turned away and walked back to his office. "A franchise it's not."

INT. GIRL'S BOARDING SCHOOL DORM — NIGHT

We see a suite, two bedrooms, each with twin beds, off of a small common room, all of it messy and girly. Two sixteen-year-old girls, CARRIE and MOLLY, are sitting on the floor of the common room smoking a joint. A third girl, LAUREN, is listening to a Walkman, singing a Backstreet Boys song loud and off-key, and doing her nails. ANGLE ON the fourth girl, visible through the bedroom door. A dark-haired beauty, sitting in her bed in a short, white, simple, but revealing, nightgown. She is oblivious to the others. Somehow, she seems both innocent and bursting with sensuality. She is reading intently. . . . <u>Wuthering Heights</u>. She is BARBIE.

The windows behind her are wide open, although it's freezing cold and windy. WE SEE and HEAR the wind HOWLING through the trees.

CU Barbie turns to windows. Dreamy-eyed from her book. Thrilled by the romantic wind.

ANGLE ON common room. Papers flying, the three girls squealing, chasing their stuff.

CARRIE

God, Barbie, close your freaking windows!

ANGLE ON Barbie, now leaning out the window, beautiful, the wind blowing her long hair. She turns, a pale pre-Raphaelite beauty, and looks pityingly at her roommates.

BARBIE (harsh, angry)

Shut the fuck up.

She turns majestically back to the roaring wind.

BARBIE (CONT.) (whispers to herself)

Pussies . . .

~

"We're not broke," Brett said.

He'd just come out of the shower. Drops of water clung between his shoulder blades. Elizabeth reached up and put her hand there. She was still in bed.

"If you think the script is such a stupid idea," he said, "you don't have to do it. You really, really don't."

"I don't think it's a stupid idea."

Brett buttoned his shirt. Elizabeth wondered why he always wore a dress shirt when he wasn't going anywhere.

"But *you* obviously do," she said.

"No. I think you're being stupid *about* it."

"That's what people do here. Pretend they hate what they're doing. In case it's stupid."

"That's what stupid people do everywhere," Brett said.

He was dressed now, walking away from her, framed by the doorway to the hall. Elizabeth sat on the edge of the bed. She saw her mother, lying down at the doctor's office, scared and filling up with chemicals. She saw her grandmother, her face decaying as she tried on new hats.

Brett! You can't talk to me like that! she thought.

"You're not helping," she said. She wanted him to help.

Brett stopped and turned toward her. He must have seen something in her face.

"Baby," he said, putting his arms around her. "My baby."

Elizabeth felt tears coming.

"Shit," she said, "all I do is fucking cry."

Brett comforted her. As if he could comfort her. But he couldn't, could he? And she realized that, at this moment, that was the reason she cried.

Elizabeth wished she wouldn't get so angry at Brett. What had he done? Nothing. Nothing at all. He deserved better. She would be nicer. Even Emma Bovary tried to be a good wife. In her fashion. She read poetry to Charles in the moonlight, hoping he would respond.

Brett walked out the door, then came back. "It's a mistake to confuse enthusiasm with weakness," he said.

"What are you talking about?"

"I don't know." He walked away, the damp from his back, between his shoulder blades, coming through his blue oxford shirt. "You, I guess."

* * *

Elizabeth drove toward her parents' house with Harry, strapped into his car seat in the back and sucking on his pacifier. Their house is like my office, she told herself. I will do my work there. *Madame Bovary* will metamorphose into *Mrs. B,* a beautiful butterfly changing into an awkward, squirming caterpillar. She looked at Harry in the rearview mirror. He had brown, wavy hair like hers. He had brown eyes that were darker than hers and that sparkled with excitement and curiosity. When he scowled or smiled, he looked exactly like her. But now, gazing out the window, his face in repose, he looked like Brett, a calm and reasonable presence.

"Look!" Harry said through his pacifier, pointing out the window at barefoot teenagers in wet suits carrying their boards toward the beach.

"Surfers," Elizabeth said.

She thought that maybe Brett was right. He often was. She wanted to write *Mrs. B* and she should stop pretending she didn't. She had become an academic because she liked to read novels and she didn't know what else to do. It was not as though little children grew up wanting to be academics. They wanted to be firemen. Or stand-up comedians. Now, a miracle had occurred, a hand had reached out from the sky beckoning her from the thorny patch of critical theory and academic political infighting. Do not bite the hand that comes from the sky. Elizabeth liked working with Daisy better than she had with any of her university colleagues. They never called her Cookie. They never told her something she'd written sounded as bad as dialogue from an episode of *CHiPs.*

Brett was right. The hand had beckoned and then graciously plucked her out of her thankless job and plunked her down in paradise. And, in addition to liking Daisy, who was so mysterious and so direct, in addition to liking Volfmann, who was so complicated and so brutish, Elizabeth liked Mrs. B. Yes, she was wet and romantic. Yes, she was self-indulgent and what Elizabeth's father would have called a status seeker. But what was it she was really seeking? Happiness. That's all. Just like everyone else.

Life, liberty, and the pursuit of happiness. Emma Bovary, founding father. No. Happiness, passion, intoxication. Like everyone in America. Funny that someone so French, so much a creature of the nineteenth century, could turn so easily into someone so American, and so contemporary. Searching for happiness just like everyone else.

Am I searching for happiness, then? Elizabeth wondered.

"Juice?" Harry said.

She looked at him in the rearview mirror and thought how happy he made her. That wasn't the happiness Madame Bovary sought. Perhaps she should have.

"We're almost there, sweetheart," she said.

As for passion and intoxication — weren't they often horribly inconvenient? Just look at what happens to poor old Madame Bovary.

"Juice!"

Dead. Graphically, hideously dead by her own hand. The wages of a commonplace, romantic imagination.

"Juice, juice, juice," Harry sang softly.

I want a truly modern, truly American Madame Bovary, she thought. The wages of a commonplace, *therapeutic* imagination. Emma and Charles and Leon and Rudolph, too, all at the couples' counselor together while the child attends Gymboree!

"Juice, juice, juice . . ."

As she turned off Ocean Avenue she realized that she had not been to the beach once since coming to California. It had not even occurred to her. Harry had never been to a beach anywhere. She should be sitting in a beach chair, working and watching Harry dig holes and chase gulls.

"Do you want to go to the beach, honey?" she said.

"Juice," Harry said.

Elizabeth tried to work at her parents' as often as she could. She felt the need to be near her mother, partly to be helpful if necessary, partly to breathe her mother's air, to see what she saw, to hear the leaf blower and the mockingbird that Greta heard. Sometimes, Harry would play with his grandma. Other times, he simply wrapped himself around Elizabeth's legs like a puttee. When he did play with his grandmother, Elizabeth worried that he tired Greta out. After all, he tired Elizabeth out, and she wasn't getting chemotherapy. Greta never complained, though. She wasn't a complainer. That fact had always been an important component of her personality, of her character.

"Your mother's not a complainer," Elizabeth's father would say.

"My Greta, she never was a complainer," Grandma Lotte would say.

"How is anybody supposed to know what the hell is the matter if you never complain?" Elizabeth said.

Greta looked up at the umbrella. There was a spiderweb at the top. It seemed to be holding the umbrella open. The sun had shifted and her left leg was exposed. She was too tired to move her leg, and she could as easily have moved the sun as moved the chaise. She heard Elizabeth's sandals flip-flopping from the house. Elizabeth appeared and tilted the umbrella until it shaded all of her again. Greta felt her daughter's lips on her forehead. She saw the dark circles beneath Elizabeth's eyes. She felt her own eyes flutter as she attempted to keep them open. She heard Harry calling.

"Mommy! Where's my mommy?"

She saw Elizabeth blink, then turn her head.

"Okay. I'm here with Grandma." Greta heard Elizabeth say this, though she spoke softly, too softly for Harry, surely, who was now wailing from inside the house.

Greta closed her eyes. If she closed her eyes, Elizabeth would think she was asleep and could go to Harry without guilt. She wanted to thank Elizabeth for fixing the umbrella. But all she could do was close her eyes and release her.

EXT. PERFECT FARMHOUSE — EVENING

A celebration. Music, dancing, champagne . . . little children running among the elegantly dressed guests . . .

EXTREME CLOSE-UP of a magnificent three-tiered wedding cake . . . the camera pans slowly up as if scaling a huge mountain . . . on the top WE SEE the figurines of the bride and groom . . .

Suddenly, a HUGE KNIFE slashes into the cake . . .

Lotte held out her hand for the mug of hot water. She forced her finger through the handle. "What that filthy arthritis did to my fingers . . . it should be executed . . ."

"So where's Norma?" Elizabeth said.

Lotte looked away. People had no sense of privacy anymore. "Oh, she had to leave. You know how they are."

"Grandma, did you fire her?"

"The tea is too hot, darling."

"It's not tea."

"It's water, Grandma!" Harry said.

Elizabeth sat on the sofa and hung her head.

"Why, why oh why, did you fire Norma?" she said.

"Her food stank. To high heaven! How can they eat all those

dirty spices? I don't understand these people. Come, Harry, sit with Grandma. And the amounts? I would get sick as a dog if I ate what she ate. Mountains of food. Enough for an army. It was frightening! I was frightened, Elizabeth!"

Lotte started to cry. Harry slid off the chair and reached for his toy trucks on the floor. I wasn't really frightened, Lotte reminded herself, drying her tears, but I was certainly revolted.

"Did she force you to eat her mountains of smelly food?" Elizabeth asked.

"Oh! God forbid! She made me nice chicken soup. A little fillet of sole. Mashed potatoes I like, too . . ."

Elizabeth went into the kitchen and came out eating a banana.

"It's not ripe, darling," Lotte said. "It's green. You'll get a stomachache. God forbid."

"So, like, what kind of housekeeper would you like, exactly? You have to have someone, Grandma. You can't do it yourself. That wouldn't be fair to you. You deserve a little help after all these years, don't you think?"

Elizabeth was a thoughtful girl. But the hair . . .

"Honey, why pull your hair back like that? Such beautiful hair . . ."

Elizabeth turned the air-conditioning up.

"Is that okay? I don't know how you can stand it. It's so stuffy."

She took Harry into the bedroom. Lotte heard the television. I still have my hearing, she thought. I still have my goddamned ears.

"Elizabeth, why don't you marry that nice husband of yours?" Lotte called from the living room.

Elizabeth returned. "I don't know. And he's not my husband. And why do I have to? What difference does it make? Why does everyone care so much?"

"Such a nice man."

"Maybe you need a husband, Grandma. Instead of a housekeeper."

Lotte gasped. "My husband, Morris, was my husband. No one could take his place. Men are pigs."

"There you go."

"My poor mother used to say what everyone needed was a wife. And you remember, Elizabeth, if that husband of yours ever gives you a hard time, let alone raises a hand to you, he should drop dead, you just turn on your heel and walk out. You remember your Grandma Lotte's advice."

When Elizabeth and Harry had gone, Lotte stood by the window and looked out at the street until her legs were too sore. She sat stiffly in her chair and turned on the television. Cartoons. She fumbled with the remote, attacking it with her index finger, which was so thick and bent these days it seemed to her to have gotten on her hand by mistake. Finally, the channel changed. Bastard of a television. News. And all of it bad. Morris, she thought, you should not have left me alone in this world. Anger rose in her breast. Morris! I can't live without you! Look what you did!

She pushed the remote control some more until she found a channel she liked, then dialed Greta's number.

"The skating!" she said to the answering machine. "Like ballerinas!"

Sometimes Elizabeth and Harry stayed for dinner with Greta and Tony and Josh, particularly when Brett was out of town. He flew to Washington every few weeks, and Elizabeth had at first looked forward to eating with her parents. There had been a time when dinner at her mother's had been a treat, a break from her own boring, moderately successful, low-fat, jarringly spiced cooking to her mother's soothing, tasty stews and roasts. Now she stayed out of loyalty, for her mother insisted on cooking but had no appetite. Greta found the aroma of food offensive and nauseating. Boiled potatoes or white rice were acceptable. Sometimes a poached chicken breast. Elizabeth made milk shakes and smoothies and Greta tried to drink them, just to be agreeable. She never got very far, but Elizabeth would watch every sip with a kind of hysterical satisfaction.

"Good!" she would say. "That's so good! Thank you."

And her mother would smile weakly back at her. "Good," she would answer, putting the glass down with obvious relief, pushing it, still almost full, away from her. "Thank you."

To Catch a Thief. The King and I. The Philadelphia Story. The Killers. Whatever was on. Elizabeth knew much of the dialogue by heart. She would sit in her parents' den after dinner and wait eagerly for certain scenes, anticipating each gesture leading up to them. But often she would be distracted by something she had never noticed. In the small-town sheriff's office, when Edmond O'Brien, the insurance inspector, asks about Burt Lancaster's suicide, he stands in front of a window. Outside the window, several men are washing a fire truck. Elizabeth stared at the fire truck and the men and the rags they rubbed across it. She had never seen the fire truck there before. How could that be? How could movies be infinite?

Her father was out of the house even more than usual, using work as an excuse, but when he was home, he sat with her and watched movies. He looked grim and strained and smiled inappropriately, his hands heavy in his lap, his eyes soft-focused on some private scene. Elizabeth remembered how, when she was very small, she used to think the Sick was an exotic person of great importance and stature, like the czar. But now that Greta was the Sick, where was Tony's hearty reverence, his loyal comrade-in-arms energy? Instead, he held his own hands, as if he were his own patient.

He doesn't *really* know, she told herself. Worry is not knowing.

Lotte asked, "Where's Greta?"

She motioned Elizabeth to the refrigerator, in which there was a plate covered with plastic wrap that held a slice of white bread, the crusts removed, topped with a thin slice of porcelain pale turkey. Lotte had prepared it ahead of time for Elizabeth.

"I miss my Greta," Lotte said. Her voice became increasingly petulant, childish. "Where is my Gretala today?"

Gretala is home puking, Elizabeth wanted to say. She's getting chemotherapy because she, too, has cancer, but she doesn't want to worry you because she is generous and brave, Grandma, so get off her back.

"Mom's got the flu," she said, instead. "Remember? She doesn't want you to catch it."

"The flu? Again? My God, my God . . ."

"Well, really just a cold. Mom has a cold. She's fine. She's resting today, that's all. *I'm* here."

"You, you're a wonderful, wonderful girl. Why aren't you home with your family?"

"I am with my family. You."

"Your mother should take better care of herself."

Elizabeth nodded. She tried to eat the turkey sandwich. Her grandmother was very proud of her turkey sandwiches.

"No crusts," Lotte said. "Pretty snazzy." She motioned for Elizabeth to drink her tea. "The flu . . ." She shook her head, her forehead wrinkled with concern. "It's a sad thing," she said. "Frightening . . ."

"She's okay, Grandma. Really."

". . . a sad thing, Elizabeth, to be so dependent," Grandma Lotte continued. Her voice slid into a wail. "To *count* on your daughter the way I do . . ."

Elizabeth stared at Lotte, speechless.

"You cannot rely on anyone," Lotte said, shaking her head sadly.

As Lotte muttered and clucked her tongue and ran through the errands she could entrust only to Greta, Elizabeth pulled herself together, nodded occasionally, and stopped listening. She wondered if the Flu was a lie or a white lie. It was Lotte who had originally introduced her to the concept of a white lie. One afternoon when Elizabeth was a little girl, she had been home with Lotte at her grandparents' house in St. Louis. The phone rang.

"You get that for Grandma," Lotte said. "Good Tizzie. If it's Renie Blum, tell her Grandma's in bed with a migraine headache . . ."

"But —"

". . . and she can't play cards tonight."

"But you're not," Elizabeth said, as the phone rang, jangling, louder and louder, it seemed, threatening her moral standing with each new peal.

"I *could* be," Lotte said. She pushed Elizabeth to the kitchen wall where the phone was mounted.

It *was* Renie Blum. Elizabeth held the receiver, hesitated, watched her grandmother gesturing for her to get on with it.

"She's lying down. In bed," Elizabeth said. She didn't particularly like Renie Blum, who smelled of cigarette smoke. "Grandma has a headache." And Elizabeth thought playing cards was a waste of time, having heard as much from her mother many times over the years.

"Oy! A migraine?"

"Yeah. Grandma has a migraine headache and she's lying down in bed and she can't go out tonight."

Renie made worried sounds.

"She said to say she's very sorry," Elizabeth added.

Grandma Lotte sighed with relief as she hung the phone up for Elizabeth, who could not reach the cradle.

"But it was a *lie*," Elizabeth said. "You made me tell a lie." And she began to cry. She had lied before. What child hasn't? But since this was not her idea and did her no good, it seemed a wasted lie, a sin squandered, throwing good money, or in this case bad money, after bad.

"I lied!" She wailed and sobbed, and Grandma Lotte, looking confused and rather annoyed, held her in her arms and explained that it was a white lie.

"Grandpa and I were invited to the club. So I can't see Renie tonight, can I? Should I hurt her feelings and explain that to her? Renie might think I was insulting her, you see? You don't want me to hurt her feelings, do you?"

Elizabeth sat on Lotte's lap, her eyes swollen, her nose stuffed. "I lied," she said. But she was tired of crying, tired of Lotte's powdery scent, her iron-strong arms with their soft, paper-white skin.

"You told a *white* lie," Lotte said. "A white lie is a lie you tell to protect someone else's feelings."

Lotte offered Elizabeth the coveted red Life Saver. "It's a *nice* lie," she said, patting her granddaughter.

"The dirty goddamned bitch of a flu," Lotte said now. "*Your mother* should know better."

She crossed her arms.

"Hitler should feel the way I feel . . . *with* a daughter with the flu, that gangster."

She glared at Elizabeth.

"*Adolf* Hitler," she said.

Elizabeth was now the one who usually took her grandmother for radiation treatments. The first time that Greta called and said she didn't think she could manage to do it, Elizabeth told herself how pleased she was that Greta was able to ask for a little help. But she was also shocked. Her mother had never, as long as she could remember, begged off of anything.

In the waiting room of the radiation clinic, caked red deformities sat crusting on faces, necks, arms, and legs. Grandma Lotte, incredibly, seemed not to notice.

"It's so hot, a person could expire," she said.

"Take off your sweater, Grandma."

Lotte looked at her, hurt.

"It looks so great," Elizabeth added quickly. "It *would* be a shame to take it off."

"A crime," Lotte said.

Elizabeth tried to make her grandmother comfortable on the hard table where the preliminary laser measurements would be made. The soft-spoken Pakistani radiologist asked Lotte to lie motionless. He explained that he would have to mark her face with tiny blue dots — tattoos. Lotte began to cry. Elizabeth herself felt the room swirling, the darkening blur of fear, her throat closing. She gripped the hard X-ray table with one hand, stroked her grandmother's arm with her other, until, ordered out by the radiologist, she found a water fountain and took a Xanax.

Eventually, they put Lotte's face in a mold.

"Lie absolutely still, madam," the radiologist said.

"Aachoo!"

The mold slipped to the left. A blink. It slipped to the right. A moan. Another sneeze. Over and over, the mold shifted, and the radiologist made adjustments. After several visits, all was ready, and the treatment began in earnest. Elizabeth helped Lotte onto the table. She looked at her grandmother's face. The little blue dots were dwarfed by burgeoning scarlet swellings.

"Tattoos," Elizabeth said, "are very hip."

Lotte faced the ceiling, the soft creases of her cancerous skin shining with the trail of tears.

"Next we'll have to get your nipples pierced."

"Feh!" Lotte said.

Elizabeth had wanted to gather her grandmother up in her

arms and rock her like a baby. She had wanted to put a pillow over Lotte's distorted face and smother her. I can't take it, she thought. Too much sickness. Too much responsibility. And I can't take it that I can't take it. It's pitiful. I'm pitiful. I'm not the one who's sick. I'm the one who whines and complains about caring for those I love. You don't have cancer, Elizabeth, she told herself. So shut the fuck up. You're blessed with health. You're blessed with people you love enough to want to help. That's nothing to sneeze at.

"Haa-aah-CHOO."

Lotte's mask flew off.

And Elizabeth trembled with love and rage.

"It's okay, Grandma," she said, letting Lotte clutch her hand with her iron grip.

I'm not a nurse! she thought. I am not a fucking nurse.

And she squeezed her grandmother's hand back.

Greta opened her eyes. She had fallen asleep on the sofa. The pattern of the upholstery loomed, huge, preposterous, beyond her nose. She felt the cat at her feet.

"Ooh, you sweet thing," she murmured, pushing her feet beneath the warm body.

"How do you do?" someone said. "Greta, I presume."

Greta sat up, slowly, the way she had accustomed herself to moving these days. She saw a woman sitting at the foot of the couch. The woman held a cigarette. A silky loop of smoke wafted idly over her head. The woman eyed her with heavy lidded eyes. Held a hand out to shake.

There was no cat on the couch. Greta's feet were wedged beneath the woman's buttocks. Greta could feel the curve of the flesh, the warmth.

She leaned forward to take the woman's hand, smiling politely. It was her house, after all, and this woman was her guest. She wondered if she should pull her feet out from beneath the guest. It might bring attention to her feet and to their placement. And would it be rude? Greta had always thought of herself as hospitable.

As a compromise, she pulled her feet out in what she hoped was a hospitable manner.

"I thought you were the cat," she said.

The woman continued looking at her in her odd, sidelong way. "I read that cats cause schizophrenia," she said.

"That explains a lot," Greta said, feeling disloyal to her cat as she spoke, coughing suddenly on her own saliva, on her own words. Poor Moochie, who kept her feet warm at night and followed her loyally through the house like a small mewling dog. She tried to stop coughing, but the effort only triggered more. She was coughing in earnest, the kind of embarrassing cough usually reserved for the theater or a library.

The woman seemed suddenly to notice her cigarette.

"Oh, shit. Sorry." She looked around for an ashtray. "Shit."

She got up and Greta heard her turning on the water in the kitchen sink. She called out, "Stay put."

Stay put. What an interesting expression. Stay put. As if we had been purposefully "put" where we were. And we could choose to continue in that place. Or not.

The woman came back without the cigarette and with a glass of water. She was somewhere around thirty-five, Greta thought. Maybe a few years younger. She handed Greta the glass and sat on the coffee table facing her. Greta sipped gratefully, although she no longer drank water, certainly not tap water, and thought the woman almost mad for offering it.

"What a fucked up piece of shit I am," Greta's unexpected guest kept saying. "Schizophrenia? I mean you've got fucking lung cancer!"

"You really shouldn't drink this," Greta said, pointing to the glass.

"Water?"

"Colon," Greta added, "by the way."

They looked at each other, both embarrassed, and then burst out laughing. Greta felt as if she hadn't laughed in months. She was sure she hadn't. She felt their self-conscious laughter unaccountably accelerate. She watched herself and this strange woman laugh at nothing.

"Who . . . who the hell are you?" she said when she finally could speak.

The woman wiped her eyes with her shirttail, flashing a strip of stomach.

"Daisy," she said. "Daisy Piperno."

In the car, Elizabeth looked out the window and tried to figure out where she was. Josh was driving. Harry was asleep in the back.

"So who sleeps more?" Josh asked. "Him or Mom?"

Elizabeth looked back at Harry in sudden fear.

"He's just a *baby*," she said, her voice shrill. "He's *supposed* to sleep."

Josh turned to give her a disgusted look. "What is *with* you?"

Elizabeth slumped in her seat. "Where are we?" She had no idea, although she had taken this route to Grandma Lotte's so many times.

"Like, Century City, I guess," he said. "Did Grandma fire the new one? Yet?"

Elizabeth shook her head no.

They rode in silence the rest of the way.

Inside Lotte's lobby, they found Lotte waiting for them.

"Why should you come all the way up to the apartment?" she said. "We can sit right here. Let *them* pay for the air-conditioning. We'll have our visit."

Harry sat on Lotte's lap, sulky from his interrupted nap, his pacifier in his mouth. Elizabeth sat on the couch and massaged Grandma's large hand, hoping that would somehow exempt her from having to make conversation. Josh sat on Lotte's other side. He was better at small talk, less self-conscious than Elizabeth.

The chairs in the lobby were not very comfortable. Elizabeth wanted to leave and felt guilty for it. Her grandmother was wearing a turquoise sundress. She was also wearing her bedroom slippers. Not a good sign.

"I got lice once," Grandma Lotte was saying, part of a conversation Elizabeth had long lost track of. "Mama washed my hair with lye."

Harry pulled his pacifier out.

"Jacob got lice," he said. "At his school. He's a big boy."

"You could eat him up," Lotte cried. She clapped her hands and Harry watched, wide-eyed, as her bracelets crashed before his eyes.

Elizabeth envied Grandma her slippers. She wanted to take her shoes off. Had they stayed long enough? It was never long enough — a horrible, ungenerous thought which she tried to shake. She wondered if they were meeting in the lobby because Grandma had, indeed, fired her latest housekeeper. She knew she should find out. But she preferred not to.

Greta noticed her surprise visitor, Daisy Piperno, unconsciously reach for a cigarette from her bag, then pull her hand away from the pack.

"Daisy Piperno," Greta said, enjoying the sound of the name. "The hot young director, yes?"

"I'm a director, anyway."

"And young," Greta insisted. "And certainly very . . ." For a moment, she felt as though she were lost inside her own body, light-headed and confused.

Daisy, leaning back into the couch, resting one ankle on the other knee, her sandal dangling from her foot, said, very softly, "Thanks. You're pretty hot yourself."

By the time Elizabeth and Josh and Harry came back from

Lotte's, Greta had made ice tea and taken Daisy to look at her garden in the back of the house. They had a pleasant discussion about native grasses, about which Daisy knew quite a bit.

"I sat on your mother to wake her up," Daisy said. "Then I blew secondhand smoke at her. She's quite resilient."

"She never complains," Elizabeth said.

Greta watched them go into Tony's study to work.

"She makes *dee*-vine ice tea," she heard Daisy say.

I do, actually, Greta thought. First make strong tea. Let it cool, or it will get cloudy. Put a lot of ice in it. Add lemon last. A lot of lemon . . . Greta realized she was thinking of food, or at least a beverage, was thinking of taste, with pleasure.

Josh was running through the house with Harry on his back.

My children are home, Greta thought. And my grandson. I have a devoted husband. I'm feeling better today. I can drink ice tea. I have enough energy to make ice tea. I'm very lucky.

She grabbed Josh and Harry and kissed their foreheads.

Elizabeth looked back at her mother. She must be feeling better. She was back in her old uniform. In her jeans and white T-shirt and bare feet, and so thin from the chemo, Greta looked like a kid. Greta was so happy today. Her mother's happiness filled the house like an exotic perfume. Elizabeth tried to share in it, to breathe it in, to push away the thought of how easily it could disappear.

Moochie the cat jumped up beside her on the couch. He curled up between her and Daisy. He began to purr. She watched the cat hair float through the air, past her laptop screen, past Daisy, lit by the deep afternoon sun.

EXT. DECK OF EXPENSIVE MALIBU BEACH HOUSE — EVENING

> Barbie is curled in a chair, like a cat, or a snake. She blows languid smoke rings. The cigarette dangles in her hand, glowing in the deep blue of evening.

Below her, on the beach, a fabulously handsome guy jogs toward her. He is LEO, an actor who lives several houses down. He looks up.

Their eyes lock.

Barbie blows another smoke ring. It hangs between them as he passes, running slowly down the beach.

Greta looked at the open door leading to Tony's study where the two girls sat, hunched solemnly over a laptop computer.

"Why does everything I write sound like parody?" Elizabeth was saying.

"Well, this scene *is* parody in the novel," Daisy said. She flipped through her paperback translation of *Madame Bovary* and read out loud. "'This is how they wanted to be, each of them imagining an ideal toward which they would now readjust their past lives.' It's parody, that's why it's parody."

Greta came closer and stood in the doorway. Daisy looked up and saw her there and held her gaze for what seemed to Greta a long time, then turned back to the novel.

"Besides," Daisy read, her voice holding the words, then gently letting them go, or so it seemed at that moment to Greta, "'the spoken word is like a rolling machine . . .'" She looked up at Greta again. "'. . . that draws feelings out.'"

"Mom?" Elizabeth had noticed her. "What's up?"

"Anyone for ice tea?" Greta said.

She looked Daisy up in the telephone book. She had no idea why. She didn't plan to call her.

There it was: Daisy Piperno. Only one with that name, certainly. She examined the number, feeling weirdly guilty, as if she were spying on the girl.

When Elizabeth arrived that day, Greta said, "How is your work going?"

Elizabeth shrugged.

"Is Daisy a help?"

"At least she has some idea of what she's doing."

"Don't you?" Greta said.

Elizabeth gave her a warning look.

Greta offered her a cup of coffee, which seemed to mollify her. "Where's Harry?"

"I made Brett take him to the beach."

"That's nice."

Elizabeth looked up from the newspaper, making sure there was no undercurrent to Greta's words.

"It's *nice*," Greta said.

"I *can't* do it myself."

Greta thought she ought to change the subject. "Is Daisy meeting you here today?"

"I *want* to. You think I don't want to go to the beach? I can't *do* everything," Elizabeth said. She got up, almost in tears, and left the kitchen.

"What's she ragging on about?" Josh said, as Elizabeth almost knocked him over in the doorway.

"Shut up!" Elizabeth yelled from the other room.

Greta watched Josh pour coffee, watched the milk slosh out of the cup onto the counter. What *is* she ragging on about? she wondered. Why does Josh tease her so much? *Is* Daisy coming today? Josh put the empty carafe back on the coffeemaker's burner.

"Sink," Greta said.

She went into the study and sat on the arm of the chair Elizabeth was curled up in.

"I'm such a wacko," Elizabeth said, wiping tears from her face.

"You're high-strung," Greta said.

Elizabeth looked up, gratefully.

"You're not supposed to be consoling me," Elizabeth said. "I'm selfish and self-indulgent and I'm not helping you."

"I'm feeling better today," Greta said. "Get it while the getting's good."

She stroked Elizabeth's hair while Elizabeth tapped on her laptop.

"Isn't Daisy coming today?" Greta said. "I liked her."

"Nope."

Elizabeth tapped away. Greta rubbed her daughter's head, feeling the shape of Elizabeth's skull, familiar beneath her hand.

Lotte knew what she knew. You didn't have to be Dr. Ruth, that little midget, to see it. Anyone with eyes in their head could tell: There was something off about the marriage. They weren't even married. That was the first clue.

Elizabeth held Harry, who had slipped and fallen. He sobbed into her breast as she knelt before him, her arms encircling his little body.

"I'll go get the car," Brett said.

"*Do* that," Elizabeth said, her voice bitter and sarcastic.

Lotte saw that Brett looked shocked. What had he done? He had offered to get the car so they wouldn't have to walk. What was wrong with that? Stupid man. Nothing was wrong with that. But who was left holding the crying baby? Couldn't he see that?

"Harry, you want to come with Daddy to get the car?" Brett said.

Well! Lotte had always liked this Brett. He had a head on him, after all.

"Don't be ridiculous," Elizabeth said.

Something was rotten in the state of Denmark, Lotte thought. Just as I thought, she thought. I know what I know.

Brett shook his head, set his mouth, and began to walk out.

"Daddy!" Harry cried. He ran after Brett. He pulled on his sleeve. "You said!"

Brett picked him up and carried him out.

Lotte thought, I keep my own counsel. Then she said, "You've got a mouth on you, young lady."

Elizabeth looked ashamed. "I just lose my patience sometimes."

"Just so you don't lose your husband."

"Grandma! Anyway, he's not."

"A nice, handsome man like that. Earns a nice living. Doesn't drink. Doesn't gamble . . ."

Elizabeth was crawling on the floor, picking up Harry's toy trucks. She wasn't paying any attention. No one listened to old people. Lotte banged her cane on the floor. With the carpeting, so beautiful, so thick, and the extra padding, the installation had cost a fortune, there was no sound. Elizabeth put the toys in her bag, then sat on the couch beside Lotte. She threw her head back and sighed. The poor girl. She was exhausted. They exhausted themselves. Children, jobs . . . Lotte grabbed Elizabeth's hand in both of her own. She squeezed it, kissed it, nibbled on it, then held it in her lap and looked at Elizabeth.

"Well," she said, smiling, patting her granddaughter's hand comfortingly. "Mark my words."

～

Tony got in bed and opened the book he was reading. It was an enormous history of New York City. He'd been reading it for a year and not yet made it out of the seventeenth century.

"Do you miss New York?" Greta said.

"I don't miss Brooklyn."

"Brooklyn is nice now. Nice again. I hear."

Tony adjusted his reading glasses. Greta could feel the heat of his body warming the bed. She looked at her hands holding the novel Tim had brought her and tried to ignore the cloudy accusation that seemed to be with her all the time now, swaying like a ghost: I waited too long to go to the doctor.

But I was so busy with my mother, she said to the ghost.

Tony's foot brushed hers, startling her.

"Anyway, you're from Queens," she said to him.

"Born in Brooklyn."

"Fraud."

"Well, I don't miss Queens. That's for sure."

Greta turned off her light.

"But Queens is the new Brooklyn," she said. "I hear."

She wondered if she missed St. Louis. The heavy summer days, wet and languid with humidity, the trees drooping with green. The trees. There were no trees like that here. Yes, she missed the trees.

"Funny you have no accent," she said.

Tony was asleep, the book open on his belly.

Daisy Piperno had an accent, but Greta had not quite located it. She was usually good at accents. She had worked at shedding her own, but liked them in others, found them evocative and touching. And Daisy had such a distinctive one — a lilting, musical sound. Greta tried to place Daisy's accent, to name the senseless, easy singsong.

She marked the place in Tony's book by turning down a page, although he hated that. She reached over and switched off his light. She kissed his sleeping lips and turned on her side.

You're pretty hot yourself, Daisy had said in her funny undulating croon. Greta felt sleep closing in. *You're pretty hot . . .* The words glided gently up, gently down, a ripple of iambs, almost Scandinavian. Greta closed her eyes. Sleep would be so good. Not the oppressive suffocating sleep of chemotherapy, but an airy, scented release. *Pretty hot yourself . . .* Greta opened her eyes and smiled. Mary Richards, Bob Dylan, the Coen Brothers, and the first Mall of America. *You're pretty hot yourself . . .* Daisy Piperno was from Minnesota.

four

Lotte's cancer was turning out to be an unusually virulent skin cancer. The radiation had been a disaster. Did it stop the tumor? No. Did it stimulate the growth of the tumor until it bulged from her face like a large tuber, a red misshapen vegetable, the bastard? Naturally. Lotte sat in her comfortable chair and tried to put the tumor out of her mind, fat chance, as she studied the catalogs. Her favorite was Victoria's Secret. Forget the lingerie, though. She was too old for that, those prostitutes. But that Victoria carried gorgeous sweaters. And Lotte liked that blazer with gold braid around the sleeves. Classic, without being dull. She sighed. She should have stuck with the surgeon in the first place. Well, now he would have his chance.

"Hi, Grandma."

She looked up to see Elizabeth.

"Darling, darling," Lotte murmured as Elizabeth bent over to kiss her. Lotte stroked Elizabeth's head with its lovely hair, hidden away, such a waste.

"Scared?" Elizabeth said.

"There are no atheists in the foxholes," Lotte said solemnly.

Elizabeth nodded her approval of the blazer.

"The navy," Lotte said.

"I assumed."

"The red is vulgar. Not always, mind you."

"No," Elizabeth said obligingly. "Red can work."

Lotte held Elizabeth's hand, feeling the youthful skin. She kissed her granddaughter's fingertips, the way she used to when Elizabeth was younger. When she was younger, herself.

"So, Grandma, don't worry," Elizabeth said. "He's a good surgeon."

"Top man," Lotte said.

Lotte ordered the blazer over the phone while Elizabeth made herself a cup of tea.

"I have exquisite taste," she told the woman taking her order.

Elizabeth helped her dress. Lotte watched her arms slide into the arms of her turtleneck. She closed her eyes and felt it cling to her face as Elizabeth pulled it over her head. The cotton, a very fine cotton, glided across her lips. Now it was on. Now Elizabeth was adjusting it. Now she would go to the hospital and lie on a hard table and that handsome prick would cut her face with a knife. Downstairs, the doorman wished her luck. "You look like a million bucks," he said. Her Morris used to say that. Lotte tried not to cry.

"See that?" she said to Elizabeth. "An old bitch like me, sick as a dog?" She wondered if she should have ordered the blazer. She might die on the operating table.

"I bequeath that jacket to you, sweetheart," she said.

"Oh, Grandma."

"*Man tracht, Gott lacht,*" Lotte said. "Man plans, God laughs."

"After your operation, I'll take you out to dinner in your new jacket."

Lotte smiled. She liked an outing, liked an excuse to wear her new clothes. For a moment she forgot that she was going to the hospital to have a piece of her face cut off and then, perhaps, to die.

"But what will *you* wear, sweetheart?" she said, turning to look at her granddaughter, so grown-up, driving a big car, a truck almost, and she'd heard on the radio they were dangerous, the dirty bastard SUVs.

"Why are you driving Mommy's car?" she said.

"Brett needed ours."

"Where is Mommy, anyway? Who's driving your mommy?"

"Josh is meeting us," Elizabeth said. "Mom can't come, Grandma. I told you. What if she's contagious? From the flu?"

"Some flu," Lotte said.

Elizabeth's such a big girl now, she thought, watching her get her own money out of her own pocketbook to pay for parking. "Oh! *My* bag! Where's my bag?"

Elizabeth held it up.

"Thank *God* you found it," Lotte said. She clutched it. She unzipped it. She pulled out a wadded-up Kleenex.

Elizabeth laughed. "As long as I can remember," she said. "Tissues and Life Savers."

Lotte said nothing more about Greta. She suspected Greta must be gravely ill and that they were protecting her from knowing. Good. Let them protect me. I deserve protection. She wondered if God laughed at the believers in the trenches. No wonder she had never approved of religion, those dirty hypocrites in their synagogues and churches. But her poor Greta. No flu lasts so many weeks. Then again, who knows? Maybe it was a lingering flu. Maybe Greta was not deathly ill. Maybe no one was protecting Lotte. No one does protect you in the end, she thought.

"I know just the thing!" she said suddenly. "The silk cardigan with the zipper. The taupe. With your black pants?" She nodded assent at her own suggestion. Lotte in her navy blazer, her grand-daughter in the taupe silk. "Very flattering," she said.

Josh and Elizabeth sat on the same couch in the hospital waiting room that Elizabeth had been sitting on with her father when they waited to hear the news about Greta. Elizabeth shivered in the air-conditioning. Josh put his arm around her.

"What did you tell her about Mom?" he asked.

"Flu. The same old fucking flu. She didn't exactly press me, ei-ther. She just called Mommy from my cell phone in the car, told her not to worry, said she hoped Mom would feel all better soon. It was almost like two normal people talking."

"She knows something's up," Josh said.

"And doesn't want to know."

"I'm with Grandma."

Elizabeth waited with Josh outside the recovery room. They wore yellow, wrinkled scrub suits that looked dirtier than their street clothes. Elizabeth wondered what Lotte's face would look like now.

"One at a time," the nurse said, and led Elizabeth through a room of coughing, sleeping, vomiting, groaning bodies.

Lotte lay on a stretcher. She was naked. Her body was a bluish white. Elizabeth tried not to look at her pubic area, the hairs white and sparse. She pulled a sheet over her grandmother. She glanced at the nurse as she did so: Okay? The nurse nodded yes. Lotte was breathing bubbly snores.

"Grandma?"

Lotte opened her eyes.

"It's me — Elizabeth."

Lotte had a bandage covering most of her face. Elizabeth took her grandmother's hand in both of her own.

"Mama?" Lotte said.

"She's fine," Elizabeth said, then realized Lotte was not asking about Elizabeth's mother.

Elizabeth waited for her grandmother in the room she would occupy. A woman in the next bed moaned softly, then cleared phlegm from her throat. The chair was a dull blue leatherette and had a high back. The bed was made up with tight cheap white sheets. The muffled sound of an ambulance could be heard beyond the grimy windowpane. The room itself seemed fairly clean, though. Elizabeth sat as the afternoon became darker. Her grandmother had looked so frail and so skinny. She had clasped Elizabeth's hand with such force.

A nurse came into the room with an enormous bunch of flowers. She switched on the harsh overhead light.

"Someone's lucky day!" she said.

Lucky day? She'd had her nose cut off!

Elizabeth looked at the card. Laurence Volfmann? How nice, she thought. Of course the twin secretaries had sent them, but he must have asked them to. She had barely mentioned the operation to him. He had remembered. It would make Lotte so happy. TO A TRUE TROUPER! said the card. It was an incredibly generous and thoughtful gesture. The arrangement was as ornate and almost as large as one of Greta's gardens. And he doesn't even know Grandma. But he does know me, Elizabeth thought. And as she pictured Volfmann in the dark suit and lilac tie she'd last seen him wearing, she found herself repressing an excited smile.

She turned the light out and sat in the dark wondering why Volfmann wasn't married. She knew he'd had an extremely costly divorce a few years ago. Maybe that was the reason. That's what I should tell people when they tell me to marry Brett. Too many alimony payments!

Why didn't she want to marry Brett, really? None of her friends had a kid when Elizabeth found out she was pregnant with

Harry. They had assumed she would get an abortion or get married. But both of those choices were unthinkable for Elizabeth. She wanted to have the baby, Brett wanted the baby, and she wanted to raise the baby with Brett. She just didn't want to get married. And the more Brett pressed her, the less she wanted to get married. If only she had an easy explanation she could have given him. Or even a complicated explanation. But all she had was an image: she saw herself walking down the aisle, and at the end was . . . the end.

Elizabeth had encountered that image when the subject of marriage came up from the time she was a little girl. Why? she wondered. Her mother always seemed so happy with her father. Greta never complained, worked at what she loved, and though Tony was not the most attentive husband, he was warm and he obviously adored Greta. So, what had given Elizabeth this idea? Perhaps she had seen *Madame Bovary* as an infant.

Volfmann's flowers sent an almost narcotic perfume through the room. Elizabeth leaned her head back and forced herself to imagine walking beside Brett toward a rabbi, toward a justice of the peace, toward a ship's captain, a judge. No, it was no good. She could not imagine living without him, but she could not imagine marrying him, either. What would happen if she and Brett did split up, though? How do you divorce someone you're not married to? Well, that's the point. You can't. So you have to stay together.

She looked at the outline of Volfmann's floral arrangement, silhouetted by the light coming from the parking lot. A girl could go for a guy who sends flowers to her grandma, she thought. And, Elizabeth reminded herself, if you're not married, you can't commit adultery.

That was Madame Bovary's mistake. Becoming Madame Bovary.

"I'll be at the hospital later," Tony said the day after Lotte's surgery. "I'll get your mother some peaches."

Greta was often taken by surprise by Tony in this way. Her mother was impossible, swore like a sailor (which Tony still hated, after all these years), told him the same stories over and over. Her mother, most important, was *her* mother, not his. And yet, even when she wasn't in the hospital, Tony would drive all over Los Angeles looking for the ripest peaches. He would go to Malibu to get her the smoked mussels she liked.

"You don't have to do that," Greta said.

"The Elderly appreciate little gestures."

"The Elderly will be thrilled. It would be awfully nice, if you really want to."

Greta listened to Tony sing "Joe Hill" as he gathered his things.

"Oh, but she won't be able to eat solids yet," he said. "Maybe lemon meringue pie. She likes that."

He waved good-bye. She heard the garage door noisily jerk open. Tony's car started up. She turned on the dishwasher. He was a good husband. She knew that. He was an even better son-in-law, chivalrous and charming, seeming to sense how much the attention of a man meant to Lotte.

She envisioned her mother, trapped in a metal bed, a thin, faded hospital gown slipping, unnoticed, from her shoulders; the looping intravenous tubes hanging, hopeless and immodest, like nylons hung to dry in the bathroom. Greta suddenly and almost desperately wanted to go to the hospital herself. Lotte was her mother. She had to go to the hospital and see her mother. It was that simple.

She found her keys and got in the car. She started it up and jumped as the radio came on full blast, a Burger King ad in Spanish. She switched the radio off. She was grateful to Tony. She was sick to her stomach. She was angry and full of self-pity and ashamed. Her mother needed her and she did not have the strength to back the car out of the driveway. She needed her mother and her mother was lying helpless in a hospital bed unable to eat peaches. She rested her head on the wheel until she was able to switch the car off. She walked slowly into the house, tripping on the cat, who sprawled in a patch of sun, and lay down.

As she eased slowly away from consciousness, Greta could almost smell the fragrance of the ripening peach her mother could not eat, of lemon meringue pie, of the lemon she squeezed into a tall glass of ice tea; and then the citrus scent of Daisy Piperno's breath, warm and intimate, as she leaned forward to bestow a good-bye kiss on Greta's cheek.

"Bye, you," Daisy had said. And Greta had inhaled the balm of her words.

The nurse called Elizabeth that afternoon.

"Your grandmother is agitated," she said. "Very agitated."

Elizabeth recognized angry panic in the nurse's voice and rushed to the hospital, much to Harry's dismay.

"Don't go," he wailed. He lay on the floor and held her right ankle in his hands. With each step she dragged him across the floor with her, a kicking, curly headed ball and chain. "Don't go, Mommy. Mommy, don't go."

She picked him up and they clung to each other. Keep me here with you, she thought. Don't let me go. She promised to call him on her cell phone from the car and he finally calmed down. She kissed his flushed face and tore herself away, leaving him whimpering in Brett's arms, the mucus in his nose and the pacifier in his mouth making breathing a gulping arrhythmic effort that Elizabeth could hear even in the driveway.

"Hi, Harry," she said when she called him five minutes later.

"Hi, Mommy."

"I'm on my way to Grandma's now. At the hospital."

"I know," he said, patiently, as if she were astonishingly literal minded. "Bye, Mommy!"

When she hung up, Elizabeth thought of his hands around her ankle. She wished they were still there, holding her.

At the hospital, the head nurse, who wore a pink nylon blouse that depressed Elizabeth, apologized for putting Lotte in restraints.

Elizabeth stared at the pale skinny person held down on the bed by an orange-mesh-net vest strapped across her middle. She had a large white bandage across her face. Her white skin was bunched up beneath transparent tape. What was left of Grandma Lotte's nose? It's like the invisible man, Elizabeth thought, and felt immediately guilty.

"Untie her," Elizabeth said.

Lotte's hands were tied down, too. She struggled and moaned.

"She's agitated . . ." the nurse said.

Elizabeth bent down and began undoing the straps herself.

"I'll watch her," she said.

She watched her grandmother for hours. She wrestled her back to bed when Lotte flailed and tried to escape whoever was chasing her. The rest of the time, Elizabeth watched Lotte sew. Lotte pulled the imaginary needle through the imaginary cloth. Again and again. Sometimes she bit off the imaginary thread. Sometimes she turned her head to the next bed, where a woman was moaning.

"Elizabeth!" she whispered. "They took Harry! They have Harry. I hear him crying. Harry!" She was no longer whispering. "The baby! They've got the baby!"

Elizabeth stroked her hand and told her no baby was crying. It was the woman in the next bed.

"Yes!" Grandma Lotte said.

"Yes," Elizabeth said in her most soothing voice.

"Yes!" Lotte repeated. "The woman. The woman who stole the baby! She's got Harry!"

Lotte began thrashing at the sheets, trying to get up.

"You just had an operation," Elizabeth said, holding her down. "You're in the hospital. Everything is fine. Harry is fine."

Sometimes Grandma Lotte stopped worrying about Harry and

went back to sewing. Other times she cried in fright at a thunder-storm she thought she was caught in. For a while she swore vi-ciously at a group of sinister Hasidim who were apparently closing in on her.

"Hypocrites, bastards, get away from me, dirty rotten pious sons of bitches . . ."

Once, she touched the bandage and said, "My face," in a voice deep with tenderness and defeat.

When the surgeon visited, he said the operation was a success.

"But why is she sewing? She's hallucinating. She's so scared . . ."

"The dementia is from the anesthesia. She'll be herself tomor-row. Won't you, dear?" he said to Lotte.

Lotte bit off an imaginary hanging thread and spit it out loudly.

When Tony arrived, he offered Lotte the lemon meringue pie, but she put her hands up to shield her face.

"The bastards!" she screamed.

Elizabeth tried to apologize.

"She doesn't know what she's saying . . ."

But her father was already waving a hand, dismissing the pos-sibility that anyone would really call him such a thing. He was comfortable in his own decency, Elizabeth had noticed. Sometimes it made him seem smug.

"Dementia," he murmured, as he opened Lotte's chart.

Elizabeth envied him his expertise. He knew something, was an authority on something. And he could do good in the world just by doing his job. Like a nun.

"You can walk into a hospital room, look at a chart, and under-stand what it says, what it means. I envy you," she said.

"It's been a while," he said, still flipping through the chart. He looked up. "You can walk into a room and open *Madame Bovary* and understand what that means."

"That's not a profession. That's . . . entertainment."

Lotte began singing, *That's entertainment!*

"For Christ's sake," Tony said suddenly.

Again, Elizabeth began to apologize for Lotte, but then saw that her father was staring at the chart.

"The bastards," he said.

Lotte nodded in satisfied agreement.

Elizabeth stared. Her father swore so rarely. He left the room carrying Lotte's chart.

Lotte, still singing, stopped her imaginary sewing and began to imaginary crochet. Elizabeth recognized the stitch.

"Sweater?" she said.

"You like the color?" Lotte asked.

Tony returned after about a quarter of an hour.

"They gave her a sleeping pill that makes people nuts," he said. He shook his head, disgusted. "Lotte?" he said, leaning over her. "You'll feel better soon."

"Dirty bastard hypocrites," Lotte cried out. "Pooh! Phoo! G'way!" She waved her hands, as if at flies.

"Right on," Tony said.

Elizabeth cringed. She found her parents' occasional '60s slang excruciating. Please don't say "Bummer," she thought.

"Bummer," he said. "But now the dirty bastard hypocrites are on their way out, Lotte old girl. I've taken care of it."

"Isn't it handy to have a son-in-law who's a doctor?" Elizabeth said.

Lotte smiled as she looped yarn around the crochet needle. Elizabeth put her head on her father's shoulder. He was the calm one in the family. He and Josh. He and Josh and Greta.

He put his arms around her.

"Thank you, Daddy."

"She'll be okay."

There was a silence as they both took in the sentence and the spaces around it.

Everyone will be okay, Elizabeth wanted him to say.

She waited.

Perhaps it's me who's supposed to say that, she thought.

"They both will," she said.

Her father hugged her closer.

"Poor Elizabeth," was all he said.

Lotte listened to the rain. It never stopped. If she died, she would see her father in heaven. He would be angry at her. With his fiery red hair, he would stamp his foot, stare silently, and chew on his cigar. Lotte saw herself cowering. She had always been her father's darling. Or so she liked to claim. But if she was his darling, why was he so angry at her? She didn't want to die. She didn't want to see her angry father. She could see the fury in his eyes. She listened to the rain. It sounded like tap dancing. She moved her feet to the rhythm. She was a talented child. Of America.

When her father left, Elizabeth sat in the only chair. The yellow curtains were pulled, like shower curtains, around the bed, the bedside table, and the chair with Elizabeth in it. She hoped Brett had given Harry dinner. Would her grandmother get dinner? She shifted irritably, accidentally kicking the bed. There was a knock on the door and she watched as Josh's friend Tim gingerly pushed open the curtains. She wondered if she should get up, if this was like greeting a guest at one's house. Was she the hostess? She didn't move.

Tim squatted beside her. He was wearing baggy blue jeans with an ink stain in the back pocket and a white T-shirt, also with an ink stain in the pocket. She was glad to see him. A family friend, she thought, and the sound of that was comforting.

"How is she?" he whispered.

"She sews a lot. It's unnerving."

They watched Lotte sleep.

"You don't have to whisper," Elizabeth said.

"Oh," he whispered. He got up, smelled the large bouquet of flowers from Volfmann, looked at the card. "Your boss?" he said. He raised his eyebrows.

"Yeah, the whole casting-couch thing," she said. But she felt herself blush.

"Where's your mom?" he said.

Elizabeth put a finger to her lips to silence him. She didn't want Greta's name so much as mentioned in front of Grandma Lotte.

"I'm in charge," she said. "Like Alexander Haig."

"Oy," Lotte said, her eyes still closed. "That dirty son of a bitch."

"They called me to come in because Grandma was agitated."

With her eyes still closed, Lotte licked the frayed end of her imaginary thread and carefully directed it through her imaginary needle.

Tim raised his eyebrows.

"What are you making, Mrs. Franke?"

Lotte did not respond. She was tying a knot.

"'Agitated' means she's hallucinating because they gave her Halcion. She thinks the lady in the next bed stole Harry. She told the morning nurse she had a fat ass."

"Was that a hallucination?"

Lotte suddenly began to sing.

Toot-toot-tootsie good-bye . . .

"I had to come untie her," Elizabeth said. She liked the noble sound of having rescued her grandmother.

Tim peered down at Lotte, who sang and moved her feet beneath the blankets until her dinner was brought in on a tray. Tim and Elizabeth stared at the Salisbury steak.

"Disgusting," Elizabeth said.

"Really? I like Salisbury steak."

"Is that why you stayed in school?" She couldn't even remember what his field was.

"Can I have it?"

Elizabeth wrinkled her nose.

"You can have the string beans," he said graciously. He sat on the arm of the chair and scooped up brown goo with the plastic fork. "I do research in school, too, you know. Throw subatomic particles at each other. See what happens. It's awesome."

Elizabeth was sure it was awesome but now wished he would go so she wouldn't have to make small talk. She preferred to watch her grandmother sink gradually into dementia in solitude.

He wiped his mouth with the little napkin and opened Lotte's carton of milk. "Teaching's awesome, too," he said.

"Your whole life is just full of awe," Elizabeth said.

Tim, who had been smiling, stopped. He shrugged. "Yeah," he said. "It is."

"I'm sorry," she said. She felt her face get hot and, probably, red. She looked down.

"I know you think I'm infantile," Tim said.

"Puerile."

"Oh." He sighed. "Right."

The phone rang. It was Greta.

"How is she?"

"Sewing and singing," Elizabeth said. "Daddy came and changed her pills. Tim's here."

"I've always had a crush on you," Tim said.

Elizabeth covered the receiver with her hand. *"What?"*

I've got a cruuush on youuu, Lotte sang.

"Honey?" Greta was saying. *"You still there?"*

Tim stood up.

Sweeeeetie pie! Lotte sang.

The woman in the next bed groaned.

"My poor baby," Greta was saying. *"I should be there. Not you. You have a family to take care of."*

"This is my family, too," Elizabeth said. "And I'm taking care of it. Relax, Mommy. Please. I'm in charge."

"Well, bye, I guess," Tim said.

Elizabeth hung up.

"You guess?" she said. But Tim was already gone.

When Elizabeth got home, Harry was asleep. Brett was in bed reading the *New York Times* on his laptop.

"I'll be there in a minute," she said. She went into Harry's room and sat on the edge of the bed. Tim had always had a crush on her? She still thought of Tim as a kid in ninth grade. That was how old he was when they met. She had come home from college and there was her brother shooting hoops in the driveway next door with this skinny boy wearing glasses. But now he was not in ninth grade, he was not skinny, he was not even wearing glasses. She pushed his words out of her mind. Her grandmother sewed what was not there. That was enough imagination for one night.

"Harry?" she said. "Are you awake?"

She put her hand on his shoulder. She shook him gently. She longed to hear his voice.

"Why can't I?" he murmured, still asleep. "Why?"

"No reason," she said softly. "No reason at all."

Elizabeth lay down next to him, letting her shoes drop to the floor as she swung her legs onto his bed and, lost in the peace of his breath and his scent and the touch of his skin, she fell asleep.

Greta lay in bed missing her mother. I'm fifty-three years old. I'm a mother myself. A grandmother. My mother has lived a long, full life. These things are supposed to comfort me. They don't. I want my mother. Her mouth twisted like a child on the verge of tears. I am a child, she thought. I am still my mother's child.

Tony was out. He had helped organize a benefit dinner and had left the house looking handsome and prosperous in his tuxedo.

"I wish you could come," he'd said.

But Greta could tell he was glad to get away. He had never been very good with sick people. Broken bones, yes. The Sick with a capital S, yes. But the terrified patient, desperate and clutching — that need had always frightened him.

She heard the car pull up, the garage door open and close. She heard Tony come into the bedroom. She pretended to be asleep as she listened to the swish of his clothes, the clank of the hangers. He went into the bathroom. She heard him pee, flush, wash, brush his teeth. He got into bed and fell asleep instantly, and she turned over and thought of Daisy. She thought she ought to rent Daisy's movie, *Doll*. It didn't sound very promising, a girl in love with her doll, but you never knew. When she was little, she had imagined that she was a princess and all the princes in all the neighboring kingdoms would come seeking her hand and she would turn them all down until she met the one who passed the secret test: he would smell just like her security blanket. She realized later that the smell she loved was partly her own, partly the cat's, and mostly, simply, dirt. But the point, she said to herself now, is why the hell not a doll? She herself had never even liked her dolls, much less fallen in love with them. But there was a plush monkey she had been enamored of. He had red corduroy overalls and his feet were white rubber made to look like high-top sneakers. His hands and face were rubber, too. To each his own, she thought. She leaned over and sniffed Tony. He smelled like Neutrogena T/Gel.

Lotte stared at the ceiling. The rain hadn't stopped, but she knew now it was a hallucination. A pale beam of fluorescent activity showed between the door and its frame. There were hundreds of men in black coats stained with food. Some wore fur hats. Their beards depressed her.

"Go away," she said. "You're not even here."

She listened to the rain and wondered if she had already died.

"But I'm not ready," she said. "I'm just not ready."

The men had kidnapped Harry, but they were just a dream. The rain was just a dream. The hospital was no dream. The cancer was no dream. And I am no dream, either, Lotte thought. She examined the blanket she had crocheted for Harry, for when the kidnapping was over. It was navy blue with red-and-white yarn drawn diagonally across the seams. She tried to put a hand up to touch her face, but she couldn't move it. She began to cry, but the men in their hats and dirty black coats ignored her.

five

Elizabeth made Barbie Bovaine come not to Milwaukee, as Daisy had at first suggested, but to Los Angeles. Where better for a romantic to wind up? Flaubert wrote that Emma Bovary "felt that certain places on the earth must produce happiness, just as a plant that languishes everywhere else thrives only in special soil." L.A., with its huge blossoms, its roses bigger than roses, its swollen oranges bulging from its chubby trees — this was special soil in which all kinds of plants flourished. Here the desperate narcissus could burst into its doomed narcissistic bloom.

"So, okay," Daisy said, "Emma wanted the romance and passion she thought resided in the lives of the rich, the aristocratic, the urban sophisticate. And Barbie wants the romance and passion she thinks reside in celebrity."

Elizabeth nodded slightly, not sure, now that someone else had summarized her idea so plainly, if she still wanted to claim it. They were in a conference room, seated around a large, polished table: Volfmann, Elliot, Elliot's two assistants, who had trailed him in like ducklings, Daisy, and me, Elizabeth thought. She looked from one face to another, trying to pick up some reaction. But everyone looked down. Everyone but Volfmann, whose eyes were closed. His chin rested in his hand. He tapped the bridge of his nose with his forefinger. It was a gesture Elizabeth found interesting because it seemed so unconscious.

"Obvious parallel," he said. He opened his eyes. "Obvious is good sometimes."

"How about this time?" Daisy said.

"Good. Obvious is good this time. Celebrity is seductive."

Elliot pursed his lips and wrinkled his brow.

"What?" said Volfmann.

"Rarefied?" he said, his head cocked to one side, pursing his lips even tighter. "Not accessible to ordinary people?"

"An obsession with celebrity?" Elizabeth said. "Rarefied? Are you kidding?"

"Gossip is good," Elliot said. "Fictional gossip? Not good."

"*A Star Is Born?*" Elizabeth said, "*Sunset Boulevard? The Player? The Jazz Singer,* for Christ's sake . . ."

Daisy put her hand on Elizabeth's. "Okay," she said.

"*The Big Picture,*" Elizabeth muttered.

"Anyway, it's not about celebrity," Daisy said. "It's about celebrity worship."

"Elliot?" Volfmann said. "Celebrity worship? Closer to home?"

By the time the meeting was over, Barbie and Chuck had successfully moved from Milwaukee to Beverly Hills. Daisy had called Elizabeth "Cookie" twice and "Pussycat" once, kicked her under the table, and squeezed her hand to shut her up, then thanked Elliot for clarifying the concept of celebrity worship. Volfmann laughed, but Elliot didn't seem to notice. Volfmann then shook Daisy's hand and said, "At ease, Ms. DeMille."

"That was awfully nice of you to send flowers to my grand-mother, by the way," Elizabeth said to Volfmann as they were leaving. She could not think of him as Larry no matter how hard she tried.

Elliot, already in the doorway, turned and gave her a curdled, knowing glance.

"The vaudevillian," Volfmann said. "She okay?"

One of the 1930s secretaries appeared. "Your lunch is canceled. The brush fires. The traffic is impossible . . ."

"I was supposed to have lunch with the assistant director of *The Fog*," he said. "Shit. I was so up for it."

Why would he be having lunch with the assistant director of a crappy 1980 John Carpenter movie? "You were?"

"I grew up in Boston."

"You did?" What did that have to do with it?

"The guy is an expert in *carte de visite*. Which I kind of collect. How often do you get to talk to a museum director about your *pischedike* hobby?"

"The *Fogg*," Elizabeth said. "The museum. In Boston."

"You know anything about *carte de visite?*"

She shook her head. No. Although she had seen the 1980 John Carpenter movie.

"They're sort of the nineteenth-century version of baseball cards. Or, say, autographed photos of movie stars. But never mind, come on," he said. "You're the ringer."

He led her to the elevator, which took them upstairs to the executive dining room. It looked like a dining room in someone's house. A movie star's house, Elizabeth thought. They sat at the large table, which was set for two. A waiter appeared and Volfmann ordered a margarita.

"Their specialty," he said.

Elizabeth ordered one, too. She never drank during the day, but she was still reeling with embarrassment from her Fogg confusion. My Fogg fog, she thought. Ha ha. Maybe the alcohol would help.

"So, about the demographics . . ." Elizabeth said, wanting to sound serious, to make the lunch worth his while.

"Did you ever read Henry James on *Madame Bovary?*" Volfmann said. "He hated Flaubert. Too graphic. Too vulgar. Imagine what he'd make of movies."

The waiter appeared with two enormous margaritas and waited to take their order. Elizabeth stared longingly at the menu, at the lobster. Always the most expensive dish, though there were no prices on this menu. Should she indulge? Her mother had taught her it was impolite to order the most expensive item on a menu when someone else was paying. It had been a long time since she'd had lobster. Maine lobster. It sounded so good. But, with only the slightest hesitation, she ordered chicken.

"Lobster for me," Volfmann said.

Elizabeth looked out the window at the mountains.

"So, okay, rubbing elbows with celebrity," he said. "Have you ever rubbed elbows with celebrity, Elizabeth?"

"With you?" she said.

He laughed. "You're getting good. Your, you know, people skills. Not as good as that Daisy, God knows. But, now, any minute people are going to be saying, 'Yeah, she's good in the room. Just get her in the room.'"

Elizabeth could not help smiling when he praised her. She concentrated on her drink. Soon, another drink appeared. She wondered how she would drive home.

"Now," Volfmann continued, "before you fuck this idea up and give me some condescending satirical piece of crap . . ."

"But I'm the one who had the idea to —"

"To write some condescending satirical piece of crap to expose celebrity, right? God, you people. Go write an editorial. Ten years ago, how about. This is a *movie*. Emma Bovary suffered. She made a lot of people suffer. Your fucking characters have to fucking suffer. You, young lady, have to figure out one thing before you can hope to get this right."

Elizabeth drank from the large glass. This man is disturbing my warm sense of well-being, she thought.

"You have to figure out how to be . . ."

What? she thought. Ahead of the curve? Original? Formulaic? Edgy? Fresh? Ironic? Commercial?

"Earnest," he said.

Elizabeth stared at him. Earnest? "Why did you hire me if you think I'm such a fool? I still can't figure that out."

"You're not a fool, that's the problem."

Her glass was empty except for melting ice cubes.

"It's hard to be earnest and not be a fool," Volfmann said. "You're not a fool, so it's hard to be earnest, isn't it?"

Elizabeth nodded, feebly, as if he were her shrink, as if he'd said, You liked being breast-fed, didn't you? Yes, she nodded. All right, yes, I admit it.

"You can't worry about being a fool," said Volfmann.

Elizabeth looked at him, at his dog face as he raised his glass and gently touched her glass with it. Maybe he wanted to sleep with her.

God, I hope so, she thought.

She sucked on an ice cube. Too much hospital, too much cancer, too much tequila.

"Emma Bovary was a fool," Volfmann was saying. "Her husband was a fool."

He put his hand on hers. Manicure, sure as shit, she noticed. He smiled at her. She smiled back.

"Everyone is a fool, Elizabeth," he said. "Otherwise, what's the point?"

≈

Lotte had been in the hospital for two weeks. Greta visited on the days when she had the strength. The sight of her mother, bandaged and disoriented like a shell-shocked doughboy, was a jolt.

"Mama, Mama," she said, kissing Lotte lightly on the forehead.

"The rain," Lotte said sadly. "The rain, the rain, the rain."

Greta saw less of Elizabeth and Josh during that time. They were always at the hospital guarding Lotte from hallucinated Hasidim and real nurses with real orange-mesh vests. No time left for me, Greta thought. Poor little me. I have cancer, too, people! She laughed when she thought this, but she meant it, too. After years of pleasant independent privacy, Greta had come, so quickly, to expect and to enjoy her children near her, fighting, asking for food, leaving coffee cups in the living room.

When Greta spoke to Elizabeth on those days they didn't see each other, she was careful to be brave. But don't sound brave, she reminded herself. Sound normal. You don't want to burden Elizabeth. Any more than you already have. Sometimes she went outside and tried to garden, scratching at the soil a little, plucking a dried leaf, watching the sprinklers. She had so little energy. The metallic taste in her mouth was so strong she wondered why she couldn't see it. She spent the nights on the couch. She tried the bed, but Tony seemed larger than ever. His legs strayed to her side, proprietary and intrusive. She wanted to scream at him, to chase his body from her bed with a broom, a shrew shooing a stray cat. Instead, she went into the living room. On the couch, she pulled a green afghan over her, one her mother had crocheted years ago.

She considered calling Daisy Piperno. I'm so bored, she thought. Maybe Daisy would cheer me up. Tim stopped by after visiting his mother next door, which was very sweet of him. He'd always been her favorite of Josh's friends. And Laurie, an antique dealer who found most of her pieces abandoned on the street, came by the next day with a rocking chair she'd picked up on Beverly Glen and a footstool from Studio City. Then on Friday afternoon, Tony took the afternoon off, as always, but instead of playing golf, he drove Greta to the hospital and she sat by Lotte's bed for an hour while Lotte slept.

That night, she went on the Internet to order books. She ordered a book about California wildflowers that she already owned. She had it sent to Daisy Piperno. Daisy lived in Silver Lake. Greta knew her address from the phone book. "It occurred to me that you might enjoy this," she typed into the computer in the space marked "Personal Message." Not a very personal Personal Message, she thought. Then she lay back down on her couch, pushed her feet beneath the afghan and the purring cat, and felt the room swirl deliriously around her, as if she were dancing, waltzing, round and round a ballroom.

~

Harry kneeled in the dirt. His face was pressed against the slats of the fence. His hands gripping the wood, he peered seriously at the walkway.

When did the word "lifestyle" first occur? Elizabeth wondered. Fairly recently, she was sure. Emma Bovary wanted a lifestyle before lifestyles existed.

Harry had not moved. His concentration was somehow touching, full of hope. He was waiting. Elizabeth wondered how long he would wait like that. She wondered what he was waiting for.

"What's out there?" she asked, staying back on the steps, though. In case he didn't want anyone around. He sometimes looked up from his playing and sent Elizabeth and Brett packing. "I'm busy right now," he would say, politely.

"Garbage trucks," he said.

"You want to go look out back at the alley? That's where the cars and trucks go. This road is only for people."

"And dogs?"

"Right. Dogs, too."

"And cats," Harry said, louder. His face was getting red beneath the dirt. "And garbage trucks!" he yelled.

He sat down and began digging a hole with a spoon.

In the age of industrialization, there was the cliché. Flaubert was obsessed with cliché. But what, in the age of lifestyle, do we have that has the same relationship to lifestyle that the cliché had to the age of industrialization and the rising middle class? Brand names. That was what her article in *Tikkun* had been about. Branding, like God, named the universe, divided the wheat from the chaff, and didn't even have to rest on Sunday. Better yet, branding, like the clichés Emma Bovary devoured in her romance novels, was for everyone. Brand names grasped the unusual, the exotic, the romantic, the world available to the privileged few and held these treasures out, in a gesture of democratic largesse, to the rest of us.

But now what? Elizabeth thought. How would she clothe this fancy-pants idea in flesh and blood and dialogue?

"Need help?" Elizabeth said.

Harry had her hold an empty clay flowerpot while he spooned soil into it. He told her about a cat wearing a bell. He had seen it in the yard yesterday.

"That's so the birds will know it's coming," he said.

Elizabeth watched him dig. Children were so patient. No wonder they put them to work in factories. Inside, Brett was doing push-ups. She could hear him counting them out. Which was more boring? Push-ups or spooning dirt into a flowerpot? The parrots who lived in the tree next door sat on the telephone wires above and screeched. Harry pointed at them, excited. Then, suddenly, he rolled over into her lap. He grabbed his dirty pacifier from the ground and put it in his mouth. Elizabeth put her arms around him and they sat like that for a long time, shaded by the tall daylilies behind them, listening to the muffled sounds of other people in their houses. A little red propeller plane flew in circles overhead.

"What are you two waiting for out there?" Brett called from the steps.

"Trucks," Harry said.

Brett picked Harry up and Elizabeth followed them inside. It was almost nine, and still light outside. She gave Harry a bath and handed him a washcloth to hold over his eyes while she washed his hair. He sputtered and cried, then began to play in the water again as if nothing had happened.

"I can't sleep," he said as soon as he got into bed. She sat down on the edge of the bed. He popped in the pacifier and watched her, warily, like an opponent in a chess game, to see what her next move would be. She wanted to lie down next to him. But she had to get to the hospital by ten o'clock or they wouldn't let her in. She unconsciously shifted, slightly, as if to stand. Before she had fully registered her own movement, she saw the flicker of understanding in Harry's eyes, saw the parting of his lips as his mouth began to shape itself into a howl, and she quickly calculated the delay entailed in telling Harry a story or singing a lullaby compared to the delay caused by a full-blown, sobbing, hiccuping tantrum, as, simultaneously, she reversed her shifting movement and resettled herself on the bed.

Harry's face slackened into peaceful relief. I feel the same way, she thought. Peace. Relief. Harry needed her, and his need protected her. No one could object to a mother comforting a child. No one else could call her away. Not Brett. Not Volfmann or Daisy. Not even her mother or grandmother. The demands of a child on a mother — natural, nearly sacred — won out over the demands of a mother on a child, and certainly of a grandmother. Didn't they? Or had her mother and her grandmother become her children?

"Mommy," Harry said, putting his arms out, reaching for her, and the demands of the world were immediately, thoroughly eclipsed. She was safe. For these few moments, on this little bed, she was safe.

"Thank you," she said, lying down, settling herself next to him. He furrowed his brow for a second, thinking, then nodded. "You're welcome."

∽

Her mother had been disoriented and in the hospital for almost three weeks when Greta arrived there one morning with Josh to discover that Lotte had returned to reality.

"Mama, how are you feeling? What an ordeal you've had," Greta said.

"Status quo," Lotte said. "Status quo with a bandage. But those men in the black coats and their filthy fur hats — and in this heat! They must be out of their minds! Hideous, the imagination. Just hideous."

Then she asked how Greta was. "Do you still have that dirty rotten flu?"

Greta wondered what to say. The next day was chemo day. She would not have the strength to come back again to see her mother for days.

"No," she said at last. "Of course not."

The next day, she did manage to call the hospital, but Elizabeth picked up and told her Lotte was being bathed, then manned the phone like a telegraph operator, tapping out their messages.

"Tell Grandma to watch the ice-skating on TV tonight," Greta said. "She likes that."

"Grandma? Mom says to watch the ice-skating."

"Thank your mommy, darling. But I don't have the strength for that bastard of a television, with all their filthy violence."

"Mom? Grandma says —"

"I heard. For Christ's sake, this is skating. *Tell* her. Skating. Not violence. What violence?"

"I don't know, Mom. I'm just telling you what —"

"Tell Mommy about the little girl, you know, the kidnapping. Eyewitness News —"

"Kidnapping? Elizabeth! She watches the local news, but not ice-skating? No wonder she's hallucinating."

"Tell her, Elizabeth! What this world is coming to . . ."

After a while, Greta sent a kiss to her mother and her daughter, and replaced the receiver feeling even farther away from both of them than she had before the call.

"Charles is a plastic surgeon," Elizabeth said. She had allocated an hour for this lunch meeting. Then she had to go back to the hospital. "Chuck, I should say. So, not a chiropractor, but a plastic surgeon. Okay? But Chuck prefers treating emergency burn victims at the hospital instead of proper, private cosmetic-enhancement surgery patients. You see how that works?"

Daisy had an unlit cigarette dangling from her mouth. Elizabeth wondered if the director had started smoking Camels as a teenager, lured by the now-outlawed cartoon camel.

"*Does* it work?" Elizabeth said.

"Crude," Daisy said, nodding her head thoughtfully. "But clear."

Elizabeth let her pay the check.

"Is he a good plastic surgeon?" Daisy asked.

Elizabeth hadn't thought of that. In the novel, Charles Bovary was a poorly trained, mediocre doctor pushed by his ambitious wife to do work beyond his limited capabilities. Patients under his care went from slight limps to amputated legs.

Elizabeth watched Daisy sign the bill. She noticed Daisy was left-handed. "It's a public hospital," Elizabeth said finally.

Daisy used the butter knife as a mirror as she put lipstick on. "In Compton?" she said, nodding an affirmative answer to her own question.

~

Every afternoon, Greta would make the journey to the mailbox. Down the twisting stone steps, through the garden, through the mist of the sprinklers. She pulled open the door of the mailbox with such eagerness. Often an enormous spiderweb stretched from the mailbox to the top of the gate. Greta walked through it once or twice, her face just registering the filmy strands. Now, whenever she approached, she tilted her head until she saw the delicate silver threads catch the light. Then she brushed the lace and hard work away with her hand. No time to be sentimental, she thought. I'm in a hurry.

There were spiders in the mailbox itself, too, on the day Greta realized what it was she had been waiting for, why she was in a hurry, the reason she had swatted at spiderwebs every afternoon at precisely four o'clock.

It was dark in the mailbox. She reached in. Dangling spiders sucked themselves up their silk and hid. Junk mail fell out onto the front walk, as well as *The New Yorker,* which had, as usual, arrived in her mailbox at the end of the week instead of the beginning. She picked up the spilled magazine and catalogs. She pulled the rest of the mail out toward her, her nails against the aluminum reminding her of the metallic taste of chemotherapy. She rested the letters on top of the catalogs cradled in her arm. She loved catalogs, though she never ordered anything from them, and was happy to see so many. She flipped through the letters.

When she got to the third envelope, she suddenly understood.

No, she thought. Not me.

No, no, no, she thought.

Isn't it bad enough that I have cancer? she thought. Is this some kind of joke?

The envelope was addressed to her in messy, heavy print. The return address said "Daisy Piperno." Greta held it, stared at it. She had the impression of uninterrupted time, of all the time in the world, of a perpetual stillness, and the tug of breathless urgency. Her hands shook. She walked up the steps quickly, with difficulty.

Shit, Greta, she thought. Don't do this.

In her bedroom, she closed the door tight, although no one was home. She sat on the floor beneath the window, her back against the wall. The light was rich and yellow. Leafy shadows trembled on her outstretched legs, on the envelope in her hand.

Don't even open it, Greta.

But it's what I've been waiting for. I see that now.

Don't you have enough problems? You're sick as a dog.

It's just a letter, for Christ's sake. A little thank-you note.

Yes, yes, but it's what you've been waiting for. You said so yourself.

Nothing is going to happen.

Ah, but, Greta, you will make sure something will happen, won't you?

"Yes," Greta said out loud, opening the envelope. "I will."

The clouds made the sky look low. Slate gray. Los Angeles squatted beneath it in a heavy rain.

"I'm going to play golf," Tony said.

"In the rain?" Elizabeth said.

"I need to play golf."

Greta was sitting in a chair in the living room staring at nothing. Tony paced the way he did the day they found out about Greta's cancer. He bumped his shin on the coffee table in the same way. Elizabeth looked at the clouds and thought, Sometimes you have to wonder why another person seeks you out. For example, Volfmann. He could have hired a real screenwriter. He could have lunch with a real Hollywood person. With Barbra Streisand or Robert Altman. Lassie. Flipper. Rip Torn.

Maybe he likes you, Brett had said.

And Elizabeth had thought, but had not said, Maybe I like him.

"I'm going out of my mind," Tony said. "I've got to get out of here."

Greta said nothing. She seemed not even to have heard him. Elizabeth woke herself from her daydream about Volfmann, whose gruff voice she was imagining. It was saying, "This is marvelous, Elizabeth. Brilliant!" She woke herself and looked at her parents and wondered what the hell was going on. The two of them could have been separated by oceans, by continents.

"Mom? Hello?"

Greta turned to Elizabeth. Her face was hard and serious.

"Dad's going to play golf in the rain," Elizabeth said. "That's very weird."

"I've got cabin fever," Tony said.

Greta sighed. Tears came to her eyes.

"Mom?"

"Go ahead," she said, waving Tony off with one hand. With the other, she covered her eyes. "It's fine. I'm fine."

"I've got to get out of here," Tony said, rushing to the door. "I'm going out of my mind."

The rain came down then, loud and sudden.

"I can't help it," Tony said.

Elizabeth heard the door slam. The car start. The rain pound on the roof.

"What's eating him?" she said.

"He can't help it," Greta said softly. But Elizabeth heard the tight threat of tears even in that short sentence.

She tried to cheer her mother up. She made ice tea, but Greta barely touched it. She made a smoothie, but Greta did not even look at it.

"You're going to get better," Elizabeth said.

"It's not that."

What else could it be? "Is it Daddy?" she said.

Greta stared at her, then turned away and said she was tired and went into her room.

Elizabeth sat holding her mother's smoothie. She sipped it. She experienced a weary and grimly dispassionate sense of helplessness, and she thought, dully, My father is having an affair.

Lotte sat in her favorite chair in her own apartment. Brett's hands were strong and large and he had lowered her gently into the lounger. She watched him as he adjusted the television so she could see it.

"A gentleman," she said. "*And* a scholar."

"Yeah," he said. "That and a nickel . . ."

Lotte liked Brett. He could be superior and cold, it was true. And he never mentioned how she looked unless prompted, but once given his cues, he usually acquitted himself well. How much more could she ask? He didn't drink or gamble, like that bitch Stanley, how her poor sister had put up with him she never knew, not like her Morris, a model of a man, how God could have taken him and left all the gangsters on this earth . . .

"Tea?" Brett said.

"Just a little hot water."

Brett stared at her as if he hadn't heard her.

"Hot *water*?" he said, at last.

Lotte wondered if he was on drugs.

"Hot water," she said. "In a mug."

Brett went into the kitchen. She heard the flicker as the gas went on. She closed her eyes.

"What?" Brett said.

Lotte opened her eyes. He was standing before her with a mug.

"*What?*" she said.

"You said, 'From Jericho to Kokomo.'"

"Did I?" If he heard her, why did he ask?

Brett handed her the mug of hot water. She sipped it, grateful for the warmth. Imagine if she were still in St. Louis, how cold it would be. Of course, it was August. St. Louis was hideously hot. And the humidity!

"Sit," she said. "You're making me nervous."

Brett smiled. "Sorry." He sat on the couch. He looked bored. Well, too bad, Lotte thought. I'm bored every day. Wait till you're old, Mr. Professor.

"Can I get you anything else?" he said. "Or do you want me to turn on the television?"

"How old are you, Brett?"

"Thirty-three. Can you believe it?"

"Why aren't you married to my granddaughter? I don't understand this generation. I don't understand anything anymore." She held out her empty mug and closed her eyes. She felt Brett lift the cup from her grip.

"Elizabeth doesn't want to. You've heard her on the subject."

Lotte grunted.

"It's not really necessary. You know what I mean?" Brett said. His voice faded slightly as he went into the kitchen.

"No," Lotte said. "I don't. But as long as you're happy."

"We're happy," Brett said.

"You should live and be well." Lotte opened her eyes. He was back. She pointed at the remote control. Brett handed it to her. "That granddaughter of mine."

"Mmm," Brett said.

"Stubborn," she said.

"Yes."

"*Why* won't she wear her hair down?"

Brett laughed. "I struggle with that daily."

Lotte pointed a finger at him. He could laugh if he wanted. But Lotte was no fool. "I know what I know," she said.

Brett reached over and took the hand pointing at him in his own.

"Please don't worry about us, Lotte," he said. "Marriage is a technicality in the end, isn't it?"

"That's what all the boys say," Lotte said. She let out a whoop and slapped her thigh.

"You just got out of the hospital?" Brett said. He had a nice smile. Lotte sat up a little straighter. "You'll be dancing any minute!" he said. "You're quite a . . ."

"Pistol!" Lotte said.

Brett nodded. "Yeah," he said. "A pistol."

Lotte looked at the newspaper. She couldn't focus on it. There was very little she could focus on anymore. She remembered suddenly that she had cancer. They cut off half my nose, she thought.

"A pistol," she said, shaking her finger at Brett.

"You look pretty goddamned good, Lotte. The interns were fighting over you, I hear."

She smiled. It took Brett a while to warm up. That's all.

"Thank you for bringing me home," she said after a while. "Just make an honest woman of her and you'll be perfect. Where the hell is she?"

"She'll be here any minute," he said.

Lotte could hear he was covering something up. Trouble in paradise. She could smell it. What was Elizabeth up to? These rotten kids. Never satisfied. Never sit still. She was married to Morris from the time she was nineteen years old. Now, divorce every time you turn around.

"She had a meeting," he said.

"A meeting," she said, snorting. "And my poor Greta with her filthy flu." She grabbed his arm. "Tell me the truth."

"She's okay," Brett said. "That is the truth."

Lotte shook her head, disgusted and relieved. No one would tell her the truth. No one.

"Greta's a trouper, Lotte. You know that."

From Benzedrine to Ovaltine, Lotte heard herself saying. "It's from a song." *From Jericho to Kokomo ... Benzedrine to Ovaltine ...* She let her eyes close. After all, it had been a long day. She would take a little nap.

"I can't recall the rest," she said. "Can you?"

It was another three days before Greta was strong enough to visit her mother. She picked up Elizabeth, although it was out of her way, simply because she could, because she was driving and it felt good.

"I'm very proud of you, Elizabeth," she said, when Elizabeth got into the car. "You've had a lot to contend with."

"And you haven't?"

If you only knew, Greta thought. A lot to contend with? Or a lot to feel guilty about? Or a lot to rejoice over?

"I was talking about you, though. You've been wonderful."

"I'm not wonderful," Elizabeth said in an oddly sober voice.

They pulled up to Lotte's building. Greta sent Elizabeth in first and parked the car. She sat for a moment in the motionless car, the air-conditioning off, the windows closed, letting the heat find its way all around her.

Until Greta rang the bell and heard her mother's voice inside, she was thinking of Tony and Josh and Elizabeth, of how disappointed in her they would be, how angry. How unforgiving. She fought back tears at the thought of her family unable to forgive her.

"What is that?" she heard from the other side of the door. "The door? Is that the door? Where's my Greta? What if something happened to her? Maybe that's her . . ."

She remembered with a shock that her mother had just had her nose cut off. It would be the first time Greta had seen her without the bandages.

The door swung open. The nose was flattened, like a boxer's, and cocked rakishly to one side.

"Do you like it?" Lotte said, posing like a model, one hand on her hip.

Greta hesitated. What could she possibly say?

"I got it from the catalog, from Victoria," Lotte was saying, spinning unsteadily to show off her new sage-colored linen tunic.

"Grandma!" Elizabeth said, reaching out to steady her.

"Overnight delivery," Lotte said, banging her cane on the thick carpet for emphasis.

Greta was used to swimming laps every morning. Why? she wondered. Back and forth, back and forth. So pointless. Floating seemed pointless, too. And sinking the most pointless of all.

"Can something be the most pointless?" Greta said to someone approaching. She was lying in a chaise, the one with the cushion, a towel covering her. The pool would not cool her. The sun would not warm her. She was shivering. "Can something be 'the most pointless'?" she said again.

"Don't be so morbid," Josh said.

"Oh, it's you."

"Disappointed?"

Yes, she was disappointed. But she held up her hand and waited for him to take it. "Remember when you wanted to marry me, Josh?"

"No."

"Perhaps that's for the best."

Remember when you wanted to marry Tony, Greta? Remember when you still lived in Manhattan and he drove you out from the city for a weekend in Montauk? In a snowstorm? Remember the ice on the road, the car sliding from lane to lane of the Long Island Expressway? Remember how you felt? As if you and Tony were flying? You flew on the ice all the way to Montauk and walked in the subzero wind on the beach and thought, I want to marry him. I want to be with him forever. I want to have children with him and watch them grow up and then I want to grow old with him and shuffle along the sidewalk holding his arm, both of us dressed in matching sweat suits.

Josh sat at the foot of the chaise. "Mommy?"

"I wasn't being morbid," Greta said. "I was being pedantic."

She thought of the letter from Daisy, a quick, simple thank-you note. And yet she knew. And she knew Daisy did, too. Really, she'd thought of very little else since the letter arrived. Daisy had elbowed thoughts even of Lotte aside, she realized. But all this Daisy nonsense was just that — nonsense. A crush. An absurd crush. And it was not as if she'd never had a crush before. She'd even had crushes on girls before. One does.

Doesn't one?

But perhaps one doesn't. Unless one is . . . what? Married for many years with grown-up children? How about that? Married to the man you love? Those crushes were so long ago, she thought. In college. A million years ago. She felt an excruciating throb of love for Tony. She had never even looked at another man. When had she stopped looking at him?

"I'm driving you today," Josh said.

Greta kept her eyes closed. A week had already passed. Again.

"I hope chemotherapy isn't the most pointless," she said.

Elizabeth looked out the glass door that led from the study to the pool. Her brother seemed to be scratching a mosquito bite on his arm. Her mother lay motionless on a chaise. For one moment, Elizabeth knew her mother was dead.

Greta turned her head. Opened her eyes. "Don't scratch that, Josh!" she said. "It'll get infected."

Elizabeth sat down, shaking, and tried to compose herself. Her mother was alive. She stared hard at Greta. She would never take her eyes off her again. Her mother was alive! But then another, unpleasant thought intruded on her feeling of relief: Her father was not home to watch her mother being alive. My father ought to be home, she thought. Doesn't he see that? It's cruel to have an illicit love affair when your wife is ill. No wonder he walks with such a heavy tread. No wonder his voice is weak with gloom. No wonder he avoids eye contact.

Greta let Josh help her up. She felt his stocky strength and realized she was proud, as if the strength, the hardy tan muscles, were hers.

Elizabeth watched Josh help her mother. She heard the doorbell ring. That would be Daisy. Daisy didn't run away from the House of the C-Word the way Dr. Anthony Bernard did. She didn't rush out the door to raise funds for the Sick or play golf in the rain. She even seemed to like working at the Bernards' house. It was a pleasant house; the pool was a bonus; no one bothered them. Still, Elizabeth was grateful Daisy understood her circumstances. She wondered how she could make her father understand. He was acting out, as the therapists would say. She would have to think of some way to get him to act in.

Elizabeth let Daisy in and offered her some coffee. Daisy sat on a stool in the kitchen and watched Josh and Greta walking hand in hand along the edge of the pool.

"They're so sweet," Daisy said.

"Them?" Elizabeth stopped spooning the coffee and looked at her brother and her mother. Josh still had a T-shirt tan from Alaska. Greta had lost weight. She looked better than usual. What was it? Her hair.

"Mom, what did you do to your hair?" she yelled out the window. "It looks so good."

Greta turned toward them. "Oh," she said.

"Come on," Josh said. "We'll be late."

Greta stood another moment. Her towel was draped over her shoulders, but she wasn't wet.

"I had it cut," Greta said. "Preemptive move."

She shivered, then shrugged, smiled, and let Josh pull her along.

"Chemo," Elizabeth told Daisy, who had said nothing to Greta.

Daisy took Elizabeth's hand and kissed it, a sympathetic gesture, a graceful offer of kindness. "So many things we don't expect," Daisy said, almost to herself.

How odd she is, Elizabeth thought, so intimate and so remote at the same time, calling Elizabeth "Cookie," kissing her hand, practically moving in with her family. But Elizabeth knew nothing about Daisy at all.

"Do you think she's a lesbian?" she had asked Brett after they first met Daisy in Malibu.

"Yes."

"Why, though? I do, too. But why? She wears makeup and everything."

Brett shrugged. "I don't know. Maybe she's not. When I was in Berlin, I thought all the women in Germany were gay. Cultural signals got mixed up."

"She's American."

"Are you seeing anyone?" Elizabeth had asked Daisy once, as casually as she could, when they were talking about Barbie's courtship rituals.

"Seeing," Daisy said, giving Elizabeth one of her languidly direct looks. "That's the word for it."

Josh held Greta's hand during the drip. He'd met a girl he liked, he said.

I, too, have met a girl I like, she wanted to say.

The girl he liked was from Tom's River, New Jersey, last year's winner of the Little League World Series.

"Jesus, Josh, how *old* is she?"

"The *town,* not Samantha," he said.

The girl I like is from Minnesota, Greta wanted to say. She has an undulating accent, like music. "That's wonderful, Josh," she said instead.

Josh smiled. Greta saw she'd gotten it right. "Mom, we *just met,*" he added suddenly, as if she were the one who had brought up the subject, as if she had fixed the two of them up on a blind date.

"Of course," Greta said.

He nodded, mollified, and continued to hold her hand and talk, friendly, tapping his foot in that way he had. Greta knew to be honored. He was confiding in her. He talked about his job in Alaska for a while. It had just been temporary, anyway. To save up some money. He was glad he ditched it, glad to be back. Now that he was home, he could apply for the research grant he wanted . . .

"I hope this isn't boring," he said.

Greta congratulated herself again. A grown son willing to talk to his mother! But instead of the unalloyed pleasure she would once have felt, she found herself wishing she could talk to *him* about *her* girl, tell him, to confide in him, unburden herself to him, to confess to him; to deny the whole thing, repent and ask his forgiveness; to celebrate, drink toasts and dance on tabletops with him.

"Oh, Josh," she said. It came out as a bitter sigh.

"Mom, don't worry!" he said. "You're going to be fine. It's just these horrible months of chemo. Then it's okay. You'll be yourself."

Myself? That, Greta thought, is the problem.

six

Elizabeth thought with envy of the scene in the Vincente Minnelli version of *Madame Bovary*. Emma and Charles are invited to a ball at the viscount's. Jennifer Jones, her shoulders bare and lovely, is Emma, dancing with the handsome viscount, a waltz, around and around, her white skirts whirling, the room around them a spin of delirium, until Emma is in a kind of frenzy. Emma waltzes at the viscount's in the novel, too, of course, but it made a far greater impression on Elizabeth in the film: the reeling sexual rhythm, the spiral of breathless, physical exertion and pleasure and desire, the beauty of the swirling skirts and flushed faces . . .

Elizabeth had a quick, confused glimpse of her envy — envy that was not a desire to write a scene as good as that in the movie but to be in the scene, to be waltzing, whirling in silk and sensuality, a desire to be lost in a lavish burst of desire.

She tried to remember the last time she had danced. Years ago with Brett at a bar. They hadn't been out alone together in months, much less at a bar, much less to dance. Those days had faded into the past. But even if I can't be whirled around, Elizabeth decided, at least I can make Barbie dance. Dance, Barbie, dance. Pow, pow. Shoot the six-shooter at her exquisite feet, the bullets ricocheting in the dirt while Barbie elegantly hops and jumps.

She put Barbie and Dr. Chuck Bovaine at an Oscar party given by a studio head named Wolf. In the emergency room, Dr. Bovaine had sewn up Wolf's daughter's Jet-Ski lacerations. When Wolf and his daughter go to the office for a follow-up visit, they meet Barbie, who charms the studio head with her beauty and her gentle presence. And so the doctor and his wife are invited to the Oscar party. No. Not an Oscar party. Wolf's daughter's extravagant bat mitzvah. They would dance the hora.

EXT. BEVERLY HILLS MANSION — EVENING

> Barbie and Chuck ring the bell at the oversize front door. The too-tight waistband of his unfashionable tux cuts into his belly. She, on the other hand, has never looked more beautiful. He grabs her waist, bends to kiss her bare shoulder.

> BARBIE
> Let go of me! You'll wrinkle my dress!

A picture of Dr. Anthony Bernard pushed the picture of Dr. Chuck Bovaine aside. Elizabeth's father had a big head, too big for his body, and a big square face. She saw him bend a big square head to kiss her mother's shoulder.

"Tony," her mother said in protest, squirming away from him.

Dr. Anthony Bernard turned to a woman on his other side, a beautiful young woman who thought his big head leonine and his square face full of character. A woman named Barbie. He lowered his big square face and kissed her perfect shoulder.

"Tony," she said, sighing with pleasure. "Oh, Tony, darling."

"Fuck the shoulder kissing," Elizabeth said out loud. "Who the fuck kisses a fucking shoulder?"

EXT. BEVERLY HILLS MANSION — EVENING

Barbie and Chuck ring the bell at the oversize front door. The too-tight waistband of his unfashionable tux cuts into his belly. She, on the other hand, has never looked more beautiful. He bends down to kiss her.

Barbie turns her face to protect her lipstick. CU Barbie's face over his shoulder — an expression of bored, bland disgust. She reaches around him and removes a piece of breath-freshening gum from her mouth.

∽

Greta made the usual round of phone calls, interviewed a new batch of candidates with Elizabeth, and then, finally, chose yet another housekeeper for Lotte. This housekeeper was small but mighty. No matter how vulgar Lotte managed to be, this housekeeper seemed to regard her eccentricities as vibrant and assured — signs of life. Touched by Lotte's helplessness, impressed by her strength, this housekeeper was tireless, but brought to the apartment a sense of serenity. Most important, this housekeeper was a man. His name was Kougi.

Kougi and Lotte spent their first afternoon together discussing politics under the watchful eyes of Greta, Tony, Josh, Elizabeth, and Brett. Lotte consigned dirty gangster politician hypocrites to the lowest levels of hell. Kougi nodded soberly, adding only, "'Drop wisdom, abandon cleverness, and the people will be benefited a hundredfold . . .'"

∽

Now that Lotte was settled in, Elizabeth returned to her post at Greta's side. Greta had to explain that mint tea had replaced ice tea as the only palatable food.

"Mommy, you have to eat," Elizabeth said.

Greta was happy to have her back. She loved the sight of Harry struggling up the steps behind his mother. She loved the sound of his voice and the warmth of his body, squeezed in beside her in the big armchair. She loved the sight of Elizabeth, too. Elizabeth came into her house and criticized her and defended her with the intense abandonment that comes of love, the same vehemence she showed toward Harry.

"You're impossible," Elizabeth said.

"You're no day at the beach, either," Greta said.

Elizabeth stared at her, as though weighing the virtues of being a day at the beach.

"I'm not?" she said finally. She seemed genuinely surprised.

Harry climbed off the chair and lay beside the cat in a patch of sunlight.

Elizabeth made Greta a pot of mint tea, and then another, and then a third.

"I know you want to help, honey," Greta said. "But mint tea will not save me."

"Yes, it will," Elizabeth said.

Greta smiled at her. She held out her arms. Elizabeth put down the pot of tea and knelt in front of the chair Greta sat on. Greta put her arms around her daughter, her day at the beach.

"Don't worry," Greta whispered. She rocked Elizabeth in her arms. "Don't you worry."

Elizabeth buried her face in her mother's neck, comforted and desperate at once. My mother is here, she thought. She is flesh and blood and a soft voice. Without her, the world would have no flesh, no blood, no voice. The arid future without her mother stretched horribly before her. She pressed her face deeper into the cavity beneath her mother's chin.

"Hello!" Greta said to someone behind Elizabeth's back.

"A tableau," said a familiar voice from the direction of the front door.

"Just a lot of stress," Greta said. "Enough to go around."

Elizabeth raised her face from its warm maternal burrow.

"Were we supposed to meet?" she said to Daisy, who stood in the doorway, backlit by the bright morning sun.

"I brought your mother flowers," Daisy said. She was holding a pot of orchids. They, too, were just a black silhouette against the daylight.

Elizabeth stood up. That was so nice of Daisy. Odd, but nice.

"I thought you might be here, though," Daisy said.

Well, not so odd, then.

"They're beautiful," Greta was saying. She had taken the pot from Daisy and given her a brush of a kiss on her cheek. The flowers were a pale glowing green that held, inside, their deep pink.

"Like you," Daisy said.

I don't have to do anything, Greta told herself. I don't have to go any farther than this with it. It's a flirtation. Someone in my position deserves a flirtation. How many of us get a flirtation at this stage in life? And how well-timed, really. Chemotherapy is so tiring, so depressing. Daisy is therapeutic, that's all. A diversion. Occupational therapy.

"You don't have to butter up my mother," Elizabeth said. "It's my *grandmother* who requires constant infusions. She's driving me out of my mind . . ."

"They really are so beautiful," Greta said, ignoring Elizabeth. "You're amazing. To have remembered."

"You like them, really? I'm so relieved. I looked at, like, hundreds."

An innocent diversion, Greta thought. She met Daisy's eyes and a tremor of desire passed through her that was so unsettling she reached out for the table to support herself.

"Remember what?" Elizabeth said.

"Your mother said she would never buy flowers for herself, and the flower she would most never buy for herself was an orchid."

"Yeah," Elizabeth said. "I've never liked them much myself. Too much like flesh." Although, as she looked at the smooth greenish petals, they didn't look the least like flesh.

"Don't be so conventional," Greta said. She was beaming. "It was so thoughtful of you, Daisy."

"Yes, it was," Elizabeth said. And I'm not the least bit conventional, she thought. What kind of thing is that for a mother to say to a daughter? "And they're awfully nice orchids, as orchids go."

Her mother's face was bent over the flowers. Elizabeth wished she had brought orchids for her mother. All she had done was make pots of hot, liquid chewing gum. The pot of blossoms on their tall stems had certainly cheered Greta up. She was smiling in a way Elizabeth did not recognize. Elizabeth knew when her mother was lying, and now, although her mother hadn't said anything much at all, she felt the same airless tension that surrounded Greta's untruths.

"I never knew you liked orchids so much," Elizabeth said.

Daisy had settled on a chair outside, near the pool, where she blew big, doughy smoke rings. Elizabeth and Greta stood in the living room with the plant and watched the silver loops rolling toward the sky.

"You never asked," Greta said.

At six A.M. Elizabeth drove Brett to the airport, which was only fifteen minutes away. He was going to Washington to a hearing. Harry slept in his car seat in back.

"I hate to leave you, baby," Brett said. "I tried to get out of it. I'll be back in a few days."

"I know."

She pulled up to the curb and got out of the car to kiss him good-bye. She wanted to get to her parents' house. Her father would probably still be home. Maybe she could talk to him. Tell him the story of *Madame Bovary*. Remind him that adultery does not pay. Remind him that these might be his last days with his companion of thirty years. Thirty-two years, actually. Couldn't he wait until . . . She stopped herself. She ran her hand through Brett's hair, making it stick up. She liked it when it stuck up like that. It gave his polished beauty an absurd, more accessible quality.

"What?" Brett said.

"I'll miss you," she said. Would she? The night before, as Harry slept beside her, his bunny clutched in his arm, Elizabeth told herself it was time to take him to his own room, time to shuffle down the hall with him dangling over her shoulder. But she didn't stir. From the living room downstairs, beyond several closed doors, she heard the muffled squeal of Brett practicing his bagpipes. She looked at Harry. The sound didn't seem to bother him. She held him. And when she heard Brett come upstairs, she pretended to be asleep holding Harry. She expected Brett to take Harry from her, to pry him loose, to banish him to his own little room. She felt the heat of her anger at Brett's anticipated behavior. It spread over her entire body as he entered the bedroom. She hugged Harry. She did not move, frozen in her warm rage.

Brett had not taken Harry from her. He did not lift him up and carry him to his room. Instead, he stood by the bed for a minute. Perhaps he was gazing affectionately at them. Or was annoyed. Or staring off into space. Elizabeth, her eyes closed tight, could not tell. Then, he had simply squeezed into bed beside Harry and fallen asleep. Elizabeth could hear his breathing, heavy and rhythmic. She could hear Harry's breathing, light and clear. She had tried to hear her own breathing, but realized she had stopped, and forced herself to exhale. She hung on to Harry and his bunny. There's no room, she thought. There's just no room.

Then she fell asleep and dreamed of a small bedroom bathed in pale white morning light. A sheer white curtain billowed in the breeze. The walls were white. The floor was white. Where was this place? She was lying on a brass bed. The sheets were white. There was no one else there. She was alone in a cool, soft white room.

"I hate to go," Brett said, standing outside the car, his arms around her.

"Why did you agree to follow me out here?" she asked. "The only people you see are my crazy family."

"And my crazy family."

Elizabeth stared at him blankly. Brett's parents lived in upstate New York. His sister lived in London.

"You and Harry," he said.

"Oh," she said. "Right! Harry and me."

Once there had been a sense to the world, an order that awaited her when she opened her eyes in the morning, an order that was as real and inevitable as existence itself. But existence is not inevitable, Greta reminded herself. And order could be disrupted by an unexpected pounding of the heart. Daisy Piperno had settled herself by Greta's feet on the couch when Greta was sleeping. And Greta had awakened.

Greta dreamed that she needed to put dollar bills into a machine in order to stay parked. But all she had were quarters and dimes and nickels. She looked down at the silver in her hands and said over and over, "I don't want change, I don't want change . . ."

Silly dream, she thought when she woke up. But she was pleased with her nocturnal pun. Her hands shook when she answered the phone and when she took in the mail. She stared at the orchid for half an hour, sipping chamomile tea. Daisy had sent the tea to her the day before. When Greta tore apart the big brown envelope and found a plastic bag, full of tiny flowers, she thought it was marijuana. But then she opened the plastic bag, and the scent of chamomile burst out.

Greta had closed the bag quickly, guiltily, as if it really had been marijuana, or the dried flowers would give her away. What nonsense, Greta, she thought. You might just as well watch soap operas all day.

She put the bag of chamomile tea in the cupboard, next to the Twinings and Lipton and Red Rose.

"What's this?" Tony said that night, after dinner, digging in the cabinet. He opened the bag and sniffed.

"I thought maybe . . ."

"Right. For the nausea. Good idea."

Greta took the bag from him and inhaled the slightly medicinal smell. What shall I do? she thought. Should I talk to him about this? What is it I would be talking to him about, anyway? A dream? A pun? A bag of tea?

"Does it help?" he said.

He opened a packet of powdered hot chocolate and emptied it into a mug.

And she didn't want to worry him. He already worried about her so much, too much. She saw how uncomfortable he was, how sad, how eagerly he left the house. He had always spent a lot of time out of the house. It was probably why their marriage worked. But now he left so she wouldn't see how worried he was. How could she add to his worries? It would be unfair.

"I'm sure that's carcinogenic," she said.

"All natural. Natural and nutritionless. No worse than chamomile tea. Except the sugar. And the cocoa powder. And God knows what else. Now, Water, that's an issue. Not just in California. All over the

United States. Of course, that's partly because California siphons off everyone else's Water . . ."

The kettle whistled.

"The Extinction of the beaver population has contributed to Water Pollution . . ."

"Tony, I didn't buy the tea."

"You didn't steal it, did you? You're not turning into one of those Kleptomaniac Housewives, are you?"

Housewife? Since when was she a housewife?

"Since when have I become a housewife?" she said.

Tony had tilted the kettle over the cocoa. Some of the boiling water sloshed over the side of the mug. Greta saw sickly little marshmallows bobbing in the cup.

"What are you talking about?" he said.

"Go to hell," Greta said. "Go to hell!"

She ran to the bedroom and sat on the end of the bed. She smelled chamomile and looked down at her hand, still holding the bag of tea. She stood up and walked back across the room. She had forgotten to slam the door.

The trouble with adultery is you don't know whose side you're on. Madame Bovary was a victim, Madame Bovary was a selfish monster. *Madame Bovary* was tragedy, *Madame Bovary* was farce. A lover is an active noun, one who acts. A lover is an object, the one you take. I love you: I am your lover. I love you: I take you as my lover.

Whose side are you on?

The lovers' side.

The faithful husband's side

The wrong side of the bed.

Elizabeth took a Diet Pepsi from her mother's refrigerator and opened it. It exploded, caramel foam flopping onto the kitchen floor.

"Whose side are we on?" Elizabeth said as she mopped up the mess. "The infantile social-climbing Emma? But she's so much more than that. And so much less. She's a woman full of ambition in a world that has no room for women with ambition. She's a girl who's been taught to seek the sublime in the banal. To exchange tradition for convention, then to exchange convention for pretension . . ."

Daisy sat at the kitchen table reading the most recent pages of the script. She looked up calmly, her finger bent back, at an odd angle, holding her place on the page. "Emma Bovary doesn't know the difference between passion and romance," she said. "That's all."

"*Love* and romance," Elizabeth said. "Between *love* and romance."

"Love." Daisy repeated the word as if it were in another language, slowly, earnestly. "That's the word, all right, Cookie," she added in her more familiar manner of gentle condescension.

Daisy had turned out to be incredibly helpful. Attentive. That was the best word. She often just appeared at the door, like a neighborhood kid at the house that stocked the best snacks. If Elizabeth wasn't there yet, she would wait, patient, decorative, undemanding, a nice diversion for Greta. If Elizabeth had already left when Daisy arrived, still she would spend a little time with Elizabeth's parents. They adored her, of course. She was adorable, Elizabeth agreed. Daisy had a handful of interchangeable pet names for everyone — Cookie and Pussycat and Babe — and she brought Harry a hat from the thrift store that made him look like Humphrey Bogart.

Elizabeth mopped up the spilled soda and muttered to herself in a singsong. "Love and romance, love and passion, love and longing, love and lotsa luck . . ."

Daisy was looking at her, much the way she had the day they met at Volfmann's beach house when Harry spilled the vase of flowers. She didn't offer to help. Elizabeth felt her watching, rapt but distant, as if Elizabeth were suspended in an aquarium, and she, Daisy, on an afternoon outing.

Elizabeth said, "What?"

Daisy smiled at her.

Elizabeth smiled back. "What? What are you looking at?"

"God, you have a great smile."

Elizabeth, embarrassed now, tried, unsuccessfully, to frown.

When Greta had her next break from chemotherapy, in which her body could try to regain some of the strength lost to the poison drips, a vacation of sorts, a holiday, she determined to use the time to tend to her mother and to allow herself to be lured to her doom. For surely adultery was doom. Elizabeth was not the only person who had ever read *Madame Bovary.* And adultery with a woman — that had to be a special, double dose of doom.

How had she come to this pass? She didn't want to be a lesbian, a word that brought to mind either unstylish women in poorly tailored pantsuits or trendy college girls who would one day regret their tattoos. She had no political interest in gay rights. She was too privileged, too protected even to be much of a feminist. Her mother had always done just as she liked and Greta was expected to do the same — as little or as much as that might be. Greta tried to imagine her mother, dressed to kill, her nose flapped to the side, marching with PFLAG.

Who says I am a lesbian, anyway? she thought. Well, I do, I guess. But, people have fantasies. So what if all my fantasies are about Daisy Piperno? So what if I'm attracted to Daisy? Wolfishly, obsessively, sexually attracted to Daisy. It's not like I want to live with her. It's not like I long to adopt a Chinese orphan girl with her. I don't want to move to Northampton or go to k.d. lang concerts. I just want to sleep with Daisy. And hear her voice. And sit beside her. And touch her hand. And sleep with her. Again and again.

Which kind of makes me a lesbian.

Well, Greta thought, Northampton is beautiful, especially in the spring. To be fair.

~

Four women and three men in a swimming pool. They are very drunk. They have been drinking a disgusting concoction called a Negroni, prepared by one of the men. He is a boy, in fact. Or nearly. Look at him, in his baggy surfer swim trunks. There is no hair on his chest. His chest is smooth and rippling with muscles. He is staring at me, Elizabeth thought.

It was the boy's birthday. Josh's best friend, Tim, was twenty-six.

"Happy birthday!" They all toasted him.

Elizabeth closed her eyes. It's only Tim, she told herself. The boy next door. She let her body sink until her head was submerged. She floated in a sitting position. He's young and drunk.

She sputtered to the surface. She didn't see Tim in the water, but her mother was splashing Tim's mother, Laurie. That was good. Then her mother splashed her father. That was better. Splash away, Greta. Elizabeth tried to relax in the water, telling herself that her mother's splashing was a sign of health. Then she wondered if the pool was full of germs that might infiltrate her mother's weakened body. She wondered if her mother wouldn't be better off asleep on the sofa beneath the crocheted afghan. She wondered if splashing was a sign not of health but of hubris. Greta turned just then and splashed Elizabeth.

"Mo-om," she said.

"Don't whine, Elizabeth. It's only water!" Greta said and reached out to ruffle Elizabeth's wet hair. Elizabeth sat on the steps and crossed her arms. Her mother was ridiculous.

Brett was away, in Washington again. He would have understood that her mother could have cancer, be brave, and still be annoying. Greta was so giddy. It struck Elizabeth as unseemly.

Elizabeth put her elbows on her knees. Her chin was in the water. Would Brett understand that Tim had a crush on her? She watched as Daisy Piperno splashed Tim, who had leaped into the pool and was now floating on his back. He opened one eye. It was level with Daisy's bikini top. Tim reached out as if to pull on the strap and Daisy dove away. He laughed. Then, catching Elizabeth's eye, he stopped laughing.

"Elizabeth . . ." he said.

A beach ball hit Elizabeth on the head. She heard her brother laughing. She heard herself laugh, too.

"I have hair!" her mother cried.

"To Greta's hair!" said Tony. He was out of the pool, pouring out another of Tim's disgusting and potent Negronis. Elizabeth eyed him suspiciously. To have an affair while your wife is undergoing chemotherapy was very low. Her father was an honorable man. He couldn't be having an affair. There he was toasting his wife's hair. Could you bring yourself to toast your wife's hair if you were having an adulterous affair?

Emma Bovary could have. She would have found a way to think about it that somehow made her both the victim and the heroine. Did her father see himself as the victim and the hero? Sometimes Elizabeth thought of herself as the victim and the hero, so why not Tony? He was closer to the real victim and the real hero. He was closer to Greta.

Everyone raised a glass to Greta's hair.

Elizabeth stared at the silky dark hair under Tim's arm as he held his glass aloft. She looked at his armpit. I am fickle even in my adulterous fantasies, she thought. I have betrayed Volfmann. She realized she was drunk. She had rarely gotten drunk when she lived in New York. What a waste. It was so easy to get home in New York. Now that she was always driving, she was always getting drunk. Tim has a crush on me, she thought. He always has. He said so. She envied Tim his carefree life. A life free of the shadow of maternal death. What a self-important bore I have become, she thought.

I've got a crush on you, she sang softly.

Sugar pie, Daisy sang, just beside her.

Daisy, Daisy, Daisy. Daisy was everywhere. Elizabeth let herself bump down the steps and back down beneath the water. She opened her eyes. She saw two hands touch, two fingertips just brush each other. Like the Sistine Chapel, she thought. Like God and Adam. But who was God and who was Adam down here? In the Bernards' swimming pool? By the light of the silvery moon?

She came to the surface and watched Tim push her brother into the pool. Josh was sturdy and square. Tim was lean and long waisted. Tim could be my brother, except that he's not sturdy and square. He's shimmering, a thousand drops of water clinging to his skin, to his long legs. Tim jumped wildly into the pool, dove beneath the surface, and pulled her underwater. How many times had long legs led to adultery? she wondered as she struggled up, gasping when she hit the surface. Too many times. Long legs were never reason enough to betray the man you love.

She wondered if she did love Brett. She had loved him once. She had grown used to him, too, which was a kind of love. But now, somehow, she wasn't used to him anymore. It was as if they had just met, as if a stranger slept in her bed and peed in her toilet. He hadn't changed. They hadn't grown apart. She had simply lost the gift of being used to him.

She wondered what kind of legs Volfmann had. Bandy legs, probably. She wished suddenly that Volfmann was there with his bandy legs. He would tell her what to do. He would say, "I want adultery!" And she would say, "What about the child? I have a child! Think of the child!" And he would say, "Happiness! Passion! Intoxication!" And she would say, "Adultery is okay in the movies. But this is real life. People get hurt." And he would turn purple and bang his fist on the desk and say, "How would you know? How would you know about happiness, passion, or intoxication? Adultery may be tragedy, but your life is farce."

"Happiness, passion, intoxication," Elizabeth said, softly, sitting by the pool drinking a Negroni.

"I don't know about happy or passionate," her father said, sitting beside her on the chaise. "But you are definitely intoxicated." He put a towel around her shoulders.

"Look at Mom," she said. "She looks happy."

Greta was floating on her back. Daisy held her hands and pulled her gently around the pool.

"You're intoxicated. She's happy. Does that make me passionate?"

I hope not, Elizabeth thought.

He began to pace along the edge of the pool, first in one direction, then the other, wet footprints on top of wet footprints.

"Daddy, what's wrong?"

He laughed.

Greta watched them. She stood in the pool, conscious of Daisy near her, of Daisy's body. What were they saying? They both looked so miserable. She could still feel Daisy's hands holding hers in the water. Tony gave a short, bitter laugh. Elizabeth's expression was taut. There was panic in her face. The air was cold and made Greta shiver. She heard the sound of someone climbing out of the pool. She knew it was Daisy. She turned her head and watched Daisy walk toward the pile of towels. Greta looked over at her husband, who now stopped pacing and looked back at her. Did he know? Sometimes she thought he knew. She wanted to run into his arms and beg his forgiveness. I don't mean it, she would say. At least, I don't mean to mean it.

Tony held a towel for her. Elizabeth was also holding a towel for her. She saw Daisy. Daisy was watching them as they held their towels for her. Greta dove underwater. Where it was quiet. Where it was safe.

* * *

Elizabeth was, as her father had said, intoxicated.

"Tell your mother," Tony was saying, turning to go inside.

Tell her what? Elizabeth wondered. That you're running away? She'll see that for herself. She took a swig of her drink, hoping to become more intoxicated.

"I want to watch the ball game," he said. "I'll check on Harry. Tell your mother."

He didn't want Greta to worry. That was a good sign. Maybe Elizabeth was wrong. He wasn't having an affair at all. He was a considerate husband who didn't want his wife to worry and a loving father who wanted to lend a hand to his intoxicated daughter by being a devoted grandfather and checking on his sleeping grandson. That made much more sense than having an affair.

When Greta climbed out of the pool, Elizabeth stood up unsteadily, wrapped her mother in the towel, and wished she could wrap both her parents up and hold them safe and sound, and together.

"Daddy went to watch baseball."

Greta nodded.

"He said to tell you."

Her mother pulled on a sweatshirt.

"Daddy wanted me to make sure to tell you," Elizabeth repeated. "So you wouldn't worry."

"Worry?" Greta asked. She looked out from the hood of the sweatshirt, her lips a little blue, but her face radiant.

Tim was suddenly beside Elizabeth. He put his hand on her arm. It was warm. Or perhaps her arm was cold.

"Happy birthday," she said.

"I'm a big boy now."

Elizabeth looked down at his hand on her arm.

"You're freezing," he said.

"Here," Daisy said. She had just picked up her own sweatshirt from a chair. She threw it to Elizabeth.

A familiar scent, Daisy's soap or perfume, something faint and feminine, washed over Elizabeth as she put on the sweatshirt. Elizabeth hadn't realized she was cold, but now she felt the warmth of the garment with relief. She watched the people around her and saw their mouths move.

"Tizzie's blottoed," she heard Josh say.

They blurred slightly, all of them, as if they were still underwater, or waltzing in a ballroom, around and around.

I won't dance, she sang softly. *Don't ask me . . .*

Josh and Tim deposited her on the guest-room bed beside Harry. She watched them go with half-closed eyes.

I won't dance, she sang, in a whisper. *Monsieur, with you . . .*

Greta lived in a tunnel, a trance, a cloud, a cave. The metaphors came and went. Each day she forced the blur of life into focus. She didn't want to miss any of it. Each day she tried to soften the outlines of Daisy's hands, which were small and delicate and just a bit plump, of her lips, which were large and delicate and a bit more than a bit plump. She tried to muffle the sound of Daisy's voice. But what she wanted to mute filled the air instead, and what she tried to lose in the shadows stood out clear and pure.

I'm tired of myself, she thought.

She was filled with a pity so tender and so true that it sickened her, for it was self-pity.

"You never complain," Tony said, full of admiration.

"I'm miserable," she said. "How's that?" Tony grimaced, almost as if he'd been hit. "I'm miserable and I'm rude, too," Greta said. "Sorry."

The phone rang and Elizabeth answered it. "Hi, Grandma." She glanced at Greta.

Poor Elizabeth, Greta thought.

"Mommy's sleeping," Elizabeth said.

"Oh, for Christ's sake," Greta said. She grabbed the phone.

"It was a white lie," Elizabeth said.

"Mama?" Greta said. "I'm up. How are you? I miss your gorgeous face."

"White lies are okay," Elizabeth said.

"Your grandmother would approve, anyway," Tony said.

"Did you get the robe?" Greta was saying.

"Does that mean you *don't* approve? What am I supposed to say? I don't know when she wants to talk to Grandma."

"Relax," Tony said.

"You can put it right in the washing machine," Greta said. "Can you believe it? Silk!"

"That's all you can say," Elizabeth said. "Relax, relax, relax."

"Don't worry," Greta was saying into the phone.

"I don't want to relax," Elizabeth said. "I can't relax. How can you relax?"

"I'm really fine, Mama," Greta said. "I just don't want to give you a germ. We can't have you full of germs right now, can we? You have enough to contend with."

"You're not the only one under pressure, Elizabeth," Tony said. "Okay?"

Greta shushed them both.

"How do *you* feel today?" she asked Lotte. "Status quo?"

"Same old status quo," Elizabeth muttered.

After she hung up, Greta went into the kitchen.

"You all right?" Elizabeth asked, following.

Greta nodded and took a glass of ice tea into her room. She closed the door. She waited until she heard Tony's car leave. She waited until she heard Elizabeth and Josh dive into the pool.

"I want to see you," Greta said.

"I want to see you," she said again, repeating the words slowly, carefully, as if she were reading them.

She picked up the phone and dialed.

"I want to see you," she said into the phone.

"It's me," she said.

"Greta," she said.

"Oh, status quo," she said.

"I want to see you," she said again. And her heart pounded. "I really do."

Greta drove to the restaurant. She turned the air-conditioning up high. She wore sunglasses. The road seemed unfamiliar. The sky seemed unfamiliar. There was a sudden thump on the passenger window.

She got out of the car and saw the gull, stunned, but alive. She watched it totter, then fly off.

I am driving to my doom, she thought. I can read the seagull entrails. I am driving to my doom.

She got back in the car.

I'm driving to my doom. She smiled, hearing the words light and rhythmic and silly as a song. I'm driving to my doom! Doom, doom! She roared through a red light.

INT. HOTEL LOBBY — DAY

Very posh and stylized. Leo's credit card doesn't go through. Barbie pretends not to notice. He fishes out another, which works. She is looking at the lobby, turning in a circle.

BARBIE

Perfect . . . Perfect, perfect, perfect!

INT. HOTEL ROOM — A FEW MINUTES LATER

Barbie and Leo face each other. "I've Got a Crush on You" plays in the background.

                              LEO
      I can't believe you're really here! Are you really
      here?

FLASH BACK TO Barbie as a schoolgirl, leaning her head out the
window to feel the wild wind in her hair.

FLASH FORWARD TO Barbie now. She's frightened. This is mo-
mentous for her. This is what she has lived in hope of, what she
has despaired of ever finding. She reaches into her bag and
takes something out, holds it in her closed fist.

                        BARBIE (CONT.)
      I'm here, you're here . . .

She opens her hand slowly, reverently . . .

EXTREME CLOSE-UP of A PILL . . .

CUT TO Barbie's excited face.

                            BARBIE
      Ecstasy.

The pain had come back and Lotte refused to get out of bed. At
lunchtime, Kougi tried to entice her with bits of food, but even the
rice pudding she had taught him to make did not tempt her. Her
jaw was red and swollen when she looked in the mirror she kept
by the bed. She combed her hair and tried to put on lipstick, but
her mouth was twisted by the surgery, by the tumor.

      "Cockeyed pirate," she said out loud.

      Her face was distorted and discolored. Inside, her jaw was the
site of a thousand deaths, a thousand hammers, a thousand axes, a
spreading poison of a thousand twisted, ugly cells. The rotten cancer
was spreading. Disgusted, she dropped her mirror onto the carpet.

      "Dirty bastards," she said into her pillow.

She called Greta, but Josh answered and told her Greta was out. Out? She could go out? She couldn't come to see her sick mother, but she could go out?

Kougi dabbed at her cheek with a sterile pad. Something was oozing from the red sore on her face and he swabbed it and changed her pillowcase. She lowered her head onto the clean case and thought that even the tall bastard with the flashlight on his head, top man, world famous, was not helping her, the dirty hypocrite, but then again he wanted to see her, had called her just yesterday, taken the time from his busy schedule to call her *in person*, but then she would expect no less, and he had asked her to come into the office. She would go, of course. Such a handsome bastard. And did she have anything else to do? She snorted. Hah! What an idea! Where the hell else was she going?

She whimpered in pain, hoping Kougi would rush in, bathe her head with a cool cloth, which did absolutely nothing, but was something to take her mind off her troubles. Kougi did not hear her, though, and her whimpers turned to moans. She forgot all about Kougi. Stabbing pain. Was this what it was like to be stabbed? Over and over?

Lotte asked God to help her. She asked God to let her die. She asked God to let her live. She promised God she would go to the big-shot doctor.

"That's my social life now," she said to Kougi when he brought her some soup. "Why pretend?"

"Heaviness is the root of lightness," Kougi said. He put the television on for her. They often watched CNBC together. "Serenity," he added, counting out her pills, "is the master of restlessness."

Lotte smiled. Kougi always knew what to say.

"Therefore the Sage, traveling all day, does not part with the baggage wagon," Kougi said.

"Oy," Lotte said. "A baggage wagon, yet."

* * *

The bar was just off the beach. The solemnity of the dark room caught Greta off guard after the sunlight, the rush of bright air during the drive. Were all bars dark? She sat in a booth facing the door. She pushed her sunglasses on top of her head and the room was still dim. She drummed her fingers on the table, wishing she had a cigarette.

"Something to drink?" a waiter asked.

Greta barely noticed him. She said, "Martini." Because she was out of the habit, she forgot to say, "Vodka."

She sipped the martini.

"It's gin," she said.

There was no one to hear her. Gin makes me drunk, she thought. Which is, perhaps, just as well. She began to shiver. She had kicked off her sandals and now could not locate the left one with her foot. She bent down beneath the table. There it was. She watched her foot slide in. When she sat up, she half expected Daisy to be standing there watching her, amused, with that funny expression of detached curiosity. But Daisy wasn't there.

Daisy entered the bar a few minutes later. Greta saw her turn toward another part of the room. She stood up and walked toward Daisy, noticing her back, her shoulders, bare and smooth, the tight fabric of her pants, the curve of her thigh, a flash of skin at her ankle. She thought, I'm staring at her ass. She caught up to Daisy. She put her hand gently on the small of Daisy's back. Greta felt Daisy's skin as her shirt twisted from beneath her fingers, as Daisy turned to face her.

"Hi, you," Daisy said.

Greta kissed Daisy on the lips.

She felt Daisy's lips with her lips. She saw the surprise in Daisy's eyes with her eyes. With her own body, she sensed Daisy's body press closer to her.

Daisy let out a quiet laugh and stepped back.

Was Daisy laughing at her? But Daisy was not laughing at

Greta. Daisy was blushing. God bless you, Greta thought. You sweet, innocent little vamp. Greta had startled Daisy. This delighted her.

"I wanted to talk to you," she said when they were sitting at the table.

Daisy nodded, biting her lip in an exceptionally delicate and appealing way. Daisy leaned forward on her elbows. Her hands, which were small and ladylike, were spread out on the table.

"Daisy, I know this is crazy . . ."

Greta stopped because it rhymed. Daisy seemed not to have noticed. "Look, I . . ." Greta stopped again. "Do you want a drink?" she said. She waved at the waiter, pointed at her martini. "Martini okay? It's gin. Gin makes me drunk."

"Good," Daisy said. She had stopped blushing.

Does she mean the martini is good, or me drunk is good?

They looked at each other across the table. Daisy said nothing. Greta felt dizzy. "I'm married," she said.

"I'm not," Daisy said.

"I could be your mother," Greta said.

"No, you couldn't," Daisy said. "And you're not."

"I've never done this before," Greta said.

"I have," Daisy said.

Greta held the stem of her glass. She saw Daisy's hands on the table. She watched as her own hand moved, slid down the stem, onto the tabletop, across the table. Those were her fingertips touching Daisy's fingertips. Their hands were moving. Her hand slid to Daisy's wrist. Daisy's fingers touched the inside of her wrist. The waiter brought Daisy's drink and Greta wondered what she, Greta Bernard, married to Dr. Anthony Bernard for thirty-two years, was doing drunk in a bar at three in the afternoon straining toward the mouth of a young woman across the table from her as a waiter set down a chilled martini with too many olives.

I'm acting out, she thought. Because I have cancer. What am I trying to prove? That I'm alive? Couldn't I take up oil painting instead?

"I haven't stopped thinking about you since I first saw you," Daisy said. "Sleeping."

And then Greta thought, I have always wanted to kiss this woman. My whole life. And now I know it. And now I will. And she pressed her lips against Daisy's again, tasting a kiss that made her drunk.

~

When she kissed Daisy good-bye, outside the bar, Greta kept her eyes open, not wanting to let go of any one of the five senses of Daisy. She breathed Daisy in, she tasted gin and olives and Daisy, she felt the warmth and novelty of full, feminine breasts pressed against her own. She heard Daisy breathe and watched as Daisy, too, kept her eyes open, barely, hooded and alert.

Now Greta was driving to Lotte's with Elizabeth beside her in the car. She realized she must have made some sound, seductive and predatory, just remembering that moment, for Elizabeth was asking what was wrong.

"Wrong?" Greta said.

"I don't know. Forget it. You're in another world."

Elizabeth turned on the radio, then, almost immediately, off.

Forget it, Greta thought. If only I could. She sped up to make a yellow light and sensed Elizabeth stiffening beside her.

"And you're kind of tailgating," Elizabeth said.

"I was driving before you were born."

Greta patted her daughter's knee to reassure her. Elizabeth took her mother's hand and placed it carefully back on the wheel.

Kougi, Kougi, lend me your comb, Elizabeth sang when they pulled into the garage and parked in a visitor spot. She thought, Am I getting like Grandma?

Her mother stared at the concrete wall in front of them.

"Mom?"

"Don't hate me," Greta said.

"What?"

"Please," Greta added, politely.

"Okay," Elizabeth said. "Since you said please." And she laughed. But she wondered, too. Her mother was still gazing vaguely forward, as if they were on the road, driving.

"Mom? We're here."

Greta turned to her. "I love you and Josh more than anything in the world," she said. Then she smiled her big smile. "Okay!" she said, as if she'd just stepped out into the fresh air. She took a deep breath. "Off we go!"

Kougi answered the door wearing a yellow slicker. He had just given Lotte her shower.

"How is she?" Elizabeth said.

"Your grandmother has great inner strength," Kougi said. "And she moved her bowels today!"

He led Elizabeth and Greta into the living room where Lotte sat in a bathrobe, her cane balanced against the arm of her favorite chair.

"Elizabeth!" Lotte cried. She received her granddaughter's embrace. "You brought Greta." She eyed Greta attentively. "You look pale."

"You look great, Mother," Greta said, laughing, kissing the good side of her face.

Lotte nodded, as if to say, What did you expect? She grabbed Greta's hands and kissed them. "Your health, your health," she murmured.

"Okay, okay," Elizabeth said. "We're all here, aren't we?"

"Did you hear the news?" Lotte said.

"You had a bowel movement?" Greta said.

"No!"

"You didn't have a bowel movement?"

"Of course I did."

"Well then," Elizabeth said.

"The news is that Kougi is going to Japan."

Elizabeth thought she might throw up. "No," she said. "No, no, no."

She sat down on the couch and flung her head back, hitting the wall with a thud. She rubbed the back of her head. She could feel the egg already.

Her mother went into the kitchen.

"Oh my God, oh my God!" Lotte drew out the word "God" as if it were elastic.

"Grandma, it's okay."

Kougi came in with a tray of green tea in tiny Japanese cups.

"She bumped her head, Kougi!"

"Perhaps she has great inner strength, like you," Kougi said.

Lotte thought this idea over and liked it.

"Thank God, thank God. That's all I can say," Lotte said. "With the world the way it is, full of dirty rotten bastards, they should rot in hell."

Greta appeared with a plastic bag of ice. "You're going to Japan?" she said to Kougi, her voice weary. She put the bag on Elizabeth's head.

He nodded.

"And he's taking me with him!" Lotte said. *If you want to know who we are,* she sang out suddenly, *we are gentlemen of Japan . . .*

On many a vase and jar, sang Kougi. *On many a screen and fan . . .*

Elizabeth's mother took the bag of ice back and put it over her eyes.

"There, there, Mommy," Elizabeth said.

We figure in lively paint . . . Lotte sang.

Our attitude's queer and quaint, the two sang together. *You're wrong if you think it ain't . . .*

Elizabeth spent the afternoon helping Lotte with her bills while Greta napped on her mother's bed.

"She works too hard," Lotte said. "You all work too hard."

Kougi was not going to Japan for another year, and if Lotte was still alive in a year, then why shouldn't she go to Japan? And why shouldn't she be alive in a year, for that matter? She seemed so much better. Kougi, it turned out, could not only sing Gilbert and Sullivan, but also make Cream of Wheat with the best of them. He massaged Lotte's feet. He even tamed her depressing houseplants. The plants had first arrived in the house when Lotte began to get sick, cheerful gifts from well-wishers welcoming Lotte home from each hospital visit. Another tumor, another begonia. Lotte had never had any patience for plants before. Plants grew in dirt and were, therefore, dirty. But the gift plants lingered, collecting dust and mites, sprawling in ugly neglected tangles. Until Kougi arrived and made them beautiful again. If that were possible, why couldn't Grandma Lotte live into next year and make her journey to Japan?

Elizabeth watched her grandmother sort through her bills.

"I *am* meticulous," Lotte said.

She took out her checkbook. It was held closed by a rubber band. Scraps of paper with phone numbers and notes were stuffed inside. Lotte laboriously wrote out each check.

"I used to have an exquisite signature," she said.

"I'll do it for you, Grandma," Elizabeth said, more than once. "That's why I came, isn't it?"

"I'm not dead yet," Lotte said. She concentrated on her signature. Slowly, the pen made the familiar loops. Elizabeth watched them unfold, wobbly, but still recognizable as the handwriting of so many birthday checks. Her grandmother's hands were huge. They were pale and bony with arthritis. They labored over their task, leaving behind their old-fashioned penmanship. Lotte Franke. Elizabeth stared at the name, at the passion and ardor and diligence.

"Damn hands," Lotte said, throwing the pen on the table and shaking out her cramped fingers.

"Damn *arthritis*," Kougi said. "*Brave* hands."

"Brave hands," Elizabeth repeated.

Lotte fanned her hands out in front of her eyes and looked at them tenderly.

"The bastards," she said.

From the side of the pool of Greta and Tony's house, which sat high up on a terraced hill, Greta could see her neighbors, two women and two huskies in the driveway below. She wondered if the two dogs in the French chateau-style house next door dreamed at night of pulling sleds. But if there were any sleds in Santa Monica, she was sure the sleds would have been engaged by the doting owners to pull the dogs. Pet talk drifted up from the neighbors' driveway. "Come here, little sweet baby dog puppy, come to Mommy who loves you, little prettiest girl-girl . . ."

For the first time it occurred to Greta that the women were lesbians. She watched the women fuss over the two big dogs.

"I want a dog," she said, startling herself.

"You *do?*" Tony said.

"Do I?" Greta said, looking around at the others for help.

Tony stared at her, then gathered up his towel. He swatted an insect away. "Golf," he said, and left.

"Those women treat their dogs like children," Brett said.

"Should they treat them like adults?" Greta said.

She felt suddenly protective of her neighbors, although when she overheard them cooing at the dogs before she'd found them excessive and saccharine.

"Mom, do you really want a dog?" Elizabeth said. Greta saw she was thinking of the dog as possibly therapeutic, like ice tea.

"You have a grandchild," Brett said.

"I'm not a dog," Harry said.

"Of course not," said Elizabeth.

"I have no doubt they send their dogs off to doggie day care," Brett said. "Why do people get a dog if they have no time to spend with it?"

"Don't you want Harry to go to preschool?" Elizabeth asked Brett, alarmed.

I don't want my children to hate me, Greta thought. It's as simple as that. And they will hate me. They would be well within their rights to hate me. I will hate me. I will be hateful, the scarlet woman, the selfish and self-indulgent midlife crisis who betrayed their father.

"Elizabeth! Harry's not a dog! That's my whole point," Brett said.

They all looked at Harry, who was digging holes in the grass and burying Cheerios.

And what about their father? What about Tony? Greta thought. She watched the neighbors as they successfully loaded the dogs into the backseat of their Mercedes SUV, strapping the two huskies in with special seat belts. A decent, no, a wonderful man who has always been loyal and kind and loving. She couldn't go on with this. It was wrong. It was cruel. It was impossible.

"A dog and an SUV," she said. That would have to be enough.

"You have an SUV," Elizabeth said.

"I'm a dog!" Harry said, rolling in the grass. He barked several times, then sat at the edge of the pool and splashed with his feet.

Greta watched the two women get in the car and drive off. Brett had turned irritably away from the neighbors. It suddenly bothered Greta that neither of the women was terribly attractive.

Elizabeth got up and took Harry into the water.

Greta looked at Brett. There was a smear of sunscreen on the lens of his sunglasses.

"It must be hard not to have children," he said.

Greta thought, What will you say about me, Brett?

Nothing. Because you will never know.

"I mean, it's what life is all about," Brett said.

"Don't be smug," Elizabeth said from the pool.

A dog, Greta thought. A secret lesbian dog. For a secret lesbian. She still wasn't sure what that meant. That she was in love with Daisy? That in the few days since that kiss in the bar, as she and Daisy plotted to get together, Greta had not stopped thinking of her? That she noticed women wherever she went, even the nurses at the doctor's office, the lines of their undergarments showing through slippery nylon uniforms? She had spent so long being Tony's wife and Elizabeth and Josh's mother. Had she been a lesbian all this time? All the time she'd been married and in love with Tony? Because she *had* been in love with Tony. She had looked into his eyes and felt her heart beat wildly, felt her knees weaken.

"What do they *do?*" Lotte would invariably ask when any mention of homosexuality was made. "That's my question. That's what I want to bring out. What do they *do?*"

What do they do? Greta thought. She smiled. She closed her eyes.

"Mom, don't you think that's smug?" Elizabeth was saying from the pool.

"Don't be smug, Brett," Greta murmured obediently. But her eyes remained closed, the hint of a smile, lingering and coy, on her slightly parted lips.

In the pool, Elizabeth bobbed up and down holding Harry. His arms were around her neck. Don't be smug, she told herself. She had noticed, off and on, that the happier Brett got, the more self-satisfied he got. Was that a normal progression? A natural chemical reaction, like ice melting into water and water boiling into steam? Perhaps, at this very moment, as Brett was lounging by the pool, he was imagining himself buckling his son into a Mercedes SUV. The little boy would be just as important an element in that fantasy picture of successful adulthood as the SUV: no less, certainly, but no more.

"Harry's not a symbol," she said. "He's not a trophy of functioning adulthood."

Brett did not hear her.

"I told you, I'm a dog," Harry said.

Elizabeth wondered if she should give Barbie Bovaine a dog instead of a daughter. Indifference to one's child, even cruelty to children, had become old hat in movies. Whereas no one, ever, could bear to see an animal neglected. Except Brett.

She pondered the phrase "old hat" for a while, letting etymology distract her from an uncomfortable feeling of annoyance at Brett, which rhymes with *pet,* she concluded finally, in illogical triumph.

"Old hat," she said, letting the words roll around in her mouth.

"I have an old hat," Harry said.

"Life is full of surprises," Greta said suddenly. "Why is that always so surprising?"

In Lotte's dream, her mother had just brought home the beautiful brown silk dress for the dance. Her father chewed his cigar on the porch. A handsome young man appeared, his eyes blue and alive. It was Morris. He took her to the dance at the college. They danced one dance, two, a thousand dances. No one was allowed to cut in. It was just Lotte and Morris. He was as good a dancer as she was. Around and around they went. She was dizzy. And in love.

It wasn't a dream. It was a memory. It was real. It had happened sixty years ago. It had happened while she slept last night. They had never been apart after they'd been married. He had died on a trip they took together to Arizona, that hideous gray desert. And now she should go to Japan? The last trip with Morris was her

172 • Cathleen Schine

last trip, period. She liked to humor Kougi, he was so polite, so gen-
tlemanly, but why would she want to travel without Morris? And
pay for a hotel? She already paid rent! No, Lotte was not one to
travel anymore, foreigners being what they were, all of them so
very foreign, and the food salty and vile.

seven

EXT. FABULOUS RANCH — NIGHT

Wolf leads Barbie by the hand toward a beautifully landscaped
pool, showing her the property. He opens his arms, as if to
encompass the whole fabulous ranch.

> WOLF
>
> Like it?

> BARBIE
>
> I like it.

He pulls her, suddenly, against him . . .

EXTREME CLOSE-UP of Wolf's hands, strong and manicured, on
Barbie's waist, fingers gripping her body . . .

Their clothes drop away . . . they slip into the pool . . .

                    BARBIE (CONT.) (breathless)
    I like it . . .

MONTAGE Wolf fucks her in the pool . . . he fucks her in his
Porsche . . . he fucks her in the barn . . .

Elizabeth stared at the computer screen and wondered if Volfmann would like the scene. She could see his face. It moved toward
her, its mouth open, yelling, its eyes narrowed in anger and disgust. It moved closer. And closer. The eyes closed. The mouth was
pressed against hers.

Oh, God, she thought. Not this again. She had been thinking of
Volfmann far too much.

She stood up, a little wobbly. She walked downstairs reminding herself of how loud Volfmann was, how rude. But Volfmann's
hands, strong and manicured, kept grabbing her waist. Like it? he
asked. I like it, she said. His words were kind and brilliant. His
mouth was sad and sensuous.

She tried watching old movies on television. But every movie
was *Madame Bovary,* just as Volfmann had said. *Dodsworth, Nia-
gara, Thelma and Louise* were all *Madame Bovary. The Postman
Always Rings Twice* was *Madame Bovary. Move Over, Darling* was
Madame Bovary. Madame Bovary c'est moi, Flaubert had said. She
is me, too, Elizabeth thought.

She tried to work again, then tried television again, then reminded herself of Volfmann ranting and stamping his feet. But it
didn't help. Movies she had always dismissed as trivial and hackneyed seemed like towering achievements compared to her own
efforts. Every frame she watched was a rebuke: You didn't write
this scene; you can't write this scene; you can't write any scene half
as good as this scene; you can't write any scene at all.

She went outside. It was gray and cool. She sat on her steps and stared at the garden and wondered what sitting on the front steps looking at the garden would have made her feel if, like Greta, she were a gardener. Would she be thinking, I ought to be digging a hole, I should be planning a herbaceous border. She remembered Volfmann digging a hole in the sand with Harry when they visited his house in Malibu. She pushed the thought away. She wondered how her mother was doing. Greta had said she was going out to meet an old college friend that night and wanted to rest up, so Elizabeth hadn't gone over.

I should go to Grandma's then, Elizabeth thought.

This was an absurd way to spend a morning. Feeling guilty and imagining new ways to feel guilty? She tried to stop. Then she wondered if having an affair would make her feel guilty. In Volfmann's office, there was a back staircase that had once been used to sneak starlets in to service the studio head. I could use that staircase, she thought. Volfmann could throw me down on the desk the way he threw down the copy of *Tikkun*. She laughed. Then she felt sick.

Of course, I would feel guilty toward Brett, she thought. I already feel guilty toward Brett just contemplating adultery.

She got up and picked some daylilies.

Would adultery also make me feel guilty about my unfinished screenplay about adultery?

The sun came out and she blinked. She watched the eighty-year-old twins next door in their SKIDMORE BASKETBALL caps watering their roses. Did they commit adultery? The two graduate students in architecture who rented the house on the other side of her came out onto their front steps. Elizabeth waved hello. Did they have any weight hanging over them, a guilty daydream of sleeping with someone unsuitable, say, or a mother with cancer? It seemed impossible. They looked so light and free, so young and unencumbered. She offered them the daylilies.

Edie, the shorter blond one, took the flowers inside the tiny cottage. The other girl, whose name was Sophie, leaned over the fence. "We're going to Fred Segal," she said, "to do research." They were designing a shopping mall for their thesis and did research every weekend, coming back loaded with shopping bags. "Do you have any research to do?"

Elizabeth wondered why she hadn't thought of this before. Fred Segal was an overpriced paradise. Who could withstand the call of a morning at Fred Segal? Not Elizabeth. And certainly not Barbie Bovaine. When you got right down to it, what did a woman like Barbie Bovaine do if not shop?

Elizabeth sat in the backseat of Edie's car, happy not to be the one determining whether to take surface streets or freeways. How luxurious to let someone else make a decision. Let these cheerful girls, who were not that much younger than she was, take charge. For these few minutes, Elizabeth could be free. She was anonymous. Not the mother, the daughter, the sister, or the unmarried wife. Not the granddaughter. Not the professor or the screenwriter. Just the neighbor. She had no role to play, no duties to perform. No one required her services.

The girls were planning to divide their shopping mall into areas determined by lifestyles rather than brands. Where would Barbie Bovaine shop? In the Social Climbing Section? The Adultery Boutique? The Naive Romantic Department? The Slut Shop?

Elizabeth browsed, trying on things she thought Barbie might consider essential. A pair of sunglasses in a neoaviator style, the lenses graduated shades of pink, which she bought for herself. A pair of silk pants, bright red, embroidered with gold dragons, not really capri length, not pedal-pusher length, not clam-digger length, but some new essential length that made those other lengths look frumpy, which she decided Barbie would wait to buy until they were on sale. A sun hat was too silly, a bag too big. But several

T-shirts were just right for Barbie, and Elizabeth bought them along with a chartreuse bikini. Barbie would wear the bikini. In the pool. With Wolf.

At one of the jewelry counters, she asked to see several tourmaline rings. She put two on each hand and held them up in front of her. Rose gold. Elizabeth loved rose gold. Barbie would not go for these, she thought. She would prefer a more gaudy and expensive gemstone. But these are just right for me. She admired the stones sparkling on her hand until, through her outstretched fingers, she saw the familiar face of Daisy Piperno.

Elizabeth expected to see Daisy at her parents' house — she was always turning up there, and that was fine, nice for Greta, convenient for Elizabeth. But she did not like seeing Daisy popping up here, where Elizabeth was posing as the anonymous neighbor. It was like being stalked. Soon she would see Daisy everywhere, around every corner, like an apparition, a ghoul in a horror movie.

Daisy caught sight of her and blushed, a bright obvious red against her normally pale skin.

Why did I make her blush? Elizabeth wondered.

Daisy grabbed a small package from the saleswoman and stuffed it into her bag. She bit her lip and seemed to will the blush to recede, then looked back at Elizabeth.

"Small town," Elizabeth said. No it isn't, she thought. It's a gigantic sprawling city. Why are Daisy and I always in the same corner? Didn't Daisy have anything else to do? Daisy swimming in the pool, drinking ice tea, bringing flowers. She seemed to think up excuses to drop by . . .

"Aren't you supposed to be working?" Daisy said, composed now, back to her distant, curious manner.

"Research," Elizabeth said.

Edie and Sophie came up to them, their arms loaded with packages. Daisy introduced herself while Elizabeth stood stupidly twisting the tourmaline rings on her fingers.

Daisy is into women, Elizabeth thought.

"Research is good," Daisy was saying. She smiled at Elizabeth. Elizabeth remembered Daisy telling her what a great smile she had when she mopped up the spilled Pepsi. She heard Daisy's voice calling her Cookie. She saw the hooded eyes, felt the appraisal in the glance.

Is she *interested* in me? Elizabeth wondered. It seemed ridiculous. But why? I *am* a woman, she thought.

"Up to a point," Daisy said.

"Up to a point?" Elizabeth was the one blushing now. What point?

"Bye, babe," Daisy said. She leaned toward her, gave her a quick kiss on the cheek, then put her fingers to her own lips, then touched Elizabeth's lips.

"Oh," Elizabeth said. She was flustered. She said, "See you later?" She had meant to say, See you later, meaning, Good-bye. But she had said, See you later? Meaning, Can I see you later? She was lost in the confusion of her own embarrassment. She stared at Daisy without really seeing her.

Daisy tousled Elizabeth's hair. "Not tonight," she said. "I got me a hot date tonight."

Elizabeth mumbled something. Then she turned and hurried away.

She heard a baby cry. She heard a saleswoman call, "Miss!" She heard someone yell, "Security!" She heard a man say, "How the hell should I know?" A slender girl spritzed her with perfume. A uniformed man appeared at Elizabeth's side and took her arm.

"Excuse me, sir," Elizabeth said, "you're squeezing my arm."

But the man said nothing as he led her back to the jewelry counter.

"That's the one!" said the saleswoman.

People were gathering, staring at her. The saleswoman was pointing at Elizabeth's hand, at four tourmaline rings set in rose gold.

Ah, Elizabeth thought.

She pulled the rings off with some difficulty, having to suck on one finger and lick another. She dropped the rings gently on the counter. "How incredibly stupid. I just wasn't thinking . . ."

As the saleswoman waved the security officer away and sternly told Elizabeth to watch her step in the future, Daisy, who had been observing the whole episode with a puzzled smile, picked up one of the rings and held it to the light.

"Pretty," she said.

Elizabeth stared at the floor, humiliated.

"It was a *mistake,*" she said.

"Yes, it was," Daisy said. "They're definitely not you, Elizabeth."

Not me? Elizabeth sat irritably in the backseat surrounded by parcels and wondered, all the way home, why not.

When she got home, she opened a can of Diet Pepsi, watched Harry as he made potions while standing on a chair at the kitchen sink, and thought of Daisy tousling her hair and calling her Cookie. And what was with the finger on the lips?

The phone was ringing.

"It's for you," Brett yelled from upstairs. "Volfmann."

She imagined Volfmann on the phone, his head tilted back, his eyes closed. Then leaning across the desk and grabbing her hand. She put the cold can of Pepsi against her cheek and picked up the receiver.

"I saw Daisy at Fred Segal's," she said.

"I see how you two spend your days."

"I was doing research," she said. "I just bumped into her. Or she bumped into me."

She watched Harry pour and stir, pour and stir. He made a growling, grinding sound, then said, "Coffee."

"Was she doing research, too?" Volfmann said.

Elizabeth was afraid Volfmann had called to scream at her. Or as she had once heard him describe the process when it referred to someone else who had failed him, to ream her a new asshole. Or worse, to fire her. She tried to put off the inevitable.

"So, she doesn't have a partner or whatever they call it? A lover?"

"Why, Elizabeth, you intrigue me," he said.

You intrigue me, too, she thought, but no words came out of her mouth.

"Daisy is quite the girl about town," Volfmann was saying.

How about you? she thought. What is your status about town?

"Look, we have to talk, Elizabeth."

We do? Yes, we do, she thought. She could see him so clearly, the phone crammed between his ear and his shoulder, his elbows on his desk, his body leaning forward, his face like a serious, intelligent dog's.

How was it that she had never noticed the hoarse, deep timbre of his voice before?

"Come and meet me for a drink, okay?" he said.

She read to Harry before bedtime. She kept skipping pages and he kept noticing. He told her he wanted to be a gardener when he grew up.

"Like Grandma," she said.

"No," he said. "A gardener with a leaf blower." And he fell asleep holding her hand.

Then she drove to meet Volfmann at Shutters, a place she had never been. It was on the beach, close to her, on Volfmann's way to Malibu. It seemed an unlikely place to meet someone to fire them. It seemed an unlikely place to scream at her. It seemed more the kind of place where you use your power and status to get someone to sleep with you, she thought. She smiled.

She reminded herself that she had never been unfaithful to Brett. He was so calm and even tempered and smug and self-satisfied that it didn't seem possible, really. Even now. When it seemed possible. Still, you never know. Adultery is wildly exciting, a powerful, intoxicating temptation. I'm sure I've read that somewhere.

But only if you're married, she reassured herself.

And remember, too, that adultery is messy, filled with lies and heartbreak.

If you're married.

Adultery is ludicrous as well, a series of embarrassing comic predicaments, locked doors, naked men on balconies, girls in the closet.

If you're married, if you're married, if you're married.

So, Elizabeth thought, it is marriage, ultimately, that causes adultery. It is marriage that is to blame.

Out the window, she saw her mother driving much too fast. On her way to her dinner date, no doubt. Elizabeth waved. But Greta did not notice her, and Elizabeth thought that perhaps, all things considered, it was just as well.

Greta was meeting Daisy at a hotel. They couldn't go to Greta's house, obviously, and Daisy's sister had come to the house in Silver Lake for a visit, so the Ritz-Carlton in Marina Del Rey was chosen, as unfashionable a place as they could think of. It was unlikely that anyone they knew would show up there, but even if someone did see them, Greta could say she had bumped into Daisy unexpectedly, that she'd gone to the hotel to meet the old college friend. And then, she'd say, Daisy and I thought we'd have a drink while I waited. A drink. Getting a drink sounded awfully good to her as she entered the lobby. She could get a drink for real, quickly, before Daisy arrived, and then she could go home.

She walked up to the desk. There was an enormous and hideous flower arrangement on it.

"I need a room for tonight," she said.

The desk clerk had scrupulously combed and gelled hair. Wide tooth marks had been left behind by the comb. He had light brown hair and a thick pink neck. He asked for her credit card.

"I lost my wallet," she said. "I'll have to pay cash."

The clerk said nothing and punched something into a computer. Greta gave her name as Gretchen Bernhardt, carefully reciting the incorrect spelling.

"I don't have any," she said when the clerk asked her for ID. "I lost my wallet. So I don't have any."

Stupid charade, she thought. I'm a grown woman. Give the man your credit card. Give the man your name.

The clerk looked at her for a minute with bored blue eyes, then shrugged.

Greta had dressed with care, choosing her least matronly undergarments, the silk sweater Elizabeth had given her for her birthday, a pair of tight-fitting pants and sandals her mother had forced her to buy at Barneys. She had gotten a pedicure and had her legs waxed, too.

"I haven't had my legs waxed in years," she told the woman who was ripping the strips of fabric off her burning legs. "Now I remember why."

The woman had given her a smirky smile, which could have been interpreted in a number of ways, one of them being a suspicion that her client was about to embark on a love affair.

The silk sweater was too heavy. Greta was hot. She noticed a mousy person on her way to a conference room. I'm wearing the same sandals as that dowdy woman, she thought sadly. She stood, sweating, worrying over her shoes and wondering what she would say if someone she knew walked in. I could leave, she told herself. I could still leave, walk out of here with my virtue and dignity intact. But she wouldn't leave. Nothing could make her leave, as she well knew. She had taken a leap and could see the ground coming at her faster and faster, and as far as she was concerned, it couldn't come fast enough. Even the appearance of Tony himself would not have stopped her. *And what would he be doing here, anyway?* she said to herself, outraged at the thought of her husband arriving for a sleazy, illicit assignation in a hotel lobby.

The clerk handed her a key.

"Luggage?" he said.

Greta, still fuming about Tony, thought again that she could simply walk out. She had handed the man $250 in cash, but she really could leave, right now. The lobby blurred a little. She mumbled something and headed toward the elevator.

In the room, she pulled the curtains and sat on one of the queen-size beds. This will be my bed, she thought. Daisy can have the other. Like Ozzie and Harriet. If Daisy even shows up. She imagined the door handle turning. Daisy's sweet, plump hand would turn the knob. Above Daisy's hand was her wrist and her smooth curved arm. Greta saw Daisy's bare shoulder, felt the warmth of her shoulder beneath her own hand.

She opened the drawer on the bedside table, wondering if there would be a Bible there. Sure enough . . . She opened it and looked for the Song of Solomon. I'm a cliché, she thought. A woman in a hotel room, about to have an affair. Would she have felt better if she were more of a cliché, if she'd been waiting to have an affair with a man instead of a woman?

"Behold, thou art fair, my love; thou hast doves' eyes within thy locks: thy hair is as a flock of goats . . ." Greta smiled, picturing a flock of goats on Daisy's head. "Thy teeth are like a flock of sheep that are even shorn, which came up from the washing . . ." Woolly teeth. Didn't it also say somewhere that the beloved smelled like Lebanon? Greta lay down on the bed, her questionable shoes still on. She reached into her bag for her reading glasses so she could stop squinting. She heard her mother's voice. *Stop squinting. You'll get wrinkles in your forehead.* She put on her reading glasses. "Thy belly is like an heap of wheat set about with lilies."

The thought of a belly made her suddenly self-conscious. She was not twenty years old. She'd had two children. She imagined Daisy finding her like this, a middle-aged woman in spectacles with wrinkles in her forehead, stretch marks on her heap of wheat, and the same sandals as a dowdy woman in the lobby. And she wondered why she didn't care, why she knew it didn't matter. "Thy two breasts are like two young roes that are twins," she read, "which feed among the lilies." Greta could feel the book's binding in her hands, the bumpy black cover, as if it were skin. "Thou hast ravished my heart, my sister, my spouse. How fair is thy love, my sister, my spouse! How much better is thy love than wine! and the smell of thine ointments than all spices! Thy lips, O my spouse, drop as the honeycomb: honey and milk are under thy tongue . . ."

The telephone beside her rang.

"Daisy coming up," said the clerk.

Greta closed her eyes. Honey and milk are under thy tongue, she thought.

The immense silence of the room released a small knock on the door and Greta let Daisy in. They stood facing each other. Greta, so bold in the bar, could not move. Should she read to Daisy from the Bible? A garden enclosed is my sister, my spouse. She could read that. A spring shut up, a fountain sealed. She was feeling dizzy, her desire surely audible.

"Hello," she said.

"Hello," Daisy said.

Daisy looked so pretty. Her shoulders were bare beneath a rather bright yellow tank top. How could anyone wear that color and get away with it? Thy navel is like a round goblet, which wanteth not liquor, she thought, in spite of herself.

Daisy put her hand on Greta's cheek and moved closer.

You look so pretty, Greta wanted to say. You are so pretty. Like two young roes set about with lilies and liquor, like a goblet heaped with wheat, like soft white sheep and deep red pomegranates, like everything sweet and full and fragrant and abundant.

"You're . . . I'm . . ." she said instead.

Daisy nodded in agreement.

Greta knew she was putting her arms out, knew her hands closed around Daisy's wrists, knew she pulled this woman to her. She understood that she and Daisy were lying on the bed, that she was in the ridiculous position of undoing a bra like a teenage boy. But there was nothing ridiculous about it. She was not a teenage boy. Her belly was not an heap of wheat. Daisy's breasts were breasts, not roes, and no metaphors were needed. No metaphor would do.

At last, she thought, and it was as if her entire life had been leading her here.

"At last," she whispered.

"So," Volfmann said, standing up from the table to greet her. "You're late."

He ordered oysters and champagne.

"You've been married, right?" Elizabeth asked, the champagne going to work immediately.

"Many times."

"I think marriage leads to adultery," she said.

"Yes. Look at poor little Emma."

"Yes. Look at her."

They were silent for a few minutes.

"I almost got arrested for shoplifting," she said. He definitely wasn't going to fire her. Not with oysters.

"What did you take, Winona?"

Elizabeth looked at him in dismay.

"Nothing!" she said. "It was a mistake!"

Volfmann took her hand in his and tried to calm her.

"Okay, okay. It was a mistake . . ."

She noticed his watch. It was one she had seen in an ad and admired. It cost many thousands of dollars.

"Don't lose that," she said, tapping the watch face.

"I'll try not to," he said.

Elizabeth listened contentedly to the ringing in her ears. She ate oysters. They seemed to glide down someone else's throat. Volfmann was watching her silently, which was a relief. Better than having him holler at her for writing trash. He was oddly attractive, with his manicured nails and jowly, masculine face. That frightened her. I'm an employee, she reminded herself. But did that make her safer or less safe? And did she want to be safe? Or had she come here to be dangerous? She couldn't remember.

"What did you want to talk to me about?" she said.

He leaned forward in his sudden, avid way. "You're the only one," he said, "the only one who would understand . . ." He almost snorted in his intensity.

Elizabeth was trembling. She felt his knee brush hers beneath the table. She was paralyzed by the heat rushing through her body. She watched his lips as they moved, slowly, in slow motion, sliding over his teeth, making the shape of an O, then sliding back, then again into an elongated O. She felt herself leaning forward to kiss him even as she deciphered his words.

"Joseph Roth!" he had said.

She stopped, her mouth an inch from his. Joe Roth? Wasn't he a producer?

"I'd only read *The Radetzky March,*" Volfmann was saying, "but this new translation of his stories . . ." Volfmann was bobbing up and down in his excitement. "Joseph Roth, man, he is great . . ."

Rote, she almost said, once she understood he meant the Austrian writer, correcting his pronunciation. Joseph *Rote.*

Her face was so close she could taste his breath as he spoke. She closed her eyes.

"'Stationmaster Fallmerayer' . . ." he was saying.

"Yes," she murmured. "'Stationmaster Fallmerayer.' Delicious . . ."

Greta was awakened by the phone. Panicked (who knew she was here?), she picked up the receiver of the hotel phone and listened to the dial tone in guilty confusion until she realized the ringing came from her cell phone.

"Hello?" she said. She tried not to sound as if she had just been asleep, her face pressed into a woman's belly.

"Darling, at last. Josh finally gave me this number. You're still out? I was so worried. All day I've been looking for you, you have no idea . . ."

Greta listened to her mother and marveled at the young woman beside her. She stroked Daisy's hair and kissed her back just below her nicotine patch.

"Mama, I'm sorry you had such a bad day . . ."

Then, because the patch was a silent offering and she knew it was, Greta kissed the patch itself.

"Never mind that now. It's too late for that. I found the doctor myself. I took care of it. I don't like to take too many medicinals, but Kougi's here, so I'll try them, but imagine if I were alone . . ."

"I'll stay there tonight," Greta said. "I'll stay there every night if you need me, Mother."

She watched Daisy walk naked to the bathroom.

"You? With your flu?" Lotte said.

"Me with my flu?" Greta said, noticing the dimple at the small of Daisy's back. She had stopped listening to her mother.

"Who else?" Lotte said. "*I* don't have the flu."

"You don't?"

"Cancer is not enough? When are you coming?"

Greta watched Daisy approach from the bathroom, her body so unfamiliar, so familiar. Daisy held her arms out.

"What time?" Lotte asked.

"Greta," Daisy whispered. Her voice was sleepy. She kissed Greta on her neck.

"This is not Spain," Lotte was saying. "We go to bed at nine."

Daisy slid into bed beside Greta, holding her, whispering her name over and over.

"And the food?" Greta heard her mother's voice as she hung up. "*Very* salty in Spain."

Lotte heard the bell. She didn't even try to get up. She was taking pills, the size of them! For *horses,* they were so big. They made her sleepy. The pain was still there, in her jaw, in her neck, in her head when she took the horse pills. She just didn't mind as much.

"Darling," she said when Greta came in. "The cell phones, they always cut you off, they should drop dead with that kind of service." Her daughter kissed her and held her hand and spoke to her softly. There was no one like blood. Kougi was wonderful. But blood was blood.

"Don't cry, Mama," Greta said.

"I missed you," Lotte said.

"I missed you, too."

"I want to die," Lotte wailed. She didn't mean to wail. She didn't want to die, either. But the touch of her daughter's hand, the gentleness of her voice, the sight of her . . . "You look so nice," Lotte said. "You had a date?"

Greta looked startled, then laughed.

"I don't want to die," Lotte said. "That's the goddamned problem. I must be crazy, the pain I'm in, they should call Dr. Karoglian."

"Kevorkian. Mr. Karoglian was the Spanish teacher who accused me of cheating."

"That bastard."

"You're a good mother, Mom. Going into school and fighting for me like that."

"You're so lucky," Lotte said. She was crying again. "You *have* your mother."

Greta got up to get her some Kleenex.

"I don't have a mother," Lotte said through her tears. "I miss my mother."

"I *am* lucky," Greta said. She patted Lotte's tears carefully.

Lotte grabbed one of Greta's hands. She kissed it and kissed it. She held on to the hand with all her strength. "Very lucky," she said. "Very, very lucky." Greta gave a little laugh, and Lotte wondered if Greta thought she was still talking about Greta's good luck. But Lotte was too tired and too weak to correct her.

Over the Pacific Ocean, the sun lowered itself, slow and magnificent, and Elizabeth watched the color it left behind. Volfmann's head was silhouetted, framed by red. It was beautiful. He was beautiful. It was passionate. He was passionate. The red turned to lavender. The air was cool. "Stationmaster Fallmerayer" was a story about falling in love, he said. About marriage, about adultery, yes, but really about love. She nodded in agreement. She said, "Yes! Yes!" He grabbed her hand, squeezing it, using the other to pound the table to make a point about Chekhov. The translator of the Roth had compared the story to "Lady with Lapdog." "Yes!" Elizabeth said. "Falling in love. They fall in love. Like a thunderbolt." No, Volfmann said, his voice rising. "Lady with Lapdog" was full of hope. Desperate hope. "Stationmaster Fallmerayer" had a cheap ending. A journalist's ending. There was another bottle of champagne. They argued about endings. They argued about Henry James. Cheap ending, he said about *The Spoils of Poynton*. She disagreed with him. She forgot he was beautiful and passionate and thought, No, you're wrong, that's an undergraduate's argument, and pressed her point. He capitulated. She rejoiced. The moon left a silver shadow on the Pacific Ocean. They returned to "Lady with Lapdog." Love. Desperate hope. They agreed. He paid the check. She was exhausted. It was two A.M.

Hours and hours past when she said she'd be home. She wanted to be in bed. She was too old to stay up all night discussing literature.

"I have to go home," she said.

"Coup de foudre," he said. "I love that phrase."

Elizabeth woke up late the next morning. She had a hangover. She plunked herself down on the front steps with a cup of coffee and read the note Brett had left. Tiny white petals drifted down from a small tree she did not know the name of. A hummingbird whirred by. The air was warming up and the light turning a softer yellow. She watched a black-and-white cat stalk an invisible prey. The note said Brett and Harry had gone to the beach. She imagined them on the sand, close to the crash of the waves. Harry would run in and out of the foam, tripping on seaweed, laughing. Holding Brett's hand.

She had taken Harry to the dentist a few days before. The dentist had addressed Harry with grave sincerity.

"You are three years old," he had said. "You're a big boy. You have to stop sleeping with your pacifier. It causes cavities. And it gets in the way of the teeth that are trying to grow in."

Harry gazed up at him, wide-eyed.

"Do you understand, Harry?"

Harry nodded.

"It's very important, Harry."

"Okay," Harry said.

When Elizabeth took him out the door, he looked up at her.

"I will not give up my pacifier," he said. "I will keep it. Up to the day I die."

Elizabeth imagined Harry, an old man, brittle and bent, sucking on his pacifier. But the thought of Harry old and so eventually dying, even such an absurd thought as the ancient Harry with the plug in his mouth, made her queasy. She wondered if Brett had put sunscreen on Harry. Brett had the kind of skin that turned a lovely deep bronze in the sun. Elizabeth never tanned, always burned. The burns would peel, leaving pale, freckled skin ready to burn again. Harry's skin was more like Brett's, but even so, he needed protection. The sun caused cancer. It caused cancer that blossomed and spread. The surgeon with the miner's lamp had saved enough of Lotte's nose to paste a flap over, like a balding man covering his bare skull with several long strands. But the red had reappeared. The tumor advanced daily, inexorable rosy lumps bulging across the jaw of Grandma Lotte.

Elizabeth went out the back door and got on her bike. She'd brought the bike from New York at some inconvenience because she thought she would use it in Venice. There were bike paths in Venice. It would be exercise and fresh air. She could put Harry on the back in his special padded safety seat. But this was the first time she had ridden the bike and she wobbled toward the beach.

Brett can't even remember to put sunscreen on Harry, she thought. Do I have to do absolutely everything? Is it a crime to go out for a few drinks and sleep late? Can't he even take the child to the beach without making a fuss about it? She grew angrier and angrier as she huffed and puffed down the street. She hoped Harry and Brett had gone to the same place they usually went, just south of the last honky-tonk shop on the boardwalk, just beyond the hot-dog stand and the tennis courts. She was feeling a little desperate now, as if the skin cancer were racing her to the beach towel. She rode as fast as she could.

"Mommy!" Harry cried, spotting her first.

"Hey!" Brett said, giving her a surprised, happy smile, which changed immediately to a suspicious narrowing of the eyes. "Everything's fine," he said, his voice defensive.

Elizabeth ran her hand across Harry's smooth, unblemished cheek.

"Time for some more sunscreen, sweetie?" she said. She didn't look at Brett.

"Daddy just made me," Harry said. He started to cry. "Don't make me. Daddy made me. *Three* times." He pulled away from Elizabeth, rubbing his tearstained face with sandy fists.

"Three times?" she said in her cheerful, encouraging I-know-you-don't-want-to-have-a-tantrum voice. She gently brushed the crusted sand from his cheeks. "Well, that's definitely enough times." She hugged him. She looked at Brett. She smiled, full of gratitude, full of remorse. She hoped the gratitude showed.

"I've been taking him to the beach every day," Brett said, his voice hard and cold. "Does he ever come home with a sunburn?"

eight

EXT. OSTENTATIOUS HOUSE — DAY

Barbie, Chuck, and REAL-ESTATE AGENT stand before an enormous faux-Spanish mansion. Barbie is beaming. Chuck, slather-
ing sunscreen on his pasty arms and bald pate, looks at the big
house with obvious worry.

                    CHUCK
        Isn't it a little out of our league?

                    BARBIE
        This is our league . . . Beverly Hills . . .

                    AGENT
        Well, Beverly Hills Adjacent . . .

                      ∼

When Greta got in Elizabeth's car to go visit Lotte, Elizabeth tapped Greta's finger and said, "Hey! You get that ring at Fred Segal's?"

"Hmm? Oh." Greta looked at the ring Daisy had given her. Imagine. Just like that. A beautiful tourmaline ring. A gift. A lavish gift. And a gift she actually liked. There were some advantages to this lesbian business.

"I just saw one like it at Fred Segal's. I tried it on and everything."

"Really? I just thought I needed to cheer myself up."

Elizabeth approved of that. That seemed healthy. Optimistic. But what an odd coincidence.

"Daisy was there," Elizabeth said. "At the store. She was on her way to a date. Did you know she's a lesbian?"

"Really?" Greta said. She hoped she said it. She thought she might have actually grunted in a self-conscious, guilty, revealing manner.

"Really," Elizabeth said. She stared at her mother's hand. She wished her father had given her mother the ring. Or would he only have done such a thing out of guilt? Perhaps Brett would give Elizabeth a ring. Or Volfmann. She struggled not to blush at the thought of him. She remembered his face, through the alcohol, through her own excitement. He had leaned so close. The image of his animated face, his eyes blazing, kept grabbing her attention, startling her, as if she'd turned a corner and there he was.

"Do you think everyone leads a secret life?" she said.

Her mother was silent. She twisted her ring.

Elizabeth stopped at a light and leaned her head wearily against the wheel, accidentally honking the horn.

"Where does privacy end and secrecy begin?" Greta said.

Elizabeth sat between them. The three of them on the couch. Grandma's big feet stuck straight out. Greta had taken her shoes off and sat cross-legged. Elizabeth thought, We are out of order. Mom should be in the middle.

"Dirty bastard politicians . . ." Lotte was saying. "Lousy terrorists . . ." She moved on to salaries for baseball players (too high) and the yen (too low). "I like your ring, though," she said, reaching across Elizabeth's lap and grabbing Greta's hand.

Elizabeth saw her mother start at Lotte's touch. Greta was so easily startled these days. There was a physical, animal quality to her fear, sometimes, that saddened Elizabeth.

"Sporty," Lotte said.

Greta laughed. "Really? Which sport?"

"I was a *wonderful* basketball player," Lotte said. "Until that Ilsa Hochstedter knocked me down."

"When was that?" Elizabeth asked.

"Seventy years ago. The bastard."

Lotte closed the door with relief. She walked stiffly back to her chair and fumbled for the remote control. She couldn't find it. She smoothed her new, gorgeous linen tunic and wondered if it was worth getting up again to look. There was nothing to watch on television. There never was anything to watch. The misery, the violence . . .

She clucked and shook her head. She sounded like a chicken, which disgusted her. She examined her fingers. They were thick and crooked. Like an old woman's hands. She reached over to the table beside her and picked up the bottle of silvery nail polish there. With quick, practiced, but inaccurate strokes, Lotte slid the brush along her thickened nails. She admired the wet shimmer and rested her hands on the armrests to dry.

Greta had looked thin and white. But radiant, too, in an incongruous way. Lotte wondered if she had, God forbid, TB.

"*Ke-nein-e-chora,*" she said, pretending to spit, to keep the evil eye away. "I didn't say TB, God," she said. "Forget I even mentioned it."

"Just the flu," she added, loudly.

Poor Greta. She remembered her as a little girl, her hair blond and bouncing, her lips like a little rosebud. Running toward them at visitors' day at camp. Her arms outstretched. Her smile giddy with love and anticipation. Lotte had opened her arms to receive her lovely daughter in her forest-green shorts and yellow polo shirt, not the best color combination, but woodsy, anyway, and little Greta, running, running, had seen her mother's arms open and had faltered, just for a moment, but long enough for Lotte to notice and then realize, even as Greta changed direction by a couple of degrees and flew into her mother's arms, that the little girl, glowing with the great outdoors, had been running, really, to her father.

But she knew! Lotte thought, with satisfaction. She saw my face and she knew how much I loved her. She knew I would be disappointed. She knew who to come to! Smart little girl. Didn't want to disappoint her mommy.

Lotte was glad to have seen Greta even if she did wish her daughter had looked a little more robust. After all, she thought, there's only so much a person my age can tolerate.

She realized she had to pee. She cursed her bladder. She pushed down on the arms of the chair with her own arms. She leaned forward as the physical therapist had taught her to. She heaved herself up, but tipped back again before she could get the strength in her legs to stand upright. She tried it two more times before she could stand. It was a struggle. Every day was a struggle. Where was the cane? On the floor? Goddamned dirty bastard of a cane. That would mean sitting back down to be able to reach it, then heaving herself up again. But there it was, thank God, thank God, leaning against the chair, within easy reach. She hooked it with her bent forefinger. Why did everything go at once? The legs, the hands, the face, her poor, lovely face? At least she had all her organs cranking away. Her heart would last forever, with its valve replacement. Or so they'd said. She tried to remember the heart surgeon as she walked slowly and painfully to the bathroom. The pain in her face was maddening. She stopped to catch her breath and whimpered a little, the soft sounds filling her with tenderness for herself. Kougi would be back tonight, thank heaven, or Buddha or whoever he was always going on about. She had not allowed Greta or Elizabeth to wait with her. She was not that far gone, for Buddha's sake! Elizabeth was a good girl, she thought, but why had she gotten her hair cut so short? "I'm sick of myself," Elizabeth had explained, as if that meant anything at all. Lotte stopped at the mirror in her bedroom and fluffed her own hair, white and silky, with her free hand. People don't know what they have when they have it, she thought. If you have your health, and an independent income, well then . . .

And Lotte lowered herself onto the toilet with genuine pleasure, and with pride.

Elizabeth sat on the steps in front of her house beneath the branches of the white birch tree that grew by the gate. The dappled sunlight played on the dark earth, on the daylilies, on the spiderwebs. Brett came out and sat on the step beside her. He patted her new haircut. "It will grow back," he had said when he saw it. She took his hand. It was such a small garden and so much went on there. Whole lives. Whole worlds. Brett's hand felt unfamiliar. A hermit thrush dug in the dirt. A hummingbird stood in the air.

"Your father called," Brett said.

Elizabeth tried to swallow. The feeling that the world was receding before her eyes, then whooshing back in, like a wave, was so disconcerting. She held on to the step beneath her.

"Shit," she said.

"No, sweetie, she's okay," Brett said quickly.

It's okay, she repeated to herself. She's okay.

"Which she?"

That pronoun had become her enemy. It meant uncertainty, fear, illness, death.

"Both shes. It's okay. He was just looking for your mother, actually. She's gone out. Old Greta certainly does get out and about these days."

"Out and about," Elizabeth said. Old Greta out and about. Brett stood. His knees were at eye level. There were grass stains on his khakis. Where out and about? Her mother was out and about far more than she ought to be.

"Where does she go all the time?" she said. "It's as if she had a secret life. What if my mother has joined a cult or something?"

"That *would* be ghastly."

Somehow the word "ghastly" gave to the idea of Greta in a cult a pleasant, comic quality, as if she were a character in an English novel, as if she were merely eccentric.

"Mom is so eccentric," Elizabeth said, though she really wasn't, was she? Brett was already up the stairs and out of earshot, but Elizabeth didn't mind. Eccentric was so much nicer than sick. Than ill. Than cancer victim. Than a battler of cancer. Cancer on the presidency. Cancer survivor. Cancer had so many clichés associated with it. She would have to reread Susan Sontag's book. She wondered which word was dragged into more hackneyed phrases — "cancer" or "Odyssey"? She wondered what kind of odyssey her mother, the cancer patient, was on.

"So eccentric," she said.

Greta had begun going out almost every day. Sometimes, on a bad day, she made it only as far as her car. When that happened, she called Daisy on her cell phone. Daisy would appear in half an hour, which was just about how long it took Greta to get back into the house.

"I'm sorry," she whispered into the phone on one of these mornings. She was too tired even to speak normally.

"Go inside and lie down," Daisy said. "May I come and watch you sleep?"

Greta dragged herself back to the house and collapsed on the living-room couch. Sleeping while Daisy sat near her was one of her greatest joys. It made the time seem worthwhile, useful, full, instead of wasted. Tony was at the hospital, Josh at UCLA where he'd gone back to finish his master's degree. And Elizabeth off at some business meeting. Greta stood up from the sofa as Daisy opened the unlocked front door. Daisy walked straight to her, put her arms around her, and kissed her. Each time this happened, Greta felt a lovely, subtle shift, as if someone had opened a window.

"You just relax now," Daisy said. "I'm here." Her voice was soft and soothing. Greta lay down again and wondered how it was possible to feel so peaceful and so excruciatingly aroused at the same time.

"It's very confusing," Greta said.

"A puzzlement," Daisy said. She sat down on the couch, put Greta's feet on her lap.

"This is where we first met," she said.

"Romantic, isn't it?" Greta said with disgust.

Daisy lit a cigarette. "Oh, shit," she said. She leaned forward, revealing two nicotine patches on her back just above her waist, and stubbed the cigarette out on the sole of her shoe. "I'm sorry." She bit her lip. "You're so patient, Greta."

Greta laughed. "*I'm* patient?"

"Well, *the* patient."

Greta watched Daisy get up, then kneel beside the couch, her face touching Greta's. Daisy kissed her and Greta closed her eyes. She felt Daisy stroking her hair. Now and then Daisy would murmur some endearment. Why? Greta wondered. It wasn't clear to Greta why Daisy had any interest in her. Perhaps it was Freudian.

Daisy had a need for mothering. But it was Daisy doing all the mothering, it seemed, and anyway, Greta wasn't really old enough to be Daisy's mother. Of course Daisy lied about her age, all those movie people seemed to. She claimed thirty-five. But to Greta she revealed, after extracting a solemn oath of secrecy, her dirty secret — she was forty. Greta was fifty-three. She could have been Daisy's mother's younger sister, perhaps, but not her mother. Maybe Daisy had a thing about aunts.

"What is the feminine equivalent of 'avuncular'?" she asked. But she fell asleep, her face pressed against Daisy's, before she heard the answer.

The drive to the studio was slow and jerky with traffic, and although the gray sky was not dark enough to be gloomy, it was dreary, it was drab. Elizabeth wondered what she would find at the other end. She hadn't seen Volfmann since the night at Shutters. She had thought about him. A lot. In her thoughts he was close, his face an inch from her face, his words hot against her lips. She sat in the car in the traffic. She was filled with a vibrant unease.

When she saw him, she smiled, he smiled, she sat, he sat.

"I thought Daisy was coming, too," she said. She couldn't think of anything else to say.

"She'll be late. Sick friend."

I have a sick mother, Elizabeth thought. A sick mother and a sick grandmother.

Volfmann chucked her under the chin and said, "Buck up, kiddo."

She took the bottle of icy water he gave her. She realized she was terribly thirsty and drank most of it, a small rivulet trickling down the side of her mouth.

Volfmann grabbed a Kleenex and dabbed at her face.

"There," he said.

"I write, I drool . . . You name it," she said, too embarrassed to take her eyes off the hand holding the Kleenex. She noticed again how beautifully his nails were done. His hands smelled good, too, clean and soapy.

"Elizabeth?" he said.

She looked up into his eyes. His boxer face looked seriously back at her. "Yes?"

"Elizabeth . . ."

He walked away from her, put his hands in his pockets, then quickly took the hand with the Kleenex out of his pocket, looked at the crumpled white tissue as if he'd never seen it or one like it before in all his life, tossed it in the wastebasket, and wheeled around to stare at her.

"How old are you?" he said.

"Twenty-nine," she said.

She liked his face more than she ever had before. Its scrubbed, almost youthful glow softened his boxer-dog expression. He seemed on the verge of something, of saying something, of doing something. Her ears were ringing.

"Does it really matter?" she said. And she looked away, feeling idiotic and coy. Her age didn't matter. Of course it didn't. She wasn't seventeen. She was an adult. A consenting adult, should she choose to consent.

"No," Volfmann said, his voice ordinary and reassuring, the tone intruding on her thoughts. "You'll trim that scene at the county fair, of course," he added.

What? She gazed out at him from the confused, outraged heat of her embarrassment, helplessly, angrily blushing. Then she thought, The county fair? It was perfect the way it was. And most of it was quoted directly from the novel.

"By about half, do you think?" Volfmann was saying. He had moved back to his desk. "Or three-quarters?"

"No way —"

"Do you know how lucky you are?" he yelled. "I'm giving you a course in screenwriting, and I'm paying you for it. I don't even *look* at scripts until they're ready to shoot."

His face softened, became thoughtful, and he continued in a normal voice. "Why am I doing it? I wonder. You think it's a midlife crisis? Well, better *Madame Bovary* than a Porsche." He walked around the perimeter of his office, tapping things, stopping to idly open and close a drawer, running his fingers along the back of the long sofa, like a dog marking its territory. "So, now, economy, okay? In the scene? In every scene. And the scene has got to do more than one thing? And there's no, how can I say this? *Feeling.* There's no fucking feeling."

Volfmann stood before her, looking down at her silently. She was exhausted. She hated him. She saw a rather tender expression in his face, thought, *Go away! I don't want to like you now!;* then thought, *Yes, I do,* then, *But that scene was so good,* and said, "So, basically, it sucks?"

"Sucks, doesn't suck — what's the difference?" he yelled. "We have a story to tell!"

When Greta had suggested they go to services for Yom Kippur, Tony groaned and declared he couldn't bear to sit for hours and then listen to a rabbi appeal for funds for Israel and the new lobby for the Hebrew School. Then he seemed to remember, almost in midsentence, that Greta had cancer and might naturally seek Solace in Religion, as so many Victims of Serious Illness do.

"Well, who knows," he had added quickly. "Maybe things have changed. And a little atoning never hurt anybody."

Elizabeth and Josh looked at her guiltily, saying of course they would go if she really wanted to, but since Yom Kippur was kind of a sad day, shouldn't they go to a fun movie instead?

Lotte had simply snorted. "The bastards," she added. "The dirty rotten hypocrites."

Greta wanted to shake them, to dig her fingers into their arms and shake them. Don't you see? she wanted to scream. I have to go. I carry a heavy weight. My conscience burns with guilt. I am an adulteress, a liar, a cheat. A wanton harlot. I have betrayed all that is dear to me. I need to bare my soul.

"Sometimes, I feel so guilty," she told Daisy. "I kind of thought of going to synagogue this year. Only the Kol Nidre. I could rend my garments while I listen."

Daisy had turned out to be more than Greta had bargained for. Greta had longed for her, for her touch, for her presence. But she had somehow not imagined friendship. Now she had a lover who was her closest friend, the one she gossiped with about her lover.

Daisy put her arms around Greta. They lay in bed in Daisy's bedroom, a tiny cubicle with high ceilings. A ledge ran around part of the room on which sat dozens of papier-mâché Mexican *puta* dolls, each one with legs spread, her name painted across her bosom, real earrings hanging from her ears. Elena was a blonde. Estella, too. Gloria had black hair and green earrings. Anna, a tiny blonde, wore red. Flor's turquoise outfit had pink flowers and glitter. They all had painted shoes and little white painted socks. Greta found their garish colors and bored, harsh Kewpie faces frightening. She turned her face into Daisy, relieved by the warmth.

"I hate it that you feel guilty," Daisy said.

"But I am guilty."

"I hate that, too."

Greta thought, How dare you hate that? That's who I am, that's the only part of me you know.

"If you hate that, you hate me," she said, furious. And they proceeded to have a fight.

"Guilt is a useless emotion," Daisy said.

"What the hell is that supposed to mean? That you're uncomfortable? So am I. So what?"

"And you think you'll find solace praying? You're as bad as Madame Bovary —"

"This is not your movie, Daisy."

"*She* went to a priest. And you know what he talked about? A sick cow!"

"Who said I wanted to fucking pray, anyway? Did I ever say that?"

"And then the priest said, 'It is indigestion, no doubt . . . You must get home, Madame Bovary; drink a little tea, that will strengthen you, or else a glass of fresh water with a little moist sugar.'"

Daisy said these words in an exaggerated French accent that forced Greta to laugh, which further infuriated her, so that she tried to play out the quarrel awhile longer.

Whenever Greta fought with Tony, he became either baffled or disgusted, and left her alone while she cried. Later, he would comfort her. When she fought with Daisy, Daisy ended up crying. And Greta ended up crying. Then they both ended up comforting each other.

"It's very strenuous," Greta said, kissing the tears that trembled on Daisy's eyelashes. Daisy dabbed at Greta's nose with a tissue.

"Yeah," she said. "Women are a pain."

Greta held Daisy tight, pressing her face against Daisy's, hard; desperate, suddenly, wanting to cross the boundary of skin against skin.

"I don't know how long I can do this," she said, her voice muffled.

"Don't leave me," Daisy whispered.

Greta held her even tighter.

"It isn't you I'm thinking about leaving."

They fell asleep, as tired as if they'd had sex. When Greta woke up, Daisy was snoring gently, like a cat. Greta touched the black hair splayed on the pillow.

How did this happen? she wondered. I wish this had never happened. Thank God this happened. What is it that's happened?

Daisy opened her eyes. "Why don't you just come to *my* synagogue with *me?*" she said. "But would that be atoning? Or further sinning?"

"You're Jewish?"

For a second, Greta felt absurdly elated. As if that made it all right, as if that made everything all right, as if now her mother would approve and her children would give their blessing and Tony would say, "I'm so proud! A nice Jewish girl!"

There were times when Elizabeth, having dinner with her grandmother, watched the food Lotte had just chewed come out a gap near her nose where a scar that refused to heal was separating. Elizabeth would lean forward with a tissue and quickly wipe the stuff away, hoping Grandma Lotte wouldn't notice she was leaking orange Jell-O.

Greta lay on the couch. She felt tears running down her cheeks, but could not for the life of her imagine where they were coming from. The nausea cradled her, a malevolent, suffocating embrace.

"Maybe you really should smoke some grass," Tony said. He stood over her. "I can get some. Medical grade." She waved him away.

"I can get you some Kytril."

"Leave me alone," she said. She said it sharply, more sharply than she intended. Her eyes closed. She meant to keep them open. She had a date.

"I have an appointment . . ." she said, almost a whisper.

"You try to do too much."

If everyone would just be quiet, she thought. She opened her eyes. "Bring me the phone?"

"Let me call for you."

Tony put his hand on her forehead, first the palm, then, turning it as if he were taking a child's temperature, the back of his hand. I know you like the back of my hand, Greta thought. She tried to remember the back of her hand. Or his.

"No," she said.

She felt herself sinking into the heavy, deadly sleep. No, Tony. You can't call for me. She sensed Tony had turned, was leaving the room, but she could not make her eyes open again. She thought, Even the swooning misery of exhaustion, even the swooning misery of nausea, even the two miseries swooning together as they tremble before the ultimate swoon of death, even they cannot conquer the swooning misery of guilt.

"So, is this *supposed* to be bad?" Volfmann said.

Elizabeth was grateful they were on the phone, not in the same room. He was yelling. "It's a fucking bodice ripper."

"It's fucking straight from Flaubert," she said.

"And I've fucking told you a thousand fucking times that I didn't hire fucking Flaubert. Because Flaubert is dead! Flaubert is a novelist. A dead novelist. And I don't want a dead novelist. And if I did I wouldn't hire you. I'd hire goddamned fucking Flaubert. Jesus fucking Christ. No wonder it's bad. 'Straight from Flaubert, straight from Flaubert . . .'" He imitated her voice.

"I'm sorry," she said.

"Where's that goddamned dyke when you need her, huh? What am I paying you people for? For shit? I make my own shit. I don't need your shit."

Elizabeth said nothing.

"Shit," he said. He sounded exhausted. "Just fix it, Professor. Do you understand me?"

Elizabeth didn't understand him at all. He was inexplicably patient one day, attentive and tender; cold and abusive the next.

"I'll fix it," she said.

Was it possible she had been attracted to this snarling bully? At least she hadn't let him make her cry. That was a point of pride. She hung up, more angry than shaken, until she read the pages over. Then her anger flipped, like a switch, to shame, and she lay down and pulled a pillow over her head.

"Why are you in bed?" Harry asked. "With all your clothes on?"

"Because I'm an idiot."

"Oh."

He climbed in beside her.

"You're very sweet," she said. "Very, very sweet." She put her arms around him and thought that this was the only love worthy of the name.

"You're not an idiot," he said, patting her back just the way Greta did. "You're just being silly."

Lotte's cancer continued to spread, and she sat every day in her chair staring vacantly in the direction of the window. She stopped calling Greta. The phone pressed too painfully against her face. Kougi convinced her to try the speakerphone, but the crackling voice on the other end and her own shouting tired and depressed her. The newspaper bored her. Television was loud and vulgar and made little sense. She ordered a pair of slippers from Saks and felt better for an hour or so. Then the heaviness of the day descended back upon her shoulders. She ate Rice Krispies with slices of banana for breakfast. She ate Cream of Wheat for lunch. For dinner, she tried to swallow little pieces of poached chicken, but they made her gag and she settled for hot water with a drop of cranberry juice. Sometimes the cranberry juice gave her diarrhea, but Kougi said she had to try. She ate a Milano cookie every night. That was her greatest pleasure. Then she lay awake and prayed for all of her loved ones, one by one, going down the list. God, you cruel son of a bitch, take care of my daughter, Greta, what the hell is going on with her, damnit? Don't you let anything happen to her, and all the while dirty gangster criminals like that Ali Baba who blew up the World Trade Center, and that lousy Woody Allen, what he did to his nice wife, she's a beautiful woman, he should rot in hell . . .

Eventually, she would advance through the list until she got to herself.

Now listen to me, God. I'm old. I've done everything. I've seen everything. I've lived my life. But I'm not ready yet, goddamnit, and that's just the way it is. Amen. No disrespect intended, excuse my French.

It had to happen sometime, Elizabeth knew that. Still, she missed Harry when he started going to school.

Four houses down, in a Mediterranean-style bungalow, there lived a pleasant family with a little girl named Alexandra. Harry and Alexandra were the same age and had become friends, splashing in the blow-up pool Alexandra's parents kept in the front yard. Alexandra went to the Little Palms Play School every day from nine until one, and Harry had begged to join her there.

Elizabeth had, in fact, longed for Harry to be at school. So much better than hanging around sick people and parents who were always trying to sneak in an hour or two of work, stealing tourmaline rings, or sucking oysters with manic-depressive producers.

She watched a California jay, black and gray and a beautiful blue, sit on the branch of a skinny tree. It sat there, every day, on the same branch, at about noon and then again at four in the afternoon. And every day a squirrel would join the jay and chase it away from the branch. Then the jay would come back and dive at the squirrel, which would run away to the garden next door. They would repeat their dance for up to half an hour, then both disappear. Elizabeth watched the jay crack open a seed it held with its foot and her thoughts turned confusingly to Daniel Day-Lewis. Oh yes, painting with his left foot. That was such a good movie. *Mrs. B* would be nothing like that. Not only would her script be nothing like *Madame Bovary,* it would be nothing like *My Left Foot.* It would be nothing like so many good things.

The squirrel and the jay were noisily playing, and it was time, at last, to go and get Harry. There were a great number of feet in *Madame Bovary,* at any rate. She must remember to pay attention to them. What, for example, was she going to do with Hippolyte and his clubfoot? She couldn't give him a clubfoot. Not in the twenty-first century. Not in Hollywood. It wouldn't make any sense at all. And yet there had to be some ambitious medical project for Barbie to push her poor husband into. An ambitious medical project. Perhaps Charles Bovary could cure Grandma Lotte.

INT. HOSPITAL ROOM — DAY

> A patient, her face wrapped in bandages like the Mummy, sits in a chair holding a mirror. Dr. Chuck Bovaine stands behind her unwrapping the bandages, slowly, slowly. ELIZABETH, sitting on the bed, watches. GRETA is in the bed.
>
> The doctor pulls off the last bandage. WE SEE . . . (in black and white) Humphrey Bogart's face . . .

Maybe he could help Greta instead. She had been so moody lately, mute and lethargic one minute, beaming and vibrant the next. Obviously she was making some sort of great life-affirming push, a bulwark against death. The traffic light turned green and Elizabeth accelerated too quickly. The tires squealed. And I didn't say "death" because that's what's going to happen, you know, she thought.

Just yesterday, her mother had insisted on going shopping and then insisted they take Lotte with them. Greta, who dined out on horror stories of adolescent shopping fiascos with Lotte, who had worn cutoff jeans beneath her dress to her own bat mitzvah, and Lotte, who found it difficult to walk down to the lobby, who wore a long iridescent gray scarf wrapped loosely around her throat to hide her tumor. Shopping. Together. But it had worked out in the end. Lotte had plopped herself down in the security guard's chair at Barneys and sent Elizabeth to fetch this and that for her to examine while Greta had uncharacteristically bought up a storm. Still, it might very easily have been a disaster, as Elizabeth had pointed out on the way home.

"Perhaps we'll have a disaster next time, dear," her mother had said soothingly.

Elizabeth pulled the car into the strip mall where the Little Palms Play School was. A nursery school in a strip mall. Well, why not?

She stood outside, leaning against the car door, her eyes closed, soaking up the sun. Which will then give me skin cancer, she thought. But the sun was warm and gentle, and the glare did not penetrate the dark lenses of Elizabeth's sunglasses or the lids of her closed eyes. The air was dry and just cool enough. There was no sense of autumn in the air, no sense of any season. Elizabeth felt the lightest breeze. Her lips felt the breeze and she thought, I've been kissed. Not by Volfmann, that ancient, churlish, dog-faced gargoyle. By a handsome stranger. Or, better yet, by Tim. Tim, who had a crush on her. What a herky-jerky imagination I have, she thought. Am I really so fickle? Then she wondered: Would Tim's kiss be soft and romantic and young? Or hungry and young?

Elizabeth! Such clichés!

But is there nothing to say ever? she wondered. Nothing to feel that isn't reeking with the banality of other people's experiences?

That isn't tagged like something at a garage sale? Can't I even fantasize in peace?

She reverted irritably to Volfmann. His bottom lip pushed out just a bit. His mouth was just inches from hers. She could taste his words. She forgot she was angry at him. She forgot about clichés. She forgot her fantasy was prosaic. She kissed Volfmann and felt him pushing her back against the car.

"Mommy! Mommy!"

Elizabeth opened her eyes to see Harry, his arms wrapped deliriously around her legs, one hand dangling a dented piece of colored paper smeared with paint. Alexandra barreled after him, waving her own painting.

Elizabeth picked Harry up, buried her face in his hair. When she put him down and looked at the two of them, their hands stained purple and red and a hideous green, Volfmann ceased to exist. She smiled and praised their work and kissed them, reassured that one nursery school was much like another, strip mall or no.

"Into the car!" she said. She felt happy and carefree now. Harry and his friend Alexandra were all she had to think about. She watched the two children climb into their car seats in the back. She leaned in to buckle them up, giving Harry another kiss as she did so. She felt his cheek and closed her eyes, breathing him in. She felt a wet tongue on her cheek, a new smell.

Between Harry's face and her own a small brown dog with a worried expression had inserted himself, wriggling and wagging his tail, jumping from one of them to the next, licking all three faces.

Elizabeth pulled the dog out of the car. The children were squealing in delight.

"Here's your little dog," she said to a mother parked beside her.

"Oh, he's not mine."

Elizabeth tried the other parents, then unbuckled the children and locked the car and brought the dog and Harry and Alexandra

212 • Cathleen Schine

into each of the stores at the strip mall, but neither the Thai, taco, nor chicken restaurant had lost a little brown dog.

The dog had no collar. His ribs showed through his short coat. He looked at her with round, sad eyes and a fretful, wrinkled forehead. His body was too long for his legs, which were bowed. Chihuahua face, German shepherd coloring. His tail was too long for his body. One ear stood up and one flopped down.

No one claimed the dog. Of course no one claimed the dog. One look at the dog and anyone could tell no one would claim the dog. He was a sorry little stray, and had been a sorry little stray for a long, long time.

"You want to come home with us?" Elizabeth said.

Harry and Alexandra were delirious. They thought up names all the way home, each and every one from a television show or a movie or a book.

"Spot!" Harry said.

"He's *brown*," Alexandra replied.

"Clifford?"

"The doggie is *brown*."

Elizabeth looked at the little dog, curled up in the passenger seat. Don't pay any attention, stray dog. There will be no brand name for you. You have no breed. Why should you be stuck with a brand? We'll call you something original and wonderful, something that fits you, something literary perhaps, or what about Wotan? The Wanderer.

Wotan? But how was Wotan any less derivative than Scooby-Doo? She was as bad as the children. Couldn't she think for herself? So . . . what if she called him something plain, like, say, Jim? Yeah, and while you're at it, buy a canoe, she thought. Jim. Might as well name the dog L.L. Bean.

When you got right down to it, what name wasn't a brand? She thought what a shame it was that language had devolved from being a means of expression to being little more than a flag. Ex-

pressing oneself, once a naive occupation of her parents' generation, had somehow devolved into waving that flag, conveying one's
place in the world, or the place one would like to hold. Pity. When
everything in life was judged as an adornment rather than by its
utility, when even a dog was seen as an accessory, when even its
name was chosen as a mirror for one's own aspirations, then what
name was free, what name was personal, what name just a name?
Fido? Certainly not. Fido was retro. Dog? No — merely ironic.

Elizabeth realized she was agonizing over this more than she
had over naming Harry, which had not been inspired by the prince,
no matter what Brett thought or Lotte hoped. She gave up. "We'll
name him after the first sign we see," she said.

And so the dog was named Temple Ben Ami.

Every night, the minute Harry was carried, asleep, into his own
bed, Temple would jump in beside Elizabeth. Every night, when
Brett returned to bed, he threw the dog onto the floor and the dog
jumped back up.

"I don't want this dog in my bed."

"You can judge a civilization by how they treat their dogs."

Temple burrowed beneath the blanket, between them.

"Gandhi said that," she added.

"Gandhi drank his own urine."

Every day, Elizabeth shuttled from her mother's to her grandmother's
and back. She lived out her days and sometimes her nights with
them, yet her mother and her grandmother, as stationary and solid
as furniture, were now drifting just out of her reach, her grandmother toward death, her mother toward uncertainty. She clung to
them like a child.

The weather was unpleasant. It was hot, and the marine layer,
as the residents of Venice so delicately called the fog, seemed never
to lift. After Elizabeth dropped Harry off at nursery school, she made

214 • Cathleen Schine

the drive to her parents' in a lethargic daydream, making the turns automatically, so that when she arrived, she was momentarily confused.

"I'm losing it," she said to Josh, who was spread out on the couch reading the newspaper.

"I'm hungry," Josh said.

"I'll make you an egg-salad sandwich," Greta said, walking in from the kitchen. "Except for the smell. I forgot. I can't stand the smell." She looked a little green. "How about turkey? Except there is no turkey."

"Anyway, you're going out to lunch today," Elizabeth said. "Don't make Josh his lunch. Relax and enjoy yourself." She glared at her brother.

"Yeah, relax," he said.

"He's not a baby," Elizabeth said.

"Yeah, I'm not a baby."

"He can get his own lunch," she said.

Josh nodded agreeably. He smiled. He didn't move. Greta looked from him to Elizabeth to the kitchen and back to Elizabeth. Elizabeth started toward the kitchen, thinking of the empty refrigerator. Two eggs, perhaps, some lactose-free milk, a couple of lemons. The sight of too much food in the refrigerator made her mother queasy.

"Hey, I know," she said. "Why don't I go out and get Josh a sandwich?"

She sat on a stool at a café by the beach, waiting for her order. She was glad to be alone. Her mother had looked so good today. She had color in her cheeks. Elizabeth leaned on the table, her chin in her hands. She was toying with the idea of an ice coffee when she heard a familiar voice.

"Hi," said Tim. He sat beside her and ordered a chocolate milk shake.

Elizabeth examined his profile. His nose had a bump in the middle that she decided gave it, and him, character, though if anyone had asked her why, she would have been unable to answer. He was just a guy looking vaguely around, as if he'd lost something. He put one ankle on his knee, nearly knocking the table over. He jiggled his legs.

"I got a grant," he said.

She thought of Volfmann, his dark, angry voice. She remembered her brief fantasy of Tim kissing her. Tim was giving her a crooked, bashful smile. His cheeks had gone pink.

"Congratulations," she said.

He had very dark, long eyelashes, like a child Harry's age.

"A big, fat research grant," he said, the tentative, self-conscious smile opening into an enormous grin. "Now I can do some big, fat research." He gazed at his hands, still smiling, as if they were the future. He looked up at her. "You don't know what this means. I mean, it means I can do my work. I can't do my work like you, on a piece of paper. I need equipment . . . space . . ."

He was more emotional than Elizabeth had ever seen him. He shook his head in disbelief. He took a folded letter out of his pocket. He shook it open and stared at it.

"Tim, did you just get that? Did you just find out?"

He nodded. "I came here to celebrate. They have really good milk shakes." He offered her a sip. "You want one? My treat."

"I got a dog," she said. "A little, skinny dog. A little, skinny brown mutt with two back toes missing. He jumped in the car when I picked Harry up from nursery school. His name is Temple. Brett hates him."

"Congratulations on your dog."

She looked at the bag with Josh's sandwich in it. She was enjoying sitting at the café doing nothing, talking about nothing.

"Maybe it's the dog I should congratulate," he said. "You know, finding a home."

She ordered an ice coffee at last. "I hope Josh isn't getting too hungry."

"Can I have his sandwich?" Tim asked. "Come on. We'll get him another. He won't know."

Elizabeth glanced at him quickly, then looked away.

"Well, never mind," he said.

"Take it, take it. The celebratory sandwich," she said. She handed him the bag.

"You're a good egg," he said.

She thought, That's the kind of thing Brett might say. And she wondered why she felt, suddenly, so sad.

When Elizabeth mentioned her new dog to Volfmann, he surprised her with his excitement. He wanted to know the dog's name, how big it was, what color. His voice changed from the rough growl she had found so attractive to a low, melodious growl she found even more attractive.

"Are you a lady with a lapdog now? Or is he too big? Emma Bovary's Italian greyhound was almost a lapdog, don't you think?"

Any chance to drop a few literary allusions. And he obviously has a thing for strays.

"I'm really happy for you, Elizabeth. He just came out of the blue and found you. It's beautiful. Have you read *My Dog Tulip?* Maybe you'll fall in love, like J. R. Ackerley with his Alsatian . . ."

"He's a mutt," she said.

"Aren't we all," said Volfmann.

When she arrived home from her grandmother's one day, she found a small gift-wrapped package on the steps. At first she thought it was for Harry, but a small label said ELIZABETH. She opened it right there. Inside was a tiny brass dog, obviously old, very heavy for its size, a paperweight, probably. It was a Pomeranian. The same breed as the lapdog in the Chekhov story.

Elizabeth held the dog to her face and felt the cool metal against her cheek. Volfmann had sent her a gift. There was no card. But there was no mistaking who had sent it. And why.

"That's nice," Brett said, when she came inside and he saw the little figure.

"I got myself a present," she said. "To cheer myself up."

A lapdog in the palm of my hand. My little secret, she thought. But her own words rang uncomfortably in her ears. So you didn't tell him it was a present. It's just a white lie, she told herself. But even as she reassured herself, she realized it was not lies that were bothering her. It was the words themselves. They were her mother's words. I got myself a present, Greta had said. To cheer myself up. Then she'd held up her tourmaline ring. Her tourmaline ring just like the tourmaline rings Elizabeth had tried on at Fred Segal. When she saw Daisy Piperno.

Elizabeth had a swift, clear memory of Daisy grabbing a little gift box and stuffing it into her bag. A swift, clear memory of Daisy blushing. Daisy blushing and hiding a present she'd bought. For someone.

Elizabeth held the brass Pomeranian dog in the palm of her hand. Where does privacy end and secrecy begin? her mother had said. You are my private little gift, Elizabeth silently told the dog. My secret little gift. The ring was Greta's secret gift. Elizabeth was sure of it. She stared at the Pomeranian. Volfmann had sent her a lapdog. It was beautifully detailed. It wore a little collar. Its eyes stared back at her.

"It won't bite," Brett said, but she was afraid he might be wrong.

She called Volfmann.

"You're amazing," she said.

"I'm a son of a bitch. And don't forget it."

"I'd say you're more of a lapdog," she said.

There was a short silence.

"Elizabeth? That is a peculiar remark."

"It is?"

"Did you call for a reason?" he said.

"Just to thank you. And to say . . ." She paused. What did she want to say? "I don't know. Can we meet for a drink?"

They met at Shutters again. There were no oysters this time. Or champagne. Volfmann was drinking scotch.

"I love the little dog," she said.

"Good, good. Little dogs are good."

"I've been thinking about the story. 'Lady with Lapdog.' I guess that's what you were thinking of, too."

He was silent, just looking at her.

"That little dog means a lot to me," she said.

"You're very kind to adopt a stray, you know," he said.

"I don't exactly think of you as a stray."

He frowned. "Me? God, I hope not. How's your grandmother doing by the way? And your mother?"

"I don't want to talk about them. I want to escape them just for a little while."

"Well, we can get right to the script, then, I guess."

"No," Elizabeth said, amazed at how bold she was being with this man who yelled and stamped feet and reamed out new assholes. But not to me, she thought. He sends little lapdogs to me. "Not yet."

She'd brought the brass Pomeranian with her. She took it out of her bag and put it on the table.

"Ah," he said. "You really are my lady with a lapdog."

She tapped the dog nervously. "I'm, well, I guess . . ." She lifted the dog and looked at it, then at him. "Thank you?"

Volfmann looked at her, then at the dog she held, then back at her.

"You got that as a gift?"

"Well, yeah . . ."

His eyes were wide and droopy and sad and perhaps a little amused. Elizabeth felt suddenly sick.

"You didn't send it to me?" she said.

He shook his head no.

"You're sure?"

He shook his head yes.

She picked up the lapdog. Its pop eyes gazed adoringly at her.

"I wish I had sent you such a sweet little dog," he said. "But, no, it's not from me."

"Oh."

"*Someone* sent it to you."

"I guess."

"I told you I was a son of a bitch." He patted her hand gently.

"Yeah," she said. "You did."

With Lotte recovered from the operation, an attempt was made to provide her with recreational activity. The day of shopping at Barneys had been welcomed, but had also tired her out and she returned to her catalogs with a sigh of relief. She could not have physically endured sitting through an entire movie, in addition to which she would have hated any movie that was being shown. She couldn't bear seeing old black-and-white movies on television. They depressed her. She no longer played cards. She refused any kind of exercise. She could not sit outside because of the sun. She ate like a bird.

"Maybe you could teach me to cook," Elizabeth said. "You tell me what to do, and I'll do it and you'll supervise."

"Cooking requires split-second timing. It's an art. I'm old and sick. Anyway, I already taught Kougi."

Both Elizabeth and Greta had begun bringing Lotte delicious little morsels — raspberry tarts, cherries, chocolate-covered marshmallows. The only offering she responded to was the box of chocolate-covered marshmallows, which she ate in one sitting.

"Kougi can teach me to make matzo balls and you can supervise," Elizabeth said.

"You certainly want to learn to make those matzo balls. Did you ever hear the joke about the waiter with the matzo balls?"

"Waiter, you got matzo balls?" Elizabeth said, recognizing her cue, happy to have engaged her grandmother's interest, even for a minute.

Lotte stood up and took two creaking bowlegged steps. "No, lady," she said in a heavy Yiddish accent. "Dat's the vay I valk!" She stood there, her legs spread, her nose a sideways flap, her chin purple and swollen. Grinning, she acknowledged Elizabeth's applause, then threw her head back and gave a hoarse croak of a laugh.

Elizabeth took her grandmother to see the surgeon. He told them he would have to operate again. She followed him when he left the examining room.

"What will happen if you don't operate?" she asked.

"The tumor will keep growing."

"Right," she said. Right? No. It's terribly wrong. "But, then what?"

The doctor looked just a little annoyed and he said, very quickly, "Well, to begin with, it becomes increasingly unsightly. And there is a foul odor associated with this sort of thing."

Elizabeth waited for him to go on.

"The tumor will interfere with your grandmother's ability to eat," he said.

She nodded.

"To drink," the doctor said. "To swallow anything at all. To talk . . ."

He started to move away as if clearly that had settled things.

Elizabeth, a little dizzy with the information and, more, with the realization that it was she who finally was going to have to make this decision, or at least to decide what and how much to tell Lotte, not to mention Greta, said, "Wait, though. Wait. What about if you cut off her jaw? If you do the operation. Won't *that* interfere with those things? Because how do you eat without a jaw, you know? Or talk or . . ."

The doctor had turned back to look at her. He put his hand on her shoulder. "I want to help your grandmother," he said.

"When you help her, will she be able to eat and drink and swallow?" Elizabeth said. Why did she sound so angry?

"With the aid of a feeding tube, yes, she will."

"And talk?"

"Her speech will be negatively impacted by the surgery, naturally."

Elizabeth leaned against the wall of the doctor's hallway. From inside the examining room, her grandmother called her.

"Elizabeth! You have my pocketbook?"

"So how long does she have to live if we don't do the operation?" Elizabeth said quietly.

"A few months," he said.

"My purse, honey!"

A few months? She had expected him to say, "We don't really know," or "Just a few more years," or, at worst, "Six months to a year."

"One month, possibly two," he said.

"And how much extra time would she gain with the operation?"

"Maybe a month or two."

"And how long does the recuperation take?"

"Oh, just six weeks or so. Miss Bernard, this surgery is your grandmother's only chance. It is the only option."

Elizabeth went back into the examining room and handed Grandma Lotte her purse. Outside, they stood beneath a flowering tree and saw a hummingbird.

"Such a handsome man, the lousy prick," Lotte said. She was smiling, leaning on Elizabeth's arm. "The air is sweet as sugar today," she said, switching to her sunglasses. "As sweet as sugar."

How could Elizabeth calculate, what formula could she apply? Elizabeth held her grandmother's hand. If Lotte got the operation, she would suffer for six weeks in order to add two more weeks of suffering. Elizabeth inhaled the blossoming warmth. Or would the two weeks be like that moment, beneath a tree breathing air as sweet as sugar?

Temple barked at the mailman. He barked at the squirrel and the blue jay. He barked at Brett.

"Don't you see," Brett said, yelling to be heard over the dog, "that we're a family? Of course I came with you to be with your mother. I'm part of your family. You are my family. We are a family."

Elizabeth nodded. Her family was everywhere. It had invaded her dreams, invaded her daydreams. Why should it overlook her home? Why should Brett escape?

"We're bound together. We ought to be married," he said. The dog yapped. "It's very perverse of you."

Elizabeth told the dog to shut up. He barked at her, wagging his tail. He barked and barked and barked. Brett hollered over the barking. Elizabeth nodded without hearing. The sun was directly overhead. The birch trees were too young and slender to protect the house from the glare. Elizabeth's head hurt. Destiny is death, she thought. Is marriage my destiny? She knew Brett was talking. She knew she ought to marry him. He was the father of her child. He was the man she loved. She lived with him already. He was her family, he said.

"I'm the daughter," she said, vaguely, not certain even if she'd spoken out loud.

"You're a mother, too," Brett said.

The dog's tongue was so pink, lolling so comfortably over the sharp, white teeth. I'm the daughter. I'm a mother. How many more titles does a person need? How many more names? This is when people who love each other have to be there for each other, Brett was saying. When things are difficult. And I'm here, he said. But I might as well have stayed in New York for all you care. You pay more attention to this lousy cur than you do to me. The dog stopped barking and lay down in a patch of glare. Brett had also stopped making any sound. He was rolling up the left sleeve of his starched white shirt, then unrolling it, over and over.

"I'm not here," she said at last. "I don't know where I am. I wake up in the morning and I don't know where the fuck I am. I run around like a chicken with three heads cut off. I worry about my mother and Grandma Lotte in my sleep. I hardly see poor Harry, I'm preoccupied when I do, and *you* want more from me? You're not my child. You're a grown man. You want to be there for me? Then maybe you should get off my back."

It was more than she had said to Brett in a long time. She sensed she was being unfair, that he was reaching out to help her, but all she saw was someone reaching out, asking for something, grabbing and pulling and needing.

"Sometimes the bonds of love are so binding," she said softly.

"And sometimes you're so full of shit."

"I don't have time to get fucking married. Okay?" She burst into tears. "I'm too tired to get married. Why can't you understand that?"

"Christ almighty," he said. He left and slammed the door. The dog's tail thumped on the wood floor.

nine

It was Thanksgiving and there were torrential rains. Any rain in Los Angeles was described as torrential, which seemed accurate to Lotte. Rain. It had ruined many an outfit. On the other hand, when else would she get the chance to wear the gorgeous new raincoat she'd ordered from Saks? Calvin Klein. Simple. Elegant. Classic lines. You couldn't go wrong with the classics. Lotte admired herself in the mirror. She pointed to the bottom drawer in her kitchen.

"That's okay," Josh said. "We have platters at home." Sweet Josh. He had been dispatched to fetch the old lady. Lotte remembered Morris helping her mother into the car, so many years ago. A beautiful baby-blue Buick. Morris always had a Buick. Baby blue. Just like his eyes. Her mother had been the old lady then, Morris the young man. Not as young as Josh, though.

And my mother was nowhere near as old as I am, Lotte realized with a start.

"My hat," she said to Josh, pointing to the drawer again.

I'm so old, she thought. There must be some mistake. She wanted to set someone straight. But who? And what good would it do? It didn't seem right to her that she was so old. She felt no wiser. No calmer. She was neither satisfied with her life nor bitter about it. She just wasn't finished with it yet. Was this what her mother had felt as the handsome young Morris helped her into the baby-blue Buick? But her mother had been such a sweet, docile old lady. Lotte remembered her mother's gloves that day, clutched in one hand as she'd allowed Morris to hold the other and ease her into the backseat. She had been wearing a dark navy blue silk dress with white polka dots. Lotte's mother was never heavy, always slim, but her ankles by then had thickened a bit. Lotte remembered the shoes, thick medium-height heels. Laced. Had her mother with her gray hair and white gloves and lace-up shoes — had that soft-spoken kindly person felt the way Lotte felt? Restless? Impatient? Full of the first glimmers of schemes and plans she was too tired to even finish imagining?

"You keep your hats in the kitchen?" Josh said. He pulled out the drawer, meant for pots and pans, but much better suited to hats, as he could surely see.

"Voilà!" she said.

Josh handed her a wide-brimmed felt hat, just the color of the raincoat, a beautiful cocoa.

"Now," Lotte said, placing it on her head at an angle, "what do you think of your old grandma now?"

"You look sensational," he said, smiling broadly. "Like a model."

"A *fashion* model," Lotte said, wishing her mother were alive to see her. "Those poor skinny girls, all they do is vomit and take drugs, they should live and be well."

Greta listened to the rain pounding on the roof. Poor Lotte would be put out. It would spoil her entrance to have a dripping coat to shake out. Greta felt suddenly happy. It was Thanksgiving and her mother would be *able* to have her entrance spoiled. Lotte was alive and coming to Thanksgiving dinner.

And I'm alive, Greta thought. Alive and coming to Thanksgiving dinner. The sight of the turkey made her queasy and she was tired, deeply tired, but she was alive. She looked up at the ceiling and silently said thank you. There was no one on the ceiling to thank, but she said it anyway, and she meant it.

She looked around the room. There was Tony. He had already stained his tie, she noticed, but there he was. She could see him through the door into the dining room, carving. There was her wonderful daughter fussing over her, bringing her a pillow she didn't want. There was her grandson, a sturdy little boy, even tempered as little boys go, sweet and affectionate. He crawled on the floor with the hideous mutt Elizabeth had brought home from nursery school. The dog looked like a homeless person's dog. It lacked only a shopping cart and a pile of rags. Brett, who stood above them drinking scotch, kept moving away, but Temple followed, jumping up to be petted.

The door opened with a whoosh and Josh dragged in Lotte's wheelchair, then went out with Brett to help Lotte in. She stood in the doorway, her arms held out dramatically, her coat and hat dripping. There was a moment when those inside stared at her, wondering why she didn't come in and get dry. But Greta quickly came to her senses.

"Mama! What a fabulous coat! And your hat! Gorgeous! And perfect for the weather. Thank God you had it."

Lotte smiled. She seemed as if she might bow or curtsy. Josh gently helped her unbutton her coat.

"Oh!" she said, seeing the dog. "Is that the turkey? Pretty scrawny if you ask me."

Harry stared up at her, trying to decide if she meant it. She jingled her bracelets at him. The dog barked. Harry stood up at the prompting of Brett and went, uncertainly, for his kiss.

"I could eat you up," Lotte said, grabbing his arms with her strong hands and kissing his cheeks. "I could bite you, chew you . . ."

Greta looked up at the ceiling again. Thank you, ceiling, thank you again.

Lotte's face was white on one side and russet on the other. Her mouth was twisted now, too, and a growth the size of a small grapefruit protruded from her jaw. But it was her, it was Mother with her smooth, stylishly cut white hair, her new jacket, the one she'd ordered from Victoria's Secret, her chic pants that hung a little on her now that she'd lost so much weight.

"It's the best bird we've ever had," Tony said, coming into the living room. "You'll see!"

"That's what my Morris used to say," Lotte said. "Every year. And you haven't even tasted it yet!" She leaned back in her wheelchair, allowing herself to be rolled in by that nice neighbor boy with the long hair, content that the ritual Thanksgiving exaggeration had been observed.

"Shit!" Greta said, trying to light the candle stubs sitting forlornly in the silver candlesticks. "Stupid asshole candles."

"Watch your mouth," Elizabeth said, pointing at Harry.

"Oh, excuse us, Miss Propriety," Josh said.

"I'm *right*," Elizabeth said.

"You are," Greta said, trying to light the candles again and burning her fingers. Elizabeth smirked at Josh.

"What I should have said is, 'Fucking stupid asshole candles,'" Greta said.

"If I may," Brett said. He took the stubs out of the candlesticks. "They're upside down."

Elizabeth watched him light them. He was handy sometimes.

"Why don't we have normal, whole candles?" she said.

Tim was politely pushing Grandma around while Laurie, his

mother, insisted on transferring the vegetables into antique chamber pots she'd picked up last week "for practically nothing" at a yard sale on Pico.

"Is Kougi coming?" Elizabeth asked Grandma Lotte.

"He has a life," Lotte said.

"But then who's the other place for?"

"It's for Daisy," Greta said. "Didn't she mention it to you, honey?"

No, Daisy had not mentioned it. Nor had Greta. Elizabeth saw her mother's tourmaline ring sparkle in the candlelight. The room was so hot. She threw open a window. She leaned her elbows on the sill and pressed her face against the screen, into the wind and the rain.

"What is your problem?" Josh said. He nudged her aside and closed the window. Elizabeth pulled the dog away from Brett and lifted him into her arms. Temple growled.

"He growls?" Lotte said.

"He bites, too," Harry said proudly.

"He's had a hard life," Elizabeth said.

"He should only know from a hard life."

"Elizabeth thinks the dog is human," Brett said with obvious irritation. "Not that she would stand such behavior from a person."

"I'm the one who wanted a dog," Greta said, a little irritable herself.

"Not this dog," Brett said.

Daisy arrived last and they all sat down.

"Nice ring," Elizabeth said to her, nodding toward Greta's hand as it passed a bowl of sweet potatoes. "Huh?"

And there followed a loud, echoing beat of silence.

Elizabeth tried to reconstruct the series of events that led to her helping Lotte into Tim's car at the end of a long Thanksgiving dinner. Did she volunteer to go with Tim? Was she drafted? Did Grandma request her? Or did she offer and Grandma requested

Tim? She'd eaten too much. She'd had too much to drink. She was tired and confused.

"Don't let that bastard of a hound bite me," Lotte said.

The rain had stopped, but the street was still slick. Elizabeth held Lotte's elbow. Lotte's large, strong hand was clamped on her shoulder. The dog pulled at his leash, looped around Elizabeth's wrist.

"My pocketbook!" Lotte screamed.

Tim, who was holding Lotte's other arm and lowering her gently to the seat, said, "Here. It's here." He waved his elbow slightly, trying to show her the bag hanging from his arm.

"Oh! The bastards! These goddamn cars."

They got her seated and Elizabeth leaned in to strap the seat belt on her. Tim's cheek grazed hers as he also leaned in.

"These no-good belts, they'll kill you before they save you," Lotte said.

In the backseat, Temple jumped on Elizabeth's lap. He sat there, at full alert, staring out the window.

"He barks at bikes," Elizabeth said. "So don't be startled."

"At my age," Lotte said.

They got her home without incident. No barking. No traffic. Elizabeth felt Temple's little paws digging into her legs. Grandma said there was too much food at dinner.

"Mountains," she said.

"Well, it is Thanksgiving," Elizabeth said.

"I eat like a bird," she said.

Elizabeth walked her upstairs, although it was clear she would have preferred Tim.

"A gentleman," she said.

"I'm a gentleman," Elizabeth said, a little hurt.

"God forbid!"

Kougi was there waiting.

"Did you miss me?" Lotte said.

"Autumn evening —" Kougi said, "there's joy also in loneliness."

"Haiku," Lotte whispered to Elizabeth.

Elizabeth walked back to the car thinking that instead of sitting beside Lotte at dinner, it would have been better to sit across from her, thus sparing others the sight of food seeping through unexpected parts of Grandma's face. She tried not to cry. It was Thanksgiving. She was thankful. She could hear Temple howling in the car.

What if he'd bitten Tim?

But when she got there, Tim was whistling and the howling was Temple's accompaniment.

There was no more rain. The clouds had passed by to reveal a nearly full moon.

"Let's go to the beach," Tim said.

Elizabeth sat in the front seat. Neither one of them spoke. The dog arranged himself on her lap and growled quietly all the way to Venice Beach.

Kougi had some sort of Japanese music playing on the stereo. Lotte listened to the plink plunk of strings and the breathy, reedy flute. Was this really music? It certainly would not have done in my day, she thought.

"You can't dance to it," she said as Kougi helped her into her nightgown. She wondered if she ought to be more modest in front of Kougi. He was, after all, a man. That was one of the things she liked about him. She had missed Morris for so long. They took up a certain kind of space, and a lot of it, men did. But they left a person alone, too. My daughter is wonderful, don't get me wrong, she thought. And my Elizabeth. They dote on me.

"They dote on me," she said to Kougi.

He put her pills, one by one, in her hand.

"Aren't they pretty?" she said. Green, pink, like Lily Pulitzer. White, pale blue, like the sky.

"My husband doted on me," she said.

She swallowed the pills one by one. There's nothing like a man, she thought.

"He made me feel special," she said.

"You are special," Kougi said.

"You see? There's nothing like a man!"

She leaned back heavily into the bed. Though, God knows, I'm as skinny as a beanpole, she thought. Kougi lifted her weary legs onto the bed. She knew her cancer was spreading. She could almost feel it advancing, creeping, marching across her face. The son-of-a-bitch surgeon wanted to cut her jaw out. Half of it. She lay in bed staring at the ceiling, too tired even to go through the list of family she thought God ought to bless, although God didn't seem to give a damn what she thought, so there really wasn't much point. What should she do? Another operation? Then what? Then another and another until there was nothing left of her. She had to pee. But she was so tired. If she fell asleep, would she wet the bed? She remembered a poem Kougi had taught her:

> A urine-stained quilt
> Drying on the line —
> Suma village.

I'll just have to move to Suma, she thought.

"Your mother seems okay," Tony said.

Greta sat on the couch watching Tony, Josh, Daisy, and Laurie clean up. Sometimes she caught Daisy's glance and wondered that everyone there, everyone for miles, did not know what was going on between them. But Tony seemed perfectly comfortable. Josh was too busy talking about his new girlfriend, or telephoning her in New Jersey, to notice much of anything. Laurie might have caught on if Greta had been involved with a man. But with Daisy?

She didn't have a clue. It suddenly annoyed Greta that no one knew, that no one guessed.

"Lotte is so funny," Daisy said.

Greta looked at her with a start. Where did she come from?

"What?" Daisy said.

"No, no. Nothing."

Nothing. Nothing at all, my darling. Daisy was wearing an odd little red dress. She might have gotten it at a thrift store. Or a swap meet. Or a trendy shop. The fabric clung to her breasts, hugged her waist, then draped loosely. It was something from an early Sophia Loren movie. Or did Greta think that because Daisy had a light shawl wrapped around her bare shoulders?

"What, Greta?" Daisy said again.

"Lotte should be home by now," Greta said quickly. Couldn't they hear it? Couldn't they hear what Greta heard in Daisy's voice?

"Thanksgiving is officially over," Tony said, putting the last of the leftovers in the refrigerator. "Time to relax."

"She's dying," Greta said.

The others paused, looked at her quickly, then turned back to their chores. But there were no more chores. The house was clean. The kitchen was clean. There was some uncomfortable shifting.

"Who told you that?" Josh said finally. "Dr. Elizabeth, M.D.?"

"I think your sister would make a fine physician," Tony said.

Daisy excused herself and headed for the bathroom.

Greta felt Daisy's absence. She could have mourned Daisy's absence. She could have mourned her mother's absence. Perhaps she could have mourned her own.

"The surgeon wants to cut away portions of her jaw," Greta said. The surgeon wanted to take off half of her mother's jaw, actually. It was such an aggressive tumor, he said. A swaggering, belligerent, bloody-minded bully of a tumor that had taken over the left side of Lotte's face. Greta wondered how much of the tension in the room had to do with Lotte and how much had to do with her.

"So, see? There's hope," Josh said. "Right, Dad?"

Greta said, "The dirty bastards."

Elizabeth took off her shoes. The sand was wet and cold. The dog ran to the water's edge, then chased each wave as it broke. Elizabeth watched him snapping at the foam. Over and over. Tim stood beside her.

"I don't know what to say about your dog."

She had put Temple's expandable leash on and he ran, hard, until it pulled him up short. Elizabeth wondered what he thought he would accomplish, deliriously charging saltwater foam, then being jerked to a halt. Full of hope! Hopes dashed! Once, twice — a hundred times.

"He's so passionate," she said, "and it's so pointless."

"You think passion is supposed to have a point?"

Elizabeth reeled Temple in and petted his soaking head. He lunged at her, his teeth bared, grazing her hand, then whimpered and licked her, leaping in the air trying to kiss her face.

"I don't know what to do about my mother," she said. She let the dog charge back to the surf and followed him. The icy water circled around her bare feet. It was so cold it hurt. Why didn't it bother Temple? He wagged his tail and shook himself, then plunged back into the surf. "What am I supposed to do?"

Tim was now just behind her. The wind was blowing.

"What?" he said.

She turned. "Nothing."

Tim put his arms around her. He moved closer to her, resting his chin on her shoulder.

"Elizabeth," he said, the sound private, so close to her ear, protected from the wind and the crash of the waves. And such a new sound; a private, secret sound. His lips were touching her neck. She thought, It was Tim who gave me the Pomeranian.

"The little brass dog . . ." she said.

234 • Cathleen Schine

"Another stray for your collection," he said.

She felt his arms around her. She said, "My collection . . ."

He said, "You have so many strays to look after. But, I don't know, I saw it, I thought of you . . ." His body was pressed against hers from behind. "I thought it might cheer you up."

She thought, Tim wants to cheer me up. He got me a Pomeranian dog to cheer me up. A dog that requires no care. She felt his body against hers. And now, she thought, I will fall, leaving my life and my destiny behind. Or will I simply fall into place?

Temple dug in the wet sand. The moon shone on the water, a long wavering cord. The waves collided onto the sand. And, cheerless still, but overcome with desire, Elizabeth turned and kissed Tim on the mouth, and his hands were inside her clothes, beneath her skirt, beneath her sweater.

"Elizabeth," he whispered in her ear, softer than the roar of the waves, soft enough for her to hear. Holding her hand, he led her back to the car. In the front seat, Temple growled irritably, like a bad conscience, and Elizabeth knew what she was doing was pointless. As pointless as passion. She pulled Tim down, surprised that he was not Brett, that his weight was not Brett's, his movements were not Brett's. She tried to breathe, but this stranger, this new lover, this man she didn't know, whom she'd known for years, took up all her air. She was not Brett's wife. She was no one's wife. She gasped. She heard herself call the stranger's name. His eyes were closed and his lashes were long. He held her down, his fingers digging into her arms. Passion was pointless and the moon lit his face.

There was no doubt in Greta's mind after Thanksgiving. She'd sat there in her dining room and watched her family, admiring them, giddy with love for them, resolved to hurt them.

"It's over for me," she said to Daisy.

They were on a bench at the Santa Monica pier, the wind whipping Daisy's black hair romantically. Greta noticed how her own hair stood up ridiculously and marveled for an instant at how a person could worry about messy hair while contemplating the dissolution of an entire lifetime.

"It's over," she said. "I watched everyone move and speak and I moved and spoke. And ate. And it was as if we were all underwater."

Daisy did not respond. Perhaps that was not what Daisy wanted to hear. Perhaps she preferred the intrigue of an affair. Perhaps she had just been playing all along. The wind carried the sounds of the video arcade behind them. Gunshots. Squealing brakes. Diabolic laughter. Exploding bombs.

"I'm freezing," Daisy said after a while.

Greta put her arm around Daisy's shoulder and pulled her closer.

"I really have to tell him."

She felt sick after she said it, an empty plunge, the ashen spin of a long, long fall. She stood up, trying to breathe in the fresh sea breeze. She leaned over the railing of the boardwalk. She held on to keep her balance, her head bent, looking at the water below, in case she vomited.

Chemotherapy had nothing on the dissolution of a life. Several lives. If I did vomit, she thought, it would have to fall such a long way. Like me.

She remembered a long-ago trip to the Caribbean with Tony and the children. To St. Kitts. They had taken a day trip to Nevis and seen a rainbow on the ferry and ragged, barefoot children in the rutted streets when they got there. A taxi-driver guide invited them to his sister's restaurant for lunch, but, although overwhelmed by guilt at the poor children, they guiltily insisted on a seaside hotel that had once been a plantation. What had they had for lunch? She couldn't remember, but then Josh and Elizabeth, so young that they shared the other double bed in the hotel room, had projectile vomited at each other all that night.

She remembered them as they slept the next morning, their exhausted, scrubbed faces nose-to-nose on the fresh pillowcases, Elizabeth clutching her teddy bear, Josh his worn puppy with its long ears.

Greta smiled. Below her, a gull bobbed on the waves. She and Tony had spent the night on their knees, mopping up vomit.

"You're sure?" Daisy said. She stood beside Greta. She looked scared.

Was she sure? She kissed the top of Daisy's head, black hair blowing against her cheeks, in her eyes. Behind them, a toddler screamed at an unearthly pitch. They began walking back to their cars.

"Soon . . ." Greta said, ". . . ish."

"I've ruined your life," Daisy said.

Greta nodded.

"I did *not*," Daisy said.

She had hoped to see Harry's bar mitzvah, but perhaps that was greedy. Spring? She could try to hang on until spring. But who could even tell when it was spring in this place? In St. Louis, the buds would swell on the bony trees and flowers would crawl out of the damp earth and birds would sing and people would switch to navy blue. But here? Enough flowers to choke a horse every month of the year. Trees that belonged in the jungle. Birds? Who knew? Could you hear them singing with the windows closed? With the air conditioner going?

She was having trouble swallowing. Even water was difficult. That she should live this long! To see the world full of pierced tongues and terrorists. And those anchormen, the dirty bitches, they should drop dead. Why were they always so nasty to Hillary? Anti-Semites, all of them.

"Grandma, I think you've got it backwards. You're supposed to say the media are all Jews."

Lotte realized she had been speaking out loud. And there was Elizabeth sitting in the chair by the bed.

"Darling, darling! I didn't know you were here!" She held out her arms. Her arms were heavy but she held them out for her darling granddaughter. Sometimes the pain was so intense she noticed nothing else.

"The pain, the pain . . ." she said.

Elizabeth rubbed her feet, which were cold. They were always cold. She needed a pedicure. It was one thing that Kougi did not do well. She was too weak to go to the beauty parlor.

"That Christina Ammammabad, though," she said. "She always looks good."

She turned up the collar of her pajama top.

"See?" she said. "That's style."

"Why don't I give you a pedicure?" Elizabeth asked, as if, again, she'd listened to Lotte's thoughts.

Lotte heard the emery board.

"Did you ever do anything you were really sorry for? But you just kept doing it?" Elizabeth said.

"Who knows? Whatever you do, good or bad, sorry or not, you get punished, darling," Lotte said. "Life kicks you in the balls, Elizabeth. Always remember that!"

"Great."

"Your Grandma Lotte told you that."

"Thanks."

"So you have to kick back."

Elizabeth moved to the other foot. The nails on the foot she had finished were a little too short. Lotte could feel it, but she said nothing. She didn't want to hurt Elizabeth's feelings. The girl did her best, poor thing.

"Your Grandma Lotte," Lotte said. "On her deathbed."

Where the hell had that come from? As the words escaped her mouth, she gasped and began to weep. She had frightened herself. Now, Lotte, shut up, you silly old crow!

"I don't want another operation," she wailed.

"I know." Elizabeth came to the head of the bed and held her hand.

"But I want to get better," Lotte said. She heard herself whimper pitifully. Well, she was entitled. If they didn't like her whimpering, they could drop dead. She was a very sick woman.

"The surgery won't cure me, will it?" she asked.

She waved Elizabeth back to the toe she was painting. Such a beautiful color. Silver. Not garish, though. Subtle.

"Not really," Elizabeth said, softly, obviously embarrassed. "Just slow the tumor down."

Lotte was grateful everyone referred to the cancer as the tumor. Cancer, that bastard, it should choke.

"I'm not ready," Lotte said. She began to cry again. She began to wail again. "That dirty rotten bitch of a doctor, to cut me up for no reason, he can't pull the wool over my eyes, thinks I'm a hillbilly from the sticks? Well, he's got another thought coming! All they want is money, in their big Mercedes, they can all drop dead."

Elizabeth hugged her and soothed her and dried her eyes and her oozing face with a tissue.

"Your grandmother's a pistol!" Lotte said.

She watched Elizabeth smile, then give in to an involuntary snort of laughter.

There was no operation. Lotte did not go back into the hospital. Just morphine and some home-hospice visitors who tried to talk to her frankly and solicitously about death.

"Death? It should drop dead," Lotte said, ungraciously.

Elizabeth spent more and more time with her, often bringing her laptop and working in the stuffy apartment. She saw very little of her own mother. I need to be with Grandma, she told herself. And that was true. But Elizabeth could not face her mother. That was also true.

Greta visited Lotte, too. On those weekends when Kougi was off and they were unable to get someone else, she stayed overnight. Lotte lay in bed with her eyes closed most of the day and all night. Greta forced her to walk in the hallway sometimes. She forced her to put on a clean nightgown. And Greta cleansed the tumor, wiping away the thick yellow scum. She inhaled the sickening smell and marveled that she was able to do it. She loved her mother and wondered if what she saw before her was possible, if her mother, so large a presence, cursing and exalting, could be this quiet lady rotting beneath Greta's hand in its latex glove. Then she massaged Lotte's big hands with lotion. Then she called Daisy and arranged to meet her for a few hours on her way home from the sickbed.

"Is it true that I never complain?" Greta asked Daisy.

"Pretty true."

"I'm sorry," she said. What a burden on other people, to have to guess, anticipate her needs. How considerate of her mother, who had complained day and night.

In January, Elizabeth brought two new sweaters to show her grandmother. Lotte, barely able to make a sound, waved her heavy arm and big hand at the blue one. She made a circle with her thumb and forefinger.

Then she pointed at the brown sweater and whispered something hoarse and indistinct. She waved at the sweater, indicating disgust.

That night she died. The tumor, oozing and stinking as vigorously as the doctor had promised, had been newly cleaned and swabbed with ointments. The pillows were smoothed and piled up. Lotte pointed at the light. She wanted it put out. Kougi held one of her hands. Elizabeth the other. Elizabeth listened to her labored breaths. When she stopped breathing, Elizabeth thought, She's stopped breathing. It took a moment to realize that meant her grandmother was dead. She had wondered earlier if her grandmother's hand would become cold when she died. But now she didn't notice. She noticed only the silence.

When the ambulance came, she watched them carry Lotte out and thought, There will be a funeral. There are arrangements to be made. I will have to make them. What would Grandma want to wear? A shroud? Her navy-blue jacket from Victoria's Secret?

When Greta and Tony and Josh arrived, Greta put her arms around Elizabeth and they cried. *Daisy,* Greta thought, irrelevantly, as she held Elizabeth and breathed in the fragrance of her daughter's moisturizer and the substance of her mother's death.

∾

Greta knew what Lotte wanted to be buried in. A plain white shroud. "My clothes should go to you girls," Lotte had said once, before it was clear that she was really going to die, before the words meant anything much. "You have to amortize my investment."

And there would be no funeral. Lotte hated funerals. Anyway, all her friends were dead.

"Mommy, we have to do something," Elizabeth said. They were gathered at Greta and Tony's.

Greta heard only the word "mommy."

"Don't worry, I'll take care of it. Just a few people over to the house, okay?"

Greta looked at her blankly.

Elizabeth turned to her father for help, but he was staring at Greta with an expression of despair so obvious it frightened Elizabeth and she lifted up the dog and took him outside. The dog ran through Greta's lavender bushes and came back smelling like a sachet. Elizabeth wanted to bury her face in his fragrant coat. But he growled at her and she did not dare.

* * *

Greta went into the bedroom and sat on the floor, her back leaning against the wall, just as she had the day she realized she was in love with Daisy, the day she'd gotten Daisy's letter.

The letter had said only, "Thank you so much for this incredible book! Yours, Daisy."

Looking at the word "yours," Greta had known. An innocent note. And Greta had known.

Thank God my poor mother never had to witness this, she thought, gesturing, as if her betrayal of Tony, the end of her marriage, her passion for another woman, were all displayed on her bedside table.

Harry knocked on the door.

He came in and sat on her lap, leaning his head all the way back, peering up at the ceiling.

"What are you looking at?" Greta asked.

"Nothing," Harry said. "There's nothing there, Grandma."

On the walk street, sprinklers had darkened the cement path with water. Roots pressed the pavement up from below. Flowering vines reached out from the fences. Roses hung down over closed gates. Temple ran ahead, the two toes missing from his back foot causing him to tip awkwardly to one side, and then back again. His tail, as long as his low body, wagged hysterically. He darted from fence to fence, gate to gate, his nose scraping the ground. At every new address, he barked. He growled. His hackles stood up like plates on a dinosaur. Ferocious snouts poked out from beneath each fence. Dogs crashed at their gates, howling with frustration.

Elizabeth and Temple made it to the cross street. Temple defecated in his usual spot. He lifted his leg against the soft bark of the malaluca tree. He barked and growled at a puppy on a leash across the street. Elizabeth gave the owner, a fit middle-aged woman in exercise clothes, a wan, apologetic smile. A child rode by on a bike. Temple lunged before Elizabeth could pull up on his leash. The little girl on her bicycle wobbled but did not fall. With a blue plastic bag that had held the *New York Times* that morning, Elizabeth scooped up the neat coil of dog shit and walked back to her house.

ten

The gathering for Grandma Lotte was an elegant affair. And it was Daisy who ended up planning it. A friend of hers was a caterer and provided a tasteful spread of tiny sandwiches and tiny pastries. Tray after tray appeared on the big dining-room table. The cantor from Daisy's synagogue sang a prayer.

"You have such a beautiful voice," Greta said to him afterward. "I'm sure my mother wouldn't have objected to you at all."

Elizabeth watched Brett offer people drinks. He opened bottles of wine. He even made martinis. Did he think this was a party? She noted how harsh and unkind toward Brett she'd become. Harry sat on the floor playing with a dump truck. She wondered if he would remember Grandma Lotte as he grew up. Daisy spoke softly to the girl serving canapés who then gathered up several dirty glasses. Daisy eyed the plates, the forks, the napkins. She checked the ice. She caught the eye of a young man with a tray of full wineglasses,

244 • Cathleen Schine

made a slight movement with her chin, and the waiter moved quickly to another part of the room where a group of Elizabeth's parents' oldest friends were standing, drinkless.

Amazing, Elizabeth thought. She is directing the *shivah*. Perhaps Kougi would begin reciting haiku. Josh and Greta could discuss the landscaping and geologic qualities of the grave site. Tony could comfort the Grieving Relatives. Tim could describe the journey of the atom from the big bang to tapping toes on a vaudeville stage to the cold feet of the body lowered into the dark burial pit. Laurie might show up any minute with a French provincial coffin she found on La Brea.

Everyone in character. But what about me? Elizabeth tried to imagine what would be in character for her. She could see herself only as she was — bewildered and unhappy.

"Eat," said a voice beside her. It was Volfmann. "Here." He handed her a small sandwich.

She ate it, surprised at how hungry she was, surprised by his presence.

"You're here," she said. "You're incredibly kind. Sometimes."

"So I've been told. Sometimes." He put his hands in his pockets. "She lived a long time," he said. "But what kind of crappy consolation is that?"

Elizabeth nodded, grateful that he understood. She drank a glass of wine he handed her, then another.

"You're always getting me drunk," she said.

"Somebody has to."

In the kitchen, Greta stood in the chill from the open refrigerator. I'm an orphan, she thought. A fifty-three-year-old orphan. She laughed. But she felt like an orphan. A small, helpless orphan.

Now that Greta was an orphan, she saw that it made things easier for Tony. He had been angry at her before Lotte died. *You're so distant,* he had said. She had laughed. *Me?* she said. *That's your line.* But he was right, she had been distant. She had been far, far away. She had been lost. He could feel it. You can't live with someone for more than thirty years and not notice they have disappeared. No matter how much you work at it.

Now, though, he was exceptionally considerate. He was helpful. He was full of love. Greta saw that he loved her, and she was grateful. She saw that she loved him back. But nobody loves you like your mama do, Tony. Or was it that you love nobody like you do your mama?

Over the course of the evening, Greta passed by Daisy again and again, the back of her hand brushing Daisy's hip, her elbow grazing Daisy's bare arm, her shoulder pressed against Daisy's shoulder for an instant, a shudder of recognition and memory and promise. She watched herself from the distance of her grief, horrified.

"I was to take her to Japan," Kougi said, taking Greta's hands in his, leading her away from the refrigerator. "Miss Lotte in Japan."

Sounds like a dime novel about a call girl, Greta thought. She enjoyed the feeling of his cool, smooth hands cupped around her own.

"She was lucky to have you to take care of her," Greta said. "I was lucky to have you to take care of her, too."

She walked quickly from the room, afraid she would throw herself on Kougi and sob on his shoulder, calling out her misery for all to hear.

Greta saw her daughter across the room, pale and puffy-eyed from crying. She came up beside Elizabeth and put her hand on the small of her back. They stood quietly like that for a few minutes. She watched Brett mixing a drink at the other side of the room and wondered if all was well between him and Elizabeth. They seemed so far apart. But the distance of a room was not really distance. Death was distance. Greta should have been with her mother when she died. She should have been holding her hand, placing a cool cloth on her forehead, offering her a small, jewellike chip of ice to suck on. She shuddered.

"Are you okay?" Elizabeth said.

Greta shrugged. "Are you?"

Am I? Elizabeth wondered. She turned her face to her mother's in order to reassure Greta that she was, indeed, okay, because whether she was okay or not, her mother had cancer and so needed to think she was okay.

She opened her mouth to say, "Status quo." She closed her mouth without saying anything. Her mother was no longer listening. She saw Greta's face, noted her flushed cheeks, her eyes wide and intense, her breath soft but uneven, jagged. Greta was smiling oddly.

Why are you smiling? Elizabeth thought. What the hell are you smiling at?

Elizabeth saw that Greta was smiling in the direction of a half-dozen half-remembered faces of graying doctors and their blond wives. She was smiling past the doctors, past the doctors' wives. She was smiling at a distant shimmer of fiery, unmistakable tenderness. It was a face. It was Daisy's face. Greta was smiling oddly, her breath jagged, her face flushed, her eyes glazed, at Daisy.

The distance of a room is no distance at all, Greta thought.

Elizabeth looked at her mother's hand, which was now entwined in her own. She looked at the tourmaline ring.

"Where's your wedding band?" she said.

Greta looked at her with an expression Elizabeth had never seen before, a combination of horror and defiance. "It doesn't fit," she said. "Anymore."

* * *

Elizabeth sat on the bed in her parents' room. They slept in this bed. Together. They were her parents, her mother and her father. Whatever their secrets, they were still that. They were still married. They still slept here, in this vast king-size bed.

"What are you doing, my poor little duck?" Brett said. "All alone in the dark?" He came in and sat beside her on the bed.

Thank you for calling me a poor little duck, Elizabeth thought. It made her feel safe, it made her remember how she felt when she felt close to Brett. His poor little duck. She felt the soft, pressed cotton of his shirtsleeve against her arm.

"My . . ." she said. She stopped. "Something is going on with my mother."

"No shit." He gestured toward the living room, where the mourners were still gathered.

Elizabeth thought of the small, crooked, lustful smile. A tourmaline ring. A blushing cheek. Two fingers touching beneath the water as if the pool were the Sistine Chapel, as if they were God and Adam.

"My poor father," Elizabeth said.

"Mommy?"

It was Harry. For some reason he was crawling. He crouched on all fours in the doorway.

Elizabeth went to him and sat on the floor, gathering him up in her arms.

"It's okay," she whispered. "Everything is okay."

Greta appeared, looming above them.

"Come on, Harry, pussycat, I'll read to you," she said.

Elizabeth did not look up. Pussycat. She held Harry tighter.

"Mommy!" he said, squeezing himself out of her grip and toddling off with his grandmother.

Elizabeth couldn't speak. She could only stare at her mother's back and think, This can't really be happening, as if she were in a trashy horror movie. I am in a trashy horror movie, Mom, she thought. Did you ever think of that? Hey, you, Mom, did you ever think of anything? Like your husband, for instance? Did you ever think of the family you have to think of? Your grandchild? Your son and your daughter? Did you ever think of thinking of England?

Brett sat on the floor and put his hand out for hers. Elizabeth clung to his hand. He was the only one in all the world she could talk to about this, and she couldn't talk to him. It all seemed so unlikely. Her mother who barely had the energy or the appetite to drink a cup of tea. Now we know what's been tiring her out, Elizabeth thought, surprised at her vulgarity. It was, after all, her own mother. Her mother to whom she was so close. How could her mother be having an affair without Elizabeth knowing? With a woman no less? Her mother, with whom she had joined forces to present a united front to lie to Grandma Lotte, had lied to Elizabeth.

Elizabeth leaned into Brett, into his familiar embrace, the sharp crease of his collar, the flat perfume of starch.

More than thirty years of marriage, a farce.

"I had it all wrong," she said. "It isn't adultery that's tragedy or farce. It's marriage."

"Shut up with that shit, Elizabeth," he said. He released her and stood up. In the doorway, backlit by the bright hallway, Brett appeared enormous, far away, unavoidable yet subtle, the peak of a misty mountain. He held out his hand to help her up. She had been so unfair to him, yet there he was. That was how her father was supposed to appear to Greta. How could her mother not see that Tony was bound to her forever? How could Greta have struggled free of the bond of matrimony? How could Elizabeth have struggled free of the bond of love?

"Brett, I'm so sorry," she said, leaning against his chest. "I love you so much."

He kissed her, a little surprised by her attention. She walked, pressed against his side. She was in the hall. She heard her father whistling, making the dog sing. The cantor was laughing. The cantor was saying, "He'll have my job!" She heard her brother through the closed door of his room. He was crying. She was walking down the hall, Brett's hand in hers, hers in his.

She saw Tim walking toward them, a big, happy smile on his face. She saw him see her hand in Brett's hand.

"Hey, Tim," she said quickly, but what she saw was in the slow motion of panic, the paralyzed slow motion of a car crash, the oncoming car, the helpless consciousness of the oncoming car, the oncoming car hurtling forward in slow, slow, suspended motion.

"Hey," Tim said, looking at the floor.

Brett did not notice the car wreck. He slapped Tim on the back and went back to bartending. Elizabeth led Tim out to the pool, taking the dog with her on his leash. Tim stood there, his hands dangling at his sides. He seemed to be growing a goatee. Greta's fat white cat walked across the grass. Temple growled and barked at the cat and strained at his leash. The cat turned toward him, blinked, and walked on.

"I can't do this anymore," Elizabeth said.

"Leave the dog home when you come here."

"That's not what I meant."

Tim put his hands on top of his head. It was an odd gesture, as if he were surrendering to the Japanese at Bataan. "What?" he said. His voice was slow. As if he were slow. "What?"

She had hooked herself, like a fish, and she felt herself dangling helplessly. She had to get loose. Off the hook, she thought. That's what "off the hook" means. I never realized that before . . .

He leaned against the wall. "I know you're sad about your grandmother . . . I'm really sorry."

She nodded.

"Right," he said.

"Right." She turned to go back inside.

Tim grabbed her by both arms. "I know it was just meaningless sex, but . . ." His face grew confused and angry. "You're not supposed to dump *me*," he said. "I was planning to dump *you*. Well, let you down easy, anyway . . ."

Behind Tim, Elizabeth was staring in the open window, face-to-face, at Brett.

"But, I mean, the window of opportunity was pretty fucking minute . . ." Tim was saying.

Brett had been emptying ice into an ice bucket. He stared back at her, still holding the bag as ice cubes fell into the silver bucket, overflowing, littering the counter.

"I didn't want to be a *total* cad, for Christ's sake . . ." Tim continued.

Elizabeth heard only the rattle of the ice cubes. She saw Brett's face go from pale to white. From pale to white to a wavering milky sheen, which was the glare behind her own eyes. In slow motion, she stood, absolutely still.

"Elizabeth," she thought she heard Brett say. "You thorough little bitch."

Elizabeth woke up in the wrong bed. It was wrong in so many ways. It was not her own bed, the one she shared with Brett. Nor was it the pullout couch in the guest room that was called "Elizabeth's room" at her parents' house. In fact the only thing familiar about the bed was Temple, who had curled himself into the curve of her belly.

This is the wrong bed, Elizabeth thought. Everything is wrong. I have no bed. I've made my bed and now I must lie in it. Lie down with dogs, wake up with fleas. She had lain down with Tim and woken up without Brett.

When she stood outside with Tim and Temple and saw Brett, framed by the window, glaring at her, ice cubes clattering onto the counter, the sound as jarring as the score of a bad horror movie,

Elizabeth had seen her life glaring, clattering, melting, turning, and walking away.

The strange bed, the wrong bed, was Grandma Lotte's bed. The deathbed.

"The deathbed will be comforting," she had said after Brett scooped up Harry and left, wordlessly, without her. Josh drove her to Lotte's strangely hollow apartment. She wondered if he thought she was insane, for insisting on sleeping in her grandmother's bed like a Hindu widow consigning herself to the flames of the funeral pyre. Probably not. He slept on Grandma's couch.

"It will be comforting," he'd said.

"I miss Grandma Lotte," Josh said, coming into the bedroom in the middle of the night. His clothes were rumpled, his face creased. Crying had left him red eyed, red nosed. Elizabeth hoped he had used a sheet and pillowcase to sleep on Grandma Lotte's couch. Lotte was so proud of that fabric.

"Silk," she said out loud, as her grandmother would have. "*Hand* painted."

Josh smiled and added, "Deluxe, deluxe, deluxe."

Greta knew something had happened to Elizabeth the night the cantor came and sang so beautifully for Lotte. She asked Elizabeth about it, but, as she expected, Elizabeth shrugged her off.

"Nothing. Absolutely nothing. I was upset about Grandma."

"There's nothing you want to talk about?"

"No," Elizabeth said. "Why? Is there something you want to talk about?"

"No," Greta said.

They sat there, in Lotte's apartment, going through Lotte's papers. They sat beside each other, both of them having something to say, neither of them saying it. Funny how that was. She and Elizabeth. They talked about everything. Except those things they didn't talk about.

Looking down at her mother's shaky handwriting, Greta wanted to kiss the check stubs, to hold them to her face and tell them she loved them, loved the ballpoint scratches, the wavering traces of Lotte Levinson Franke.

"I can't do this," she said. She stood up abruptly. "I'm sorry." She walked out, got in her car, and drove home.

Greta left the emptying of the apartment to the children. It was, simply, too painful. She avoided the children. She thought of her mother lying in her coffin. She thought of her mother lying in her bed. She thought of her as she had seen her last, when she was dead, and as she had seen her as a child, when she'd thought she was dead. She thought of Lotte when Lotte was preening and when Lotte criticized her. She imagined Lotte's big feet. Lotte's big feet would turn to dust. She barely spoke to Tony. She never answered the phone. She dodged everyone, even Daisy. Especially Daisy.

Months went by. When Greta's last chemotherapy session came around, it was Tony who took her. He read an old *National Geographic* in the waiting room while she went in for the drip.

"I think all *National Geographic*s are old," he said in the car on the way home. "I think they come that way."

After dinner, Greta asked him to come into the garden with her. She needed air. She leaned on him.

"When you're up to it, we'll celebrate," he said, helping her into a chair on the terrace. But he sounded wary. He looked away from her.

And then she told him. Just told him. She couldn't see his face. But she could feel the air go out of him. She could feel him deflate. "I knew it," he said. "Of course I knew it." He knew it, but he didn't believe it. He explained to her that she was angry about having cancer. He explained that it was natural. He understood that she was acting out. He understood that it was a phase. It was his fault. She wanted his attention. She deserved his attention. He explained. He understood.

"But you can't explain it away," she said. "And you don't understand."

If only she could have given him that, she thought. If only she could have left him with the illusion that he understood. But how could he understand? She didn't understand. What she was doing, what she was feeling, was absurd, on the face of it. And what did it have, besides a face, to those outside?

They went inside. They raised their voices. They sat silently on the couch in the living room. They said the same things, back and forth. They screamed at each other and spoke in sentences that trailed off in hopeless whispers. They did this all night.

"I'm sorry," Greta said, over and over. "I'm so sorry," she said again. She said it so many times. She said it too many times. "I'm sorry, Tony. I'm sorry." It stopped meaning anything. "I'm sorry." Stopped meaning anything at all.

"You're a fool," Tony said. "You're a fucking fool."

He stood up so violently that his chair skidded backward and hit the wall. For one moment, Greta thought he might strike her, but he just turned and walked out. She heard the engine of his car. He was gone for three days.

Elizabeth sat with her feet in the pool. Josh sat beside her, lifting one foot, then the other, staring at the circles the droplets made.

"I was right," she said.

"Congratulations."

Their parents had just taken them aside for the "talk," the one so many of their friends had described so many years ago. Elizabeth and Josh had sat on the couch like two children. They had cried like two children.

"It's sickening for her to be happy when he isn't," Elizabeth said. "Poor Daddy."

"It's ridiculous."

Elizabeth put her hand in the water, then held it against her flushed face.

"But I don't want her to be *un*-happy," Josh said.

"No," Elizabeth said. She breathed in the clean, antiseptic smell of chlorine. "Well, maybe a little."

Aunt Rose and Uncle Leonard were the first in line, but that was only to be expected. They specialized in events. Funerals, weddings, a nice *bris,* bar mitzvahs, bat mitzvahs . . . They knew the ropes.

"I'm so glad you could get here," Elizabeth said.

"You remember your Uncle Leonard's sister? Lillian? Her cousin passed yesterday. We'll miss the service," Rose said. Leonard shook his head sadly. Rose looked Elizabeth straight in the eye, as if it were Elizabeth's fault. Missing the funeral. The death itself.

"And how old are you, young man?" asked the next in line, a tall bony woman with a red face. She squatted, her knees protruding awkwardly from her skirt, and still she towered over Harry. In a funny broad accent that was not quite an English accent, she said, "Four, is it?" She made a clucking noise. "A big boykie, hey?" She stood up and offered Elizabeth her large hand. "It's a new world, a new world," she said, and moved on.

Politely, Elizabeth said, "Yes it is."

For it was a new world.

"We're married," she whispered to Brett, beside her in the receiving line, handsome in a blue suit and white shirt and the new silver tie Tony had given him for this day.

"That explains all these peculiar people," he said.

But what explains this marriage? Elizabeth thought.

"I don't know what to think about you," Brett had said when Elizabeth arrived home the morning after Grandma Lotte's funeral. "I don't know what to think about you anymore."

Elizabeth didn't know, either.

"I don't know what to think about anything," she said. "Except that you and I belong together."

"Tell that to Elizabeth," Brett said to Elizabeth.

They slept in separate rooms for months, barely speaking. Elizabeth heard the eerie bagpipe sounds late at night, and on one of those nights, she tried to open the door to his room and found it was locked.

"You realize that Charles Bovary is the hero?" Elizabeth said to Daisy, with whom she was forced to continue working.

"I can see how you might think so," Daisy said.

"I can see how you might not."

Elizabeth had spent months explaining it all to Brett: They had not been married, therefore she could not have committed adultery, unlike poor Madame Bovary, who had been married and could.

"You're insane, and your insanity is self-serving, which suggests you're not insane at all," Brett had replied. "You are low." He spoke gravely, severely, for he was both hurt and deeply, profoundly offended. "You can't be so high-handed with people you love," he said. "Can't you see that?"

"Adultery . . ." she began, but he slammed his fist on the table.

"Adultery is something you taught in a class," he said. "This is my life. And yours. And Harry's, too. You want a word? Unfaithful. An adjective. It describes a person who other people had faith in. A person who broke that faith, trampled it underfoot, who spit on it . . ."

Elizabeth cried, but Brett paid no attention to her tears anymore.

Once, he threw a chair across the room and, dark with rage, yelled, "It's not acceptable!"

Elizabeth, both frightened and noting what an odd schoolmarmish choice of words he'd made in his fury, looked at the overturned chair.

"But that's what I'm trying to explain," she said. "If we'd been married, what I did would have been adultery."

He stared at her. "One of us has to move out. I can't stand this anymore. I can't stand you."

"If we had been married, what I did would have been wrong," she continued.

"It *was* wrong, damnit!"

"And that's why people get married."

Brett left the room.

"You get married so that you *will* be like Madame Bovary," Elizabeth called after him. "If in fact you *are* like Madame Bovary."

No answer.

"I thought that's why people shouldn't get married," she yelled.

Still no answer.

"But I was wrong," she yelled to the silent house.

I was wrong, she said to herself that night. She put Harry to bed and went into the bathroom and turned on the shower and cried and said, out loud, "I was wrong." But it was only when she stepped into the shower and stood, naked and shivering, and heard the faint wail of bagpipes piercing the din of the water, that the sickening plunge of comprehension hit. She had done something wrong. She had hurt people she loved. She could not undo what she had done. She was a fool.

Elizabeth and her father danced the first dance.

"Is Mommy going to dance with Daisy?" Elizabeth said.

"Worried she'll scare the horses?"

"Yes."

It was embarrassing, having a mother and a mother's girl-friend at one's wedding. No one could convince her it wasn't. No one had tried. But even if they had . . .

Brett danced with Greta. Greta thought what a good dancer he was.

"My mother would have loved this wedding," she said. "Most of it."

Elizabeth had been wrong, she was a fool, she knew it, and she made sure Brett knew that she knew it. At first, he merely agreed with her.

"Yes," he said, coldly. "You were wrong. You hurt people you love. You threw your life away. You're a fool."

On his birthday, Elizabeth had talked him into letting her take him out to dinner. They went to Chadwick's in Beverly Hills and drank wine and ate their salads in companionable silence. Elizabeth could almost forget they were estranged and wondered if maybe, just for a moment, Brett could, too. Then, she saw an elegant, heavily made-up older woman at a table in the corner.

"Oh my God," she said. "That's Madame Bovary."

Brett had looked up from his plate, and his face, so relaxed just a moment before, turned hard and cold and angry. He looked at Jennifer Jones, looked at Elizabeth, shook his head with disgust, stood up, and walked out.

But perhaps Brett was a fool, too. Or had it been that he really did love her and she really did love him and the rest was an evil memory to be exorcised every minute of every day they had left together? For neither Elizabeth nor Brett moved out of the bungalow in Venice, and gradually, almost without either of them realizing it, they stopped their frigid, discordant discussion of adultery and began talking, again, of marriage.

"I didn't want anything to end," she said one evening when Harry was asleep and she and Brett sat on the couch finishing the wine. "I think I thought if we got married, something would have to end. I don't even know what."

He laughed and tapped her forehead. "And now?" he said. "What do you think you think now?"

"I love you. I want to marry you. No end in sight."

And Brett had smiled and kissed her and repeated her words back to her.

Tony whirled Greta across the floor in a waltz. The room spun. She leaned her cheek against his shoulder. The familiar scent of three decades of marriage washed over her. She remembered their wedding. They had grinned until their mouths ached. Her parents had danced, just as she and Tony did now. We've been friends a long time, she thought, but hesitated saying it. Tony might take it the wrong way.

"I've known you a long time," he said.

She laughed. "I was just thinking that."

"I've known you long enough to know what you're thinking," he said, and they both lapsed into a sober silence.

Harry stood in front of the band and pretended to tap dance. Elizabeth watched her mother and father. She had decided to make Tony a project of hers when her parents split up, but he seemed to prefer to take care of himself. He spent all his time working or working out, dated his massage therapist for a while, then began seeing a cardiologist he seemed to like, although Elizabeth had never met her.

"My Blushing Bride," he said, coming over, kissing her forehead.

Elizabeth noticed her mother watching him walk off. She had an expression of gentle fondness Elizabeth could not remember seeing when her parents were still married.

*   *   *

"I hope your marriage is as happy as mine was and lasts twice as long," Greta said to her.

Sixty years? Elizabeth thought, watching Brett dance with Daisy. Good God.

"That's a long time," she said. She put her arms around her mother. "You *were* happy?" she asked. It was suddenly important to know, to hear it. "Really?"

"Very."

"So why . . ."

"Come on, Elizabeth," Greta said, laughing. "Not today, honey."

Greta kissed her, then wiped lipstick off Elizabeth's cheek with her thumb.

"Are you happy now?" Elizabeth asked.

"Yes."

"You better be," Elizabeth said. "After all the trouble you caused."

"I'm especially happy today."

Elizabeth smiled, in spite of herself.

She looks so beautiful when she smiles, Greta thought. My heart still soars when she smiles, just the way it did when she was a baby. She looked at her daughter, an adult in a wedding dress — simple but elegant, Lotte would have said. Over Elizabeth's shoulder Greta could see Josh and Daisy dancing. In her wallet she kept a fortune she'd gotten a year ago in a fortune cookie. "Your family is one of nature's masterpieces," it said. Then it listed her lucky numbers: "17, 28, 32, 34, 38, 43."

"I miss Grandma Lotte," Elizabeth said.

"Yes," Greta said. "I wish she had lived to see this day. Well, perhaps not all of it," she added, nodding toward Daisy.

Elizabeth watched her brother and her mother's girlfriend dance. She watched her father cut in. She sighed. "You never complained or anything," she said.

"I was saving up for a rainy day."

"I'll never forgive you for breaking up our family," Elizabeth said. She watched Tony and Daisy dancing comfortably together. "*I will never* forgive you."

Then, seeing her mother's face, feeling her mother's hand in her own, seeing her husband approach her, her own husband, realizing that love and passion and adultery — and marriage and family, too — were farcical only from the outside and tragic only when they ended, and that hers had just begun, she did.

~

Volfmann stood on the beach in front of his house. A wave arched and crashed to the sand, foamed gently around his feet, then disappeared. Then another. And another.

The Pacific Ocean, he thought. Big deal.

The next wave hit the shore, enormous and loud.

Such a fuss, Volfmann thought. And then, nothing.

The dog snapped at the foam. He splashed toward the next curling wave, then splashed frantically away as the water broke. Then he snapped, ever diligent, at the line of white foam.

Volfmann headed back to the house. He rinsed his feet with the hose. What the hell did he need a dog for? Two houses wasn't enough? He was never even home, for Christ's sake. He had to fly to New York tomorrow, then to London. A week later, he would be in China. Chasing markets. Instead of waves.

But how could he let the poor bastard be put to sleep? Okay, so the dog was a little nuts. True, true, he had a temper. He had some anger issues. You couldn't deny it. But, so what? So fucking what? I mean, how does that make the little cur any different from me? Volfmann thought.

"Temple is very unhappy," Elizabeth had said one afternoon. "He growls all day long. I can't leave him alone. If I do, he bites his back feet." She had dragged the dog in to a meeting. "Look."

Volfmann and Daisy and Elliot and his two young assistants had dutifully examined the dog's back paws. They were raw and bloody.

"And he bites children, too," she said. "And men in uniforms. Men in general, actually. And women, of course."

Temple was on the same antianxiety drug that Volfmann took.

"If it doesn't start working, I have to put him to sleep," she said.

"It doesn't work for me," Volfmann said.

* * *

Then the script for *Mrs. B* did not turn out to be all that Volfmann had hoped it would. "So, look, I'll take the dog instead," he said. "What the hell."

"Another pet project," Elliot grumbled.

"The script is not bad," Volfmann continued. "Don't get me wrong. But now I want something, I don't know, meatier. So . . . I've been thinking . . ."

Temple, sitting in his lap, curled his lip at Elizabeth and snarled. Volfmann gently stroked the dog.

"*Anna Karenina,*" he said softly. "*Anna* fucking *Karenina.*"

Volfmann stood on his deck above the beach, his cell phone to his ear.

"What am I?" he yelled. "Public television?"

He watched as his fabulous new assistant, hired for just this purpose, followed his new dog in and out of the foam. He sighed with contentment at the sight: Temple, frantically charging the waves; Kougi, placid and unruffled, holding the long, wet leash.

And there, beyond them both, rising, retreating, and endlessly rising again, was the vast Pacific Ocean, which, Volfmann noted with satisfaction, with all its noise and nonsense, never once lost its enthusiasm.

about the author

Cathleen Schine is the author of five novels — *Alice in Bed, To the Birdhouse, The Evolution of Jane*, and the international bestsellers *Rameau's Niece* and *The Love Letter*, both of which were made into feature films. She divides her time between New York City and Los Angeles.

copyright acknowledgments

She Is Me

A novel by
Cathleen Schine

A READING GROUP GUIDE

A Conversation with Cathleen Schine

In She Is Me *you write about the secrets, dramas, emotional hurdles, and comic dilemmas that wind through the everyday relationships of three generations of women in a family.*

Right. I like to look at the ways in which people take the unforeseen and incorporate it into their daily lives. To me, there is nothing more comic, more touching, more human. *She Is Me* was a particularly satisfying book to write because all these subjects — marriage, adultery, illness, family — rose up and joined together and came banging on my door. One day I was walking along Columbus Avenue trying to understand what the book was really about. And then I thought: Oh! Love. All kinds of love — between a husband and wife, between illicit lovers, between a mother and daughter.

Did something specific suggest the plot to you?

Some years ago, my grandmother, who was in her nineties, became very ill. I watched my mother, who was very close to her, struggle to take care of her and continue her normal life. Then my mother became ill, and I was running back and forth between them, and this new family dance began. We were all trying to protect each other, and suddenly we were all lying to each other. It took on the shape of a drawing-room comedy, all of us covering up and hemming and hawing and making lame excuses. We could just as well have been having illicit affairs. That's when I realized that this absurd situation, which so many people go through, was the starting point of a novel. A romantic comedy, actually.

Where's the romance?

Just where it always is — where you least expect it. *She Is Me* is about what happens when passion blooms not, say, in the secluded moment of a summer romance but in the chaos and tension of a family crisis, like a flower pushing up through a crack in the pavement.

And the comedy?

Families are funny and adultery is funny; families are tragic and adultery is tragic. Love just complicates everything that much more. Elizabeth, Greta, and Lotte's family has no boundaries — only secrets, the meat and potatoes of comedy and of passion. A secret romance is surely the most romantic of all. But there is a decidedly comic element when you're daydreaming about undressing your secret lover while you're pulling up your grandmother's corset.

Each person's life has so many different sides — the mother side and the daughter side and the career side and the romantic, sexual side. We're like these weird octagonal cells floating around, colliding. One of the most comic elements of family life occurs when those roles come crashing up against one another, when need and desire and tribal responsibility crash. That's one of the joys of writing about families.

She Is Me is a work of fiction, but readers often wonder just how much of the author is in the characters. To what degree do you mine your personal experience when you write fiction?

She Is Me includes certain events that parallel events in my life. My grandmother died of skin cancer. My mother survived colon cancer. I was married and now live with a woman. I had a dog who chased waves and bit people. But unlike, say, my first novel, *Alice in Bed, She Is Me* is not autobiographical at all. For me, the real story is always in the characters, and Elizabeth and Greta and their husbands and lovers are not disguised real people. Not only are they unlike me or my family, but they are *like* themselves. To me they're very real *and* very fictional characters.

Sometimes the connection to real life is just serendipitous: when I was writing *The Love Letter,* not sure of anything but Helen's seductive personality, I received an anonymous letter that had clearly been sent to me by mistake. Of course I used it, but, like anything I absorb into a novel, it showed up there transformed, distorted, and new. Another writer, I can't remember who, said, "Do not trust a writer. She is not your friend." I gather up bits and pieces from the lives of everyone I know, and from the lives of those I don't know. I'm an equal-opportunity scavenger.

I would say that for me, and for many other writers, the relationship between my life and my books is intimate, inescapable, and usually irrelevant.

One surprising twist in the book is Greta's decision to leave her husband for another woman. It would seem that a decision like that would take a tremendous amount of courage. Where does Greta get hers?

When I was twenty, I was in the hospital for a year and I was in a lot of pain. People would say, "Cathy, you're so brave." I tried to explain to them that it wasn't bravery. It was reality. If I could have run away from the hospital and the pain, I would have. I think Greta is in a similar situation. She's married and relatively content. That has been her reality. But her reality changes. It's frightening, it's painful, but unlike my hospital stay, it is also a door opening to her future. At first, that door seems like the door of an airplane at 38,000 feet. Greta feels like she's being sucked into the sky without a parachute. But she lands on her feet.

Greta's family is ultimately very accepting of her life change. Where does their understanding come from?

Do they really understand her? Or are they relieved that they still recognize her? Both, I think. They discover that they are still a family, although their family shape is now a little lumpy. Elizabeth and her brother need the chance to remember that they want to keep loving their mother. Greta's husband is furious and hurt, but he is also strong enough to accept the reality of their past together and the reality of their future apart. As for Lotte, well! Thank God she didn't live to see this day, what goes on in this world, it's enough to kill you, but as long they're happy, although how they could be, don't ask, they should live and be well.

The title, She Is Me, *is both ungrammatical and intriguing. How did you happen to choose it?*

It is a poor translation of something Flaubert said: "Madame Bovary, c'est moi." The youngest of my three heroines, Elizabeth, is trying to write a modern adaptation of *Madame Bovary* for the movies, so Flaubert was much on my mind. Flaubert was identifying himself with the baffled, tragic, and romantic character of Emma Bovary. I found the phrase particularly suggestive for this story because my heroines are not only bound to Madame Bovary by their own passionate confusion but also bound to one another. I think mothers and daughters can sometimes be so close, so intimate, that they have to struggle in order not to lose themselves entirely. That struggle is part of what *She Is Me* is about.

It is difficult for Elizabeth to write the screenplay. Why?

I think Elizabeth's struggle is about how to authentically translate at least some of the meaning of *Madame Bovary* into a contemporary cinematic form. Flaubert was obsessed with cliché and with the romance novels that Emma Bovary was constantly reading. She was seduced by banality. Elizabeth has to find a modern equivalent. For her *Mrs. B,* banality resides in the modern world's obsession with brand names and celebrity.

You've had two of your novels (The Love Letter *and* Rameau's Niece) *adapted into feature films. To what degree were you involved in that process, and what was it like?*

The two experiences were very different. *Rameau's Niece* was made into a movie called *The Misadventures of Margaret.* The director/screenwriter and producer were two young British guys, and it was their first feature film. They were so excited that they called every time anything remotely promising happened. *The Love Letter* was a DreamWorks film and had a much smoother journey to the screen. The people involved were wonderful and friendly, but the process was far removed from me.

I know many writers complain about adaptations of their books, about changes from the original material. I've always felt that in order to be faithful to a book, a movie has to stray and find its own way of telling that story. Watching a character you created grow and change in someone else's hands was weird, like bumping into someone you haven't seen in forty years. They're the same, but . . . they're not. It made me want to go back and remeet all my characters in that way, see what they've been up to since I last wrote about them.

In She Is Me, *love pops up in unexpected places, and not just for Greta. Lotte bonds with her male Japanese housekeeper; a stray dog jumps into Elizabeth's car and into her heart. What did you want to say about the nature of love?*

Love, as Flaubert showed us, is a cliché, a powerful cliché. We're all Emma Bovary in all her anguished banality. That's why it's so hard to find any original language to use to describe love. It's all been used. And yet when you're in love, you long for those words. That's why Greta can lie on a hotel-room bed and read the Psalms while waiting for her lover and see her own situation reflected in those ancient words. Because this banal, universal cliché is always completely fresh and doesn't follow the rules. There's a line from a Yeats poem (which I used for the epigraph for *The Love Letter*): "O love is the crooked thing." I like that.

Questions and Topics
for Discussion

1. What motivates Greta's and Elizabeth's affairs — love or lust? How do their lives mirror Madame Bovary's?

2. Lotte, Greta, and Elizabeth are all keeping secrets from one another. Why? Is it because what the others don't know can't hurt them, or is it because they are unwilling to admit their desires to themselves, let alone to one another?

3. Lotte's illness results in her disfigurement. How does her physical appearance affect her attitude? Do Lotte's fond memories of her vaudeville days keep her from facing the predicaments she and her family currently confront, or are they the example on which she feels Greta and Elizabeth should model their own lives?

4. Where do the men fit into the lives of the mothers and daughters in *She Is Me?* Are Tony and Brett pushovers, or are they the backbone of their respective relationships?

5. What does Daisy Piperno offer Greta that Tony can't? Does Greta's love for Tony diminish when she discovers what she be-

lieves is true love with Daisy, or does Greta's love for Tony just become something different from what it was?

6. What do you make of Lotte and Kuogi's relationship? How is her friendship with him a source of strength or solace?

7. What keeps Elizabeth from marrying Brett? How would marriage change their relationship? Does Harry keep them together or put a wall between them?

8. How do the relationships between Greta, Lotte, and Elizabeth resemble relationships you have with your mother or sister? How are the relationships depicted in the novel different from yours?

9. Why is Volfmann so appealing to Elizabeth? What does her attraction to him reveal about her personality? How does it reflect on her relationship with Brett?

10. *She Is Me* discusses illness and adultery very frankly, but with an irrepressible sense of humor. Are most such crises inherently funny in some way?

Cathleen Schine's Suggestions for Further Reading

These are the books I read over and over:

Anything by Anthony Trollope, especially *The Small House at Allington*
Emma and *Pride and Prejudice* by Jane Austen
Anything and everything by Barbara Pym
Our Mutual Friend by Charles Dickens
War and Peace by Leo Tolstoy
Huckleberry Finn by Mark Twain
Pictures from an Institution by Randall Jarrell
Leaves of Grass by Walt Whitman
The poetry of W. H. Auden, Elizabeth Bishop, and James Schuyler
Loitering with Intent and *A Far Cry from Kensington* by Muriel Spark

These are other books I love:

My Dog Tulip by J. R. Ackerley
The Voyage of the Beagle by Charles Darwin
Mrs. Bridge by Evan S. Connell
Hateship, Friendship, Courtship, Loveship, Marriage
    by Alice Munro
The Good Negress by A. J. Verdelle
An Obedient Father by Akhil Sharma
Amy and Isabelle by Elizabeth Strout
Moo by Jane Smiley
The Blue Flower by Penelope Fitzgerald
The Crossley Baby by Jacqueline Carey
And Now You Can Go by Vendela Vida

Hunger
A novel by Elise Blackwell

"An exquisite little book. . . . Blackwell craftily weaves history and botany through this utterly devourable narrative. . . . A compact embarrassment of riches."   — Mark Rozzo, *Los Angeles Times*

Like Family
Growing Up in Other People's Houses
A memoir by Paula McLain

"Astonishing. . . . With her poetic gift for language, an extraordinary frankness, and narrative generosity, McLain demonstrates through the impenetrable bond with her sisters the true meaning of family."
— Kera Bolonik, *Chicago Tribune*

The Fall
A novel by Simon Mawer

"A fine novel. . . . Utterly convincing, one of the most credible accounts I've ever read of two people falling in love."
— Gary Krist, *New York Times Book Review*

BACK
BAY
BOOKS

Available wherever paperbacks are sold

The Dogs of Babel
A novel by Carolyn Parkhurst

"Wonderful. . . . Parkhurst has created two compelling characters to take us through the shoals and delights of falling in love."
— Susan Dooley, *Washington Post Book World*

The Lovely Bones
A novel by Alice Sebold

"Mesmerizing. . . . *The Lovely Bones* takes the stuff of neighborhood tragedy and turns it into literature."
— Katherine Bouton, *New York Times Book Review*

All He Ever Wanted
A novel by Anita Shreve

"There's something addictive about Shreve's literary tales of love and lust. . . . She is a master at depicting passion's ferocious grip."
— Jocelyn McClurg, *USA Today*

 BACK
BAY
BOOKS

Available wherever paperbacks are sold